CAN'T DENY LOVE

Brandon sensed the moment Tanya's frigid stance of resistance melted away and she opened her mouth to allow him to slide his tongue between her lips and taste all of her. So long since their tongues had danced together, the passion dormant for five years overtook him with the force of charging bulls. As he ran his fingers through her hair, the kiss intensified as he sucked, stroked, and glided over every part of her mouth. He molded his body to the contour of hers, and the kiss took on a life of its own and every primitive part of him came alive. Hearing a moan from deep in her throat encouraged him and was quickly followed by moans of his own.

Hearing the erotic sound caused Tanya to jump back. *What am I doing?* "How dare you!"

Breathless, Brandon reached out to her. But it was too late, he saw in her eyes the second her mood went from passion to anger. However, Brandon refused to let her shut him out. "Tell me you didn't feel it."

Wiping remnants of his touch from her mouth, she quickly put her hands down when she realized they were shaking. Trying to slow her pounding heart, she held her head high in defiance and declared, "I don't know what you're talking about."

"The hell you don't." The words were harsher than his intention, but all doubt as to whether she still had feelings for him were erased by that kiss. God, his knees were weak and he felt as if he needed to sit down. He could see her unsteadiness as well. Not wanting this opportunity to slip away, he again reached for her.

"Tee, I know what happened between us was messed up, but that's in the past. We deserve another chance."

"Don't call me that," she said, angry with herself for responding to his kiss. As his hands caressed her hair, her nipples stretched against her bra and every intimate part of her craved his touch. The kisses with Martin had never been like this and she hated herself for comparing the two. But as her mind fought for control of this situation, there was no denying her body's reaction.

BOOK YOUR PLACE ON OUR WEBSITE AND MAKE THE ARABESQUE ROMANCE CONNECTION!

We've created a customized website just for our very special Arabesque readers, where you can get the inside scoop on everything that's going on with Arabesque romance novels.

When you come online, you'll have the exciting opportunity to:

- View covers of upcoming books

- Learn about our future publishing schedule (listed by publication month and author)

- Find out when your favorite authors will be visiting a city near you

- Search for and order backlist books

- Check out author bios and background information

- Send e-mail to your favorite authors

- Join us in weekly chats with authors, readers and other guests

- Get writing guidelines

- AND MUCH MORE!

Visit our website at
http://www.arabesquebooks.com

CAN'T DENY LOVE

Doreen Rainey

ARABESQUE

★BET BOOKS™

BET Publications, LLC
http://www.bet.com
http://www.arabesquebooks.com

ARABESQUE BOOKS are published by

BET Publications, LLC
c/o BET BOOKS
One BET Plaza
1900 W Place NE
Washington, D.C. 20018-1211

All Kensington Titles, Imprints, and Distributed Lines are available at special quantity discounts for bulk purchases for sales promotion, premiums, fund-raising, and educational or institutional use. Special book excerpts or customized printings can also be created to fit specific needs. For details, write or phone the office of the Kensington special sales manager: Kensington Publishing Corp., 850 Third Avenue, New York, NY 10022, attn: Special Sales Department, Phone: 1-800-221-2647.

BET Books is a trademark of Black Entertainment Television, Inc. ARABESQUE, the ARABESQUE logo and the BET BOOKS logo are trademarks and registered trademarks.

First Printing: August 2003
10 9 8 7 6 5 4 3 2

Printed in the United States of America

This book is dedicated to Lea Roy and Abbey Flowers. Thanks for all of your support and words of encouragement. Both of you are truly priceless!

Prologue

"Please, Tanya, can we talk?"

The touch of his hands on her arm sent a massive wave of awareness through her, warming her from head to toe. It had been so long since she last felt his touch. Closing her eyes, she reached deep for the strength to walk out the door and never look back.

"I can't do this," she whispered, and opened the door.

As she stepped onto the stone porch, the cold bolt of winter air against her face was a welcome feeling. Breathing deeply, she cursed herself for being so affected by him. How much longer before he moved completely out of her system? Lord knows she had tried, dating several nice, eligible men. The problem was, no one compared to him. And she hated herself for feeling that way. Realizing tears welled in the corners of her eyes, she pulled her keys out of her purse and headed for her car.

"Tanya, wait," he yelled, jogging to catch up with her.

"Go to hell, Brandon," she said, not turning around and picking up speed.

Catching up with her before she could unlock the door, he stepped in front of her.

"Please, Tanya, don't go."

Taking a deep breath, she wiped the last of her tears and stared him directly in the eye. "Get out of my way before you get hurt."

"Just give me five minutes, that's all I ask."

"No." The desperation in his voice left her unaffected. The heart racing inside her had grown hard and there was nothing he could do to change that. Pushing him out of the way with a brute force she didn't know she possessed, she opened the door and slid inside.

"I never slept with anyone while I was with you."

His words stung her like a queen bee. Stepping out of the car and slamming the door, she felt the raw anger brewing on the inside of her as barely containable. The slap was hard, fast and lethal.

"How dare you stand in my face and tell me that bald-faced lie!"

Ignoring the sting on his cheek, he felt it was time to cleanse his soul. Taking a step forward, he repeated in a low whisper, "I never slept with anyone while I was with you."

This time, he caught her wrist before she connected another blow.

"Five minutes, Tanya. That's all I ask."

Jerking her hand away, she replied, "You have no right to ask for anything. Good-bye." Opening the car door again, she said, "If you get in my way, I will run you over."

Stepping around the door, he dropped to his knees, feeling no shame. He had made a mess of their lives, and this chance meeting tonight gave him the opportunity to make things right. Whatever it took, he would get her to listen to him. "I'm begging you, Tee, just five minutes."

Her head was spinning at breakneck speed. Did he really have the audacity to stand before her and continue this charade? What did he hope to gain by all of this? What did he want from her?

Seeing the confusion play across her face, he reached up and touched her hand. "Five minutes, and then I'll walk away."

She wasn't sure if it was watching him get down on his

knees, or hearing him call her by her pet name, but she gave in and allowed herself to give him the benefit of the doubt.

"Four minutes and counting."

Rising, Brandon refused to waste one moment of his precious time. "I was scared. You were everything a man would ever want in a woman. You gave yourself completely to me and you loved me unconditionally. I had never experienced that before. All my life, women were like a commodity, to be traded when a better one came along."

"Three minutes."

"But then you came along and shattered everything I thought I believed. And when you wouldn't give me the time of day, even though I was your best friend's brother, I knew you were something special. And when we finally got together, our passion, intensity, and attraction blew me away. But when you confessed your love, I panicked. I didn't know what to do. I knew deep inside that I would probably end up hurting you, and that thought haunted me day and night. My track record was nothing to be proud of, and my thoughts became consumed with the idea that I would somehow, someway, destroy everything we built. So, in order to spare you the pain that would surely come, I figured it would be best to get out before I really screwed up. So I lied. I made it up because I believed I would eventually hurt you. But you have to believe me. I never cheated on you. Ever."

Seemingly unfazed by his confession, Tanya sat in her car. "Time's up."

"I love you, Tanya. Please forgive me. My life has been so empty without you."

Slamming the door, she gunned the engine and drove off . . . never looking back.

One

One year later

"Happy birthday to you . . . happy birthday to you!"

Tanya Kennedy forced her lips into a small, tentative smile while her friends sang the familiar song way off-key. Judging from the sounds coming from their lips, the natural conclusion any person with ears would make is that no one in that room could claim to be musically inclined. Voices went flat when they should have gone sharp, and the concept of harmony eluded everyone.

As the group of about forty finished the final words of the verse, Tanya willed her smile to remain in place, secretly pleading that a second round of notes beginning with the words "how old are you?" wouldn't start. Tonight's celebration aimed to commemorate her special day, but Tanya wanted absolutely zero reminders of the number of years that had passed since her birth.

"Make a wish and blow out the candles!" someone yelled from the back of the room.

The jumping flames from the thirty-five candles taunted Tanya and confirmed what she had been trying to avoid for the past few weeks. As with a dark cloud hovering in the skies before a storm, Tanya had anticipated this day with the same enthusiasm she would a root canal.

As she tried to make a fake laugh sound genuine, her light

brown eyes scanned the room at her group of friends and colleagues who had gathered to honor her on her birthday. On any other occasion, she would have been thrilled to see so many of her friends. But as she prepared to extinguish the flames before the wax melted into the icing, one question kept running through her mind: how much longer would she have to endure a party that forced her to celebrate an occasion she would have preferred to forget?

The ballroom at the Capital Hilton in the nation's capital buzzed with excitement. Decorated in the elegance of gold and black, buffet tables lined the walls and the floral centerpieces centered on Tanya's favorite flowers, calla lilies. A DJ spun the sounds of the latest dance grooves and had the guests shaking and moving on the dance floor. Only the chef wheeling the cake into the middle of the floor with an overexaggerated flourish caused the music to die down and the crowd to quiet.

Tanya's original plans for this day had included words like "quiet" and "low-key." Renting her favorite movies, ordering a pizza, and lounging around her house alone were the only things on her birthday to-do list. Dreading this day the past few weeks, she had implemented a "no fuss" rule and thought everyone around her agreed to abide by the rule. Unbeknownst to her, her friends had had other ideas. It started when her good friend Christine Ware pressed her to at least go out to dinner. After much cajoling, Tanya finally relented.

With Christine's husband, Damian, not due back from a business trip until tomorrow, Christine convinced Tanya that she would actually be doing her a favor by keeping her company for the evening. Christine's sweet demeanor gave Tanya no reason to suspect that the "quiet dinner" she talked about treating her to was actually a full-blown surprise party.

Mingling with the guests and accepting hugs, kisses, and well-wishes, Tanya realized she should have figured out that something out of the ordinary was up long before she arrived at the hotel.

Her first clue? Christine suggested they ride together. Typically, whenever they went out to dinner, they met at the restaurant.

The second clue? Christine suggested they dress up, since technically, she reasoned, January 4 could still be considered part of the holiday season.

However, the final piece of the puzzle should have fit together when Christine claimed to have to stop by a hotel to pick up a contract for her interior design company. Tanya thought it odd to conduct business so late in the evening on a Saturday night, and her antennae went up as soon as Christine mentioned it.

Parking her SUV in the hotel garage, Christine insisted that Tanya come inside with her, and that's when Tanya smelled a setup. *If she just had to pick up papers, why would she need to park the car? And why would she insist that I go with her?* But before she could express her thoughts, Christine had already shut the car door and walked halfway across the parking garage toward the elevators.

When the hotel manager met them at the entrance and handed Christine a set of papers, Tanya's posture physically relaxed. Obviously, Christine came to do just what she said: pick up contracts. So, when Christine prodded her to take one more minute to view the ballroom her company would be redoing, Tanya thought nothing of it. Opening the double doors, Christine motioned for Tanya to enter first.

The second Tanya walked into the pitch-black room, she instinctively knew something wasn't right. Smelling food, she could have sworn she heard someone giggle. The lights flipped on and people jumped out from everywhere. Christine called Tanya's expression "priceless" when all the guests yelled, "Surprise!"

"I tried to talk her out of it," Natalie told Tanya a few minutes into the evening.

Christine's half sister, Natalie Donovan had only known

Tanya for about a year, but in that time the two women had become the best of friends. As the controller for Christine's interior design firm, Natalie also ran a nonprofit foundation to help minority businesses manage their finances properly.

"I know you didn't want a big celebration, but there was no stopping her," Natalie continued. "I even told her it would be better to wait until Damian returned, but Christine insisted that birthdays should be celebrated on the actual day."

"Thanks for the effort, Nat. At least you tried," Tanya replied, cutting her eyes to the guests enjoying wonderful food and drinks. "You would have thought the words 'I don't want to do anything to celebrate my birthday' would have been enough of a clue, but I can see that my wishes meant absolutely nothing."

Fearing they had actually made her day worse instead of better, Natalie frowned and said, "Please don't be mad. Christine just thought that because you were dreading this day, sharing it with people who cared about you would make it bearable . . . if not enjoyable."

Giving a half smile, Tanya squeezed her hand to reassure her. "I'm not mad. Actually, I'm almost enjoying myself."

"Good."

Not wanting to continue being the wet blanket at her own party, Tanya opted to change the subject. "By the way, is Russell here?"

"Oh, please, girl," Natalie hissed, rolling her eyes in agitation. "That two-timing, no-good bum? I dumped his tired butt last week. Can you believe he actually tried to convince me that the remains of some edible panties I found on his sofa belonged to his mother?"

"Well, maybe . . ." Tanya started sarcastically.

"His mother is sixty-eight!" Natalie exclaimed.

"Some men expect you to fall for anything," Tanya said, shaking her head from side to side at the absurdity of Russell's lie. "It's as if they really think we don't have one intelligent bone in our entire body."

"I think it's more that men think we are so desperate to find a mate that we'll put up with anything they dish out . . . regardless of how ridiculous it is." Natalie paused and added thoughtfully, "I might want to get married and have a family, but I'm not so desperate that I'll settle for just anything—or anyone."

"I hear you," Tanya answered, nodding in agreement. "But I'm sure you won't have to settle. You're a beautiful person, inside and out."

Natalie, hearing those words, appreciated the compliment. At twenty-nine, she had overcome growing up with an absent father, a bitter mother, and a weight challenge that haunted her all through college. But today, comfortable in her size twelve, she no longer felt inferior when she stood beside someone like Tanya, who wore a size eight. With her black chin-length hair, sparkling eyes, and a good heart, Natalie was happier than she'd ever been. She had her career at Christine's interior design firm, and her nonprofit organization. Professionally, these were the best of times for her.

"Oh, no," Natalie cried, glancing across the room.

Following her gaze, Tanya saw Christine standing next to a fairly attractive man, waving to get Natalie's attention.

"Who is that she's standing with?" Natalie asked suspiciously.

"That's Nicholas Moore, one of the foremen at the construction company . . . and I believe he's single," Tanya answered, amused at the entire scene. It was no secret what Christine was up to.

"I swear, Tanya," Natalie said through clenched teeth while continuing to outwardly portray a smile, "if she tries to match me up with one more person, I will scream."

Laughing, Tanya answered, "Judging by the way she's looking at you, get ready to scream."

"I'm heading for the buffet." Turning her body away from them, Natalie refused to make eye contact with her half sister. "Maybe she'll get the hint."

"I don't know if I would reject him so quickly. If I remember correctly, he's not only single, but he's handsome and nice. This might not be such a bad hookup."

Natalie took another quick glance and thought about getting introduced to yet another one of Christine's picks. "He is cute," she started, beginning to ponder accepting the introduction. But Natalie quickly changed her mind when she remembered the last guy Christine thought would be "perfect" for her.

A friend of a friend of a friend, he could have been the one for her—if it weren't for the repossessions, the two ex-wives, the four children, and the fact that, even though he claimed to have been diligently looking for the past two and a half years, he had yet to land a job. "I think I'll still head over for the food."

Tanya smiled as Christine's frustration showed on her face. Not deterred, Tanya watched Christine lead Nicholas right over to the stuffed shrimp . . . right next to Natalie.

Now, hours later, Tanya stood behind the three-layer cake taking part in the most traditional part of the evening.

Taking Christine's advice to dress up, she wore a deep purple velvet lace-up top with flare sleeves and a black pencil skirt. Pinning up her shoulder-length cinnamon hair, she accented the ensemble with gold earrings and a matching necklace. Elegant and traditional, she had to admit that the clothes helped maintain some level of a festive mood.

As she prepared to blow out the candles, a sense of nostalgia and longing that had hovered over her the past few weeks began to rear its ugly head. Without warning, she felt the sting of tears in the corner of her eyes and blinked several times to keep the drops at bay.

Flashes of past birthday celebrations flooded her thoughts.

As a little girl, she remembered the silly wishes she would make before blowing out the candles, an important moment for someone so young. Tanya took her birthday wishes very seriously. Before she was a teenager, her wishes centered on the latest toy or game. But when she turned thirteen, she settled on one wish and continued to make the same one up until five years ago:

Oh, birthday candles, burning bright
I make this wish, my birthday night,
A gorgeous husband, a beautiful child,
A successful career will make me smile.
Bless me, God,
With all I've asked
You're the only one
To make my wishes come to pass.

At thirteen, she had made that wish with childish innocence. At twenty-one, she had made it with passion and a strong sense of belief that her dreams were just around the corner. At thirty, she actually believed she had found the man to make all her wishes come true. But at thirty-five, the sting of reality hit her like a Mack truck. No husband. No child. And while she had experienced a successful career as a contract administrator for Ware Construction Company, restlessness began settling in. *Making a wish is a stupid tradition anyway!*

"You better hurry up and blow out those candles before the sprinkler system goes off—all that smoke is bound to set them off!"

Laughter from the crowd bought Tanya back to the present. Leaning forward, she hesitated briefly to silently recite the wish one last time. It had been five years, but so what? Maybe this time . . .

As she blew across the cake until she ran out of steam, the

guests jokingly booed and sneered, pointing out that a few remaining candles burned brightly.

Not amused, she quickly extinguished the few remaining candles and reached for a knife. Preparing to cut the first slice, she paused when the crowd parted down the middle of the room, allowing a clear path to her.

Everyone attending her party would probably agree that the time was nearing when she could check "husband" off her wish list. With Tanya's having dated him a little over a year, Martin Carter had defined the term husband material. A graduate from a top business school, Martin not only ran a successful software development company, but newspapers and magazines profiled him continually for his contributions to charity work—not just with his money, but with his time. Having just helped Martin to his first term in Congress, Gavin Blake, his campaign manager, and now his chief of staff, made it known that adding a wife, and a baby or two, to the official publicity photos would do wonders for Martin's career.

In their recent discussions, Tanya had carefully side-stepped the conversations that leaned toward moving their relationship to the next level. There was no doubt in Tanya's mind that for Martin the next level meant the diamond engagement ring and everything that came with it. And as she stared at another year of life, Tanya had to admit that she greatly wanted those exact things. Her only challenge? She just couldn't quite convince herself that she wanted them with Martin.

Beginning his political career when he had run for freshman class president in high school, he went on to hold several offices during his college and graduate school days. He continued in the political arena by serving in local and county government, before taking the jump to being a state representative. With a platform built around his commitment to improve the public school system and putting children first, his first time running, he narrowly beat his opponent, an incumbent who had served twenty-four years.

Having escorted Martin to several political functions, Tanya had witnessed firsthand the admiration and the high opinions others had for him. Everyone respected his business mind and his political savvy, but women took their adoration one step further by taking note of his muscular frame, his smooth walnut complexion, and the fact that he was fine, single, and financially set. Tanya's coworkers offered to pay for psychiatric counseling every time Tanya considered breaking it off with him.

The lingering looks, the soft touches, and the breathy laughs of other women didn't go unnoticed by Tanya. However, instead of feeling jealous or insecure, she found their tactics humorous. It never ceased to amaze her how some women would make a spectacle of themselves—all to gain a man's interest. But to Martin's credit, he never paid any attention to those women, or their obvious passes. Tanya often wondered if that was because of his commitment to her, or the fact that he was a public, political figure.

A symposium on traffic challenges facing the metro area had promised to be a brainstorming session on handling the growing congestion in the Washington, DC, area. Contract administrator for Ware Construction Company, Tanya had spoken as a representative of the construction industry, while Martin discussed the different options that politicians were considering.

Afterward, claiming to be intrigued about her ideas on improving the traitorous rush hours, Martin invited her to dinner. But after sitting in the restaurant for a few moments, it became quite obvious to Tanya that traffic patterns and lane expansions were the last thing on Martin's mind.

While there were no fireworks or immediate sparks, Tanya found him to be interesting, kind, and considerate. Finding comfort in their developing relationship, she had invited him to Christine and Damian's wedding reception last December. Since that time, they'd been a couple—attending political functions, enjoying leisurely dinners, and taking in the sights and sounds of Washington, DC.

But as Tanya faced another year, she found herself taking stock of every area of her life. Professional and personal. As for the personal, she could no longer deny the truth about her future with Martin. Over the past year, their relationship had developed into something stable—comfortable. But there was something missing. Where were the butterflies in the stomach? The sweaty palms? The loss of breath when he walked into the room? She waited patiently for the passion—the spark—the burning fire to well up in her for him. But to this day—there was nothing.

Some would say those things didn't matter, but for Tanya they did. She'd witnessed the passion in Christine and Damian's marriage. She had even experienced those feelings herself. Unfortunately, that had been with the wrong man.

Standing beside Tanya now, Martin placed a possessive arm around her waist and smiled lovingly at her. "Before she cuts the cake, I just want to say a few words about this amazing woman."

The "ooohhhs" and "aaahhhs" from the group encouraged him, making the glint in his eyes shine brighter and the corners of his mouth curve wider. Wanting to avoid an emotional speech, Tanya attempted to continue cutting the cake. Gently, he removed the knife from her fingers and placed it on the table.

"My life has not been the same since I met this woman. She's beautiful, smart, and has brightened my days. We've had a great time getting to know each other and I couldn't have asked for a better person to fall in love with."

Tanya held her expression in place, her cheeks growing warm with embarrassment. Nudging him, she hoped he would pick up her silent signal to end his impromptu speech.

She had never liked the spotlight, and her uneasiness quickly was magnified by the man standing beside her.

Because he fit the classic mode of tall, dark, and handsome, she had tried over the past few months to focus her attention on making this relationship work. After all, she wasn't getting any younger. But it seemed like the more she forced herself to envision them together, the more she struggled. It wouldn't be fair to continue in a relationship she didn't wholeheartedly believe would work out . . . did it?

Turning her attention back to Martin, she tuned her ears to his voice. Having heard Martin give many speeches during the past year, Tanya thought it odd that if she closed her eyes, she wouldn't be able to decipher by the tone of his voice whether he was speaking about a woman he claimed to love or to a group of strangers in an attempt to garner more votes. Focusing on his speech, she felt her stomach lurch as his words registered in her mind.

"That's why I can't imagine spending the rest of my life with anyone else."

Tanya started to protest but paused and swallowed deliberately as her brown eyes widened in utter surprise. He pulled a small, black velvet box out of his jacket pocket. "Tanya Lynette Kennedy, will you marry me?"

A stickpin could have been heard hitting the floor as the room became engulfed in complete silence. Expectation weighed heavily in the air as all eyes zeroed in on her, waiting to see if she would take the unopened box presented to her. When she didn't move, Martin raised the box higher, motioning for her to take it.

Her inner voice screamed *no!* as her body responded with rigid silence. Opening and closing her mouth twice, she had no idea what to say. Tanya stared at the small box but didn't reach out to take it. Fear raced through her body like lightning. *What am I going to do?*

"Oh, my God!"

The fearful cry came from deep in the crowd, and panic flushed through Tanya. With no regard for Martin or anything else happening around her, Tanya leaped from behind the cake table and fought her way through the sea of people until she reached the source of the shriek.

"What is it, Christine?" Tanya asked, breathless and filled with anxiety.

Holding an expression crossed between pain and excitement, Christine declared, "I think my water just broke."

Tanya stared at Christine in disbelief. "Did you say what I think you just said?"

Christine nodded in the affirmative, feeling the stain in her clothes grow.

"But it's not your due date!" Tanya exclaimed, as if that revelation would change the current situation.

"Tell that to the baby!"

The commotion that followed gave Tanya a momentary reprieve as all the attention was taken off her and placed on the woman who appeared to be going into labor—two weeks early.

With Martin promising to take care of the party guests, getting Christine to the hospital and contacting Damian became the only priority for Tanya.

Tanya tried Damian on his cell phone. Getting no answer, she left a message and then tried his hotel room. No luck. She had to leave another message. With him in New York on business, Tanya checked her watch and prayed that he received the message in time to catch the last shuttle back to Washington, DC.

As she pulled out of the hotel parking lot, Tanya's sweaty palms sharply contradicted the cold January air. Her nervous anxiety level that had started to rise with Martin's marriage proposal continued to escalate with every second that passed. "Are you comfortable? Should you be lying down? How much time do you think we have?"

Laughing lightly, Christine said, "Tanya, calm down. I'm fine. And we have plenty of time before anything will happen."

Fifteen minutes later, the car turned into a stone-paved circular driveway. "I can't believe you wanted to come home first. I should be taking you straight to the hospital. If Damian knew this, he would have conniptions."

"Well, we just won't tell him," Christine answered, giving Tanya's hand a reassuring squeeze that relayed the message *Everything is going to be fine.*

Putting the car in park, Tanya worked to get the house key off Christine's key ring. "I'll leave the car running with the heat on while I run inside and get your bags."

Opening the door, Christine said, "Don't be ridiculous. I'm not going to the hospital without taking a shower and putting on some fresh clothes."

Tanya jumped out of the car, walking briskly just to keep up with her. There was no use in arguing. When Christine's mind was made up about something, there was no changing it.

Opening the front door, they stepped into the foyer and Christine headed straight for the spiral stairs leading to the second level. "My doctor's number is by the phone in the study. Can you call and tell her we'll be at the hospital in less than an hour?"

Tanya, a guest in this home many times, made her way down the hallway and into the study. Turning on the Tiffany lamp, she reached for the phone and paused. The small Post-it note on the mahogany desk glared at her, commanding her full attention. The words seemingly shot off the paper, causing her to retreat two steps. Her heart rate accelerated and the slight throb in her temple signaled the rush of blood to her head. Dropping her eyes from the name, she read the additional information just below it. *January 18, United, flight 543, 5:30 P.M.*

Was it not enough that she had to celebrate her most depressing birthday with an unwanted surprise party? Was it

not enough that she got a marriage proposal from a man
she wasn't sure she wanted to spend the rest of her life with?
Was it not enough that her friend's labor started early and she
wouldn't go straight to the hospital?

Obviously, God had decided to see just how much Tanya
could bear in one night, because this latest bit of news definitely tested what little strength she had left. With seemingly
little information, Tanya had no problem deciphering exactly
what the words on the small yellow paper meant. It had been
twelve months since he left, and five years since they'd been
a couple. But all that time apart was about to end. He was
coming back. Brandon Ware was coming home.

TWO

Broken heart. Crushed soul. Wounded spirit. That's what he had given her when he turned his back on her and never looked back. With everything she had in her, Tanya had worked hard to erase all feelings she had had for him when their relationship ended five years ago. Love? Erased. Passion? Gone. Complete devotion? Obliterated. There remained only one feeling she hadn't been able to extinguish. Pure, unhindered anger.

As she closed her eyes to calm her racing heart, his face flashed in her head and she cursed as his seductive eyes, smooth skin, and quirky grin came into focus. At six feet one, with a runner's body and a handsome face, Brandon Ware would put any Hollywood leading man to shame.

She recalled the romantic dates, the steamy nights, and the declarations of love, and the beginning of a smile tipped the corners of Tanya's mouth. But as thoughts of betrayal and lies crept up, her mouth took on an unpleasant twist and the taste of bitterness settled in.

"Tanya," Christine yelled, "did you find the number?"

Snapping out of her daze, Tanya picked up the receiver and pushed Brandon Ware back where he belonged . . . out of her mind. "Umm, yeah. I'm calling Dr. Palmer now."

Forty minutes later, Tanya impatiently waited at the administrative desk at Georgetown University Hospital while the nurse put together the set of forms that needed to be filled out. Grabbing the clipboard, Tanya stood to the side, quickly filling out all the information she knew. The faster she could get this done, the sooner she could join Christine, who'd already been wheeled to the maternity ward. Putting on a brave front, Tanya wasn't fooled by Christine's air of calmness. The last thing a woman wanted to be at a time like this was alone.

Just as Tanya handed the forms back to the nurse, her cell phone rang and her sigh of relief echoed when she recognized the number. Damian. As Tanya pushed the TALK button, the nurse loudly cleared her throat and pointed to the sign posted on the wall. PLEASE TURN OFF ALL CELL PHONES AND PAGERS. USE OF THESE DEVICES PROHIBITED INSIDE THE HOSPITAL.

"I'll call you right back, Damian. I can't use my cell phone inside the hospital."

Stepping into the crisp, winter air, Tanya shivered as she pulled her coat tighter and redialed the number. A few minutes later, she reentered the hospital humming an upbeat tune and sporting a genuine smile for the first time that evening. Damian had gotten her message and had just boarded the plane. He'd caught the last flight out of LaGuardia and would be arriving at the hospital in less than an hour.

Making a quick stop in the waiting room to grab a much-needed cup of coffee, Tanya couldn't wait to tell Christine the good news.

"There you are."

Retrieving her coffee from the machine, she hesitated before turning around to face Martin. She wouldn't be able to avoid him forever, but somehow she had hoped to put this conversation off as long as possible.

Removing his wool coat, he sat on one of the cushioned chairs, motioning for her to sit beside him. "How is Christine?"

She blew on her coffee and began to ramble. "She's fine, Martin. As a matter of fact, I'm on my way to her room now.

Hopefully they've settled her in. Damian called. He should be here within the hour. He caught the last flight out of La-Guardia. The airport is only about ten minutes from here, so I don't think he'll miss the grand event."

She shifted uneasily from one foot to the other; the nervous gesture didn't go unnoticed by either of them.

A few uncomfortable moments of silenced passed and Tanya took a sip of coffee to occupy her hands. Searching for the right words, she finally sat and turned to him. "About what happened at the party . . ."

Martin sat forward and forced a laugh. "I think the saying is 'saved by the bell.'"

Her confused expression prompted Martin to continue. "What happened at your party when I asked you to marry me . . . you were saved by the bell. Or should I say 'by the scream'?"

His weak chuckle signaled that his lame attempt at humor had failed.

Finding her nervous energy too hard to contain, Tanya walked to the other side of the room, hoping the right words would come. "Martin, I . . ."

Holding his hand up, he shook his head. "You don't have to say anything."

"I want to—"

"Tanya," Martin interrupted, "I want you to know that I love and care for you deeply. You're kind, considerate, and I want to spend the rest of my life with you."

With sincerity and truth, she answered, "I care for you too, Martin."

Moving to stand in front of her, he removed the coffee cup from her hands and placed it on the table next to a pile of magazines. Pulling her hand to his mouth, he gently kissed it. His eyes, filled with questions, clung to hers, desperately seeking to analyze what reflected back at him. "I know you care for me, but I want to know if you love me."

The empty waiting room of a hospital didn't seem to be the appropriate place to have such a personal conversation, but Tanya felt the need to answer his question with a few questions of her own. "Does your heart skip a beat when I walk into the room? Do you find yourself anxious with anticipation each time you know you're going to see me? Does the thought of living without me put the fear of loneliness in you?"

Dropping her hands, he paced in front of her, frustration evident in his stride. "What you read about in fairy tales is not real life, Tanya. What we have is solid, true, and real. Can't you see that?"

Refusing to let him off the hook, she stood her ground and said, "That doesn't answer my questions. Is what we have enough for you?"

As he stepped directly in front of her, the anger that had threatened to surface seconds ago disappeared, replaced with uncertainty. "I think the better question is, is what we have enough for you?"

Startled by having that question thrown back at her, Tanya carefully contemplated her answer.

"Miss Kennedy?"

Both turned to the voice and saw a nurse standing in the entranceway.

"Mrs. Ware is asking for you."

Reaching inside his coat, Martin removed the ring box again and placed it in the palm of her hand. Closing her fingers around it, he refused to let her give it back. "Don't answer me now. Think about what I said. I'll see you tomorrow."

Martin headed for the exit and added, "Give Christine my best."

Watching his retreat, she found that confusion reigned in her heart. He was offering everything she claimed to have wanted since she had been a little girl. Why the hesitation?

Fingering the ring box, she stared at it for several seconds. Finally, curiosity got the best of her, and she couldn't resist.

As she slowly lifted the lid, her brown eyes widened in astonishment and all the air was sucked right out of her lungs. The brilliance of the ring temporarily stunned her and her jaw literally dropped. A two-and-a-half-carat emerald-cut diamond set in a platinum band with diamonds cascading down each side glistened in the light. Good thing she stood in a hospital. A rock like that could knock a sista out.

"Miss Kennedy?" the nursed repeated.

Pushing thoughts of Martin and the decision out of her mind, Tanya snapped the box shut and dropped it in her purse. She wouldn't see him until tomorrow so she decided to take the advice of an age-old saying. *I'll cross that bridge when I get to it.*

"Good news," Tanya said, entering Christine's private room and taking a seat beside the bed. "Damian should be here in less than half an hour. He caught the last shuttle out of LaGuardia."

Propped up against a stack of pillows, Christine pointed at the monitor that spat out line-filled paper tracking her progress. "It's a good thing, because I refuse to have this baby without him. I just had a contraction that words could never describe, and I had no one to yell at or blame for my situation."

Laughing, Tanya rubbed her friend's stomach. "I don't think you'll have to worry about that. He'd charter a private jet if he had to. As the saying goes, wild horses couldn't keep him away. Damian truly loves you."

Hearing the wistfulness in her voice, Christine started to speak, and then abruptly changed her mind. When it came to affairs of the heart, Christine knew that Tanya, an extremely private person, rarely discussed her relationship with Martin—and she never spoke of her relationship with *him*. As a matter of fact, Tanya had implemented a rule after Christine and Damian's wedding reception. Neither Damian nor Christine was allowed to speak his name in her presence—

which proved challenging at times considering that he and Damian were brothers.

But over the past few weeks, Tanya's attitude had concerned Christine. Their holidays were usually filled with shopping and social gatherings, but Tanya's participation was lackluster, to say the least. Passing on a few shopping excursions and declining a dinner invitation for Christmas were very much out of the ordinary for Tanya. Christine also recalled Natalie's comment on Tanya's pensiveness when she invited Tanya to a New Year's celebration. She turned Natalie down, choosing instead to ring in the new year with Dick Clark.

Not that Tanya had been the social butterfly in the past, but turning down dinner invitations, not wanting to go shopping, and her overall funky attitude about her birthday had provided Christine with a clear understanding that all was not well with her friend. She'd hoped the party would help, but it only worked to depress her even more.

Clearing her throat, Christine decided to throw caution to the wind. If Tanya didn't like it, then so be it. Besides, she reasoned, how much could Tanya do to a woman in labor? Watching Tanya rise and walk to the window, Christine decided to find out exactly where her friend's head was. "Martin truly loves you, too."

Without turning around, Tanya sighed. "I know."

"I hear a 'but' coming."

"Let's just say your timing couldn't have been better. I have no idea what I would have said to his question."

"It's actually quite simple," Christine reminded Tanya. "You only had two choices—yes or no."

Grinning at her sarcasm, Tanya turned to face her. "If only it were that simple. If I had said yes, it would have been horrible to tell him later if the answer is really no. I could have said no, but that would have embarrassed him. Hearing you scream was a gift from God."

"So you're saying your answer is no?"

"I'm saying I don't know what to say."

Staring intently at her friend, Christine wondered how long she would fight it. It'd already been five years. Tanya had to know by now that refuting it any longer would be fruitless. "There's no denying that Martin would probably make a wonderful husband, but we both know you wouldn't be happy."

Exhaling deeply, Tanya didn't disagree with the truth in that statement. "And it's frustrating because I don't know why. Everyone thinks I'm crazy for not wanting to become Mrs. Martin Carter."

"Not everyone," Christine answered boldly. "And I beg to differ that you don't know why."

Tanya's eyebrows shot up in surprise. "What are you talking about?"

Christine thought Tanya knew very well what she spoke of, but believed that she would never willingly admit it. "How could you marry Martin? You're in love with another man."

Tanya's expression grew dark and her olive complexion deepened as the anger started to rise.

Not giving her a chance to respond, Christine continued, "How long are you going to deny the fact that you still have feelings for—"

Snapping her hand up, Tanya stepped forward and clenched her teeth. "Don't you dare say his name!"

Knowing the raw feelings of rage were genuine didn't stop Christine from continuing. "All I know is that you claim that Martin doesn't ignite a spark—a fire in you."

"That has nothing to do with that . . . that . . . that other person," Tanya spat.

Barely able to keep the laughter out of her voice, Christine ignored her overdramatic refute and answered, "Of course it does. Every relationship you've ever had or will have will be compared to *him*. And in every case, the man simply will not measure up."

Not wanting to discuss anything remotely related to *him,* Tanya answered in a tense, clipped voice that would dissuade any further discussion on the topic. "Keep your matchmaking focused on Natalie. There is no way that that person and I will ever get back together."

"He's coming back in two weeks and I have a strange inkling that Tanya Kennedy will be the first item on his agenda."

Crossing her arms at her chest, Tanya leaned against the wall and said with confidence, "I couldn't care less about his agenda or who's on it. That part of my life ended years ago, and if he thinks any different, he's in for a rude awakening."

Before Christine could respond, she suddenly leaned forward and began to moan. Stepping to her in less than a second, Tanya grabbed her hand and began to soothingly stroke her back. Having no idea what to do in this situation, Tanya called on all of her years of watching television shows and movies. "Breathe, Christine. Take your breaths. It won't be long before it subsides."

As the pain diminished, Christine leaned back and Tanya gently wiped the small beads of sweat on her forehead.

Catching her breath, Christine relaxed back against the pillows. "Forget everything I just said about love. If this is what it gets you, stay as far away from men as you can."

At that moment the door swung open and Damian Ware stormed into the room with long, purposeful strides, panic evident on every part of his face. Making a beeline for Christine, he barely acknowledged Tanya as she stepped out of his way. As he checked his wife from head to toe, his anxiety and excitement showed in his voice. "Christine, baby, are you all right? What's going on? You weren't due for another two weeks. . . . What does this mean? Is everything fine with the baby?"

Patting her husband on the arm, Christine found his hysteria amusing. "Relax, honey. Everything's fine. What's going on is that we're about to have a baby."

Kissing her sweetly on the forehead, he couldn't believe this day had finally arrived. "Are you comfortable? Do you need anything? Where's the doctor? Shouldn't the doctor be here?"

"Calm down, sweetie. The doctor is on the way. But don't worry, Tanya has done a great job of taking care of me."

For the first time, he noticed his best friend standing by the window. Removing his heavy coat, he allowed his face to crease into a sincere smile and his eyes said a thousand thank-yous. His friend since college, Tanya needed no words from him to understand the level of gratitude he had just expressed. She had always been there for him. Tonight was no different. "Thanks, Tanya, I appreciate you taking care of my girl." Squeezing Christine's hand, he gave his wife a playful wink before turning back to Tanya. "And by the way, happy birthday. And for the record, I voted against the surprise party."

"Well, that tells me how much influence you have over your wife," Tanya answered lightly. But her words were lost on Damian, as his full attention quickly refocused on his wife.

They'd been married for a little over a year, and Tanya remembered his life before Christine had entered the picture. Focused on his business, Damian was determined to build the best construction company in the area. Recovering from a broken engagement, he failed to see the value in pursuing another personal relationship.

But the day he had walked into a business reception hosted by Christine's interior design firm, everything changed. And while they had their share of trials and challenges, in the end true love prevailed. They'd been the poster children for a happy marriage ever since they tied the knot.

Watching Damian rub Christine's stomach and whisper in her ear, Tanya felt a twinge of envy. Having spent the last year dating a man who, while steady, faithful, and a good friend, did not invoke the look of pure love that she saw reflected in Damian's and Christine's eyes, she felt the rest-lessness that had been with her the past couple of weeks returning. Inhaling deeply, she discreetly rubbed away the tear that formed in the corner of her eye and quietly left the room.

Knowing it would probably be hours before anything happened, Tanya had no real reason to stay, but she was in no hurry to go. Her party guests had surely left by now, and going home to an empty town house didn't seem that appealing to her now.

She entered the waiting room again, where the only other occupant was a young man reading to a toddler. Sitting on the opposite side, she closed her eyes and contemplated her next move. Almost eleven o'clock. It wouldn't be long before her birthday would officially be over.

"Thank God," she mumbled under her breath. But that realization did nothing but highlight the feelings she had been trying to avoid not just today, but the past few weeks. At thirty-five, was it possible to be going through a midlife crisis?

Since she had graduated from college, her life had been consumed with reaching milestones that, measured by others, would equal success. A thriving career, good friends, a successful and handsome man asking for her hand in marriage. But for some unknown reason, none of those things excited her. Her work had become mundane—almost routine. Her social activities had become repetitive, and her circle of friends had decreased over the years, as their time was now occupied with husbands, children, and families of their own.

Opening her purse, she searched for her cell phone. No need to try to solve all her life issues in one night. She would call a cab, get a good night's sleep, and think about the future tomorrow. Fishing in her bag, she came across the small velvet box. Staring at the lid for several minutes, she found the magnetic pull too great to fight. Gradually, she once again raised the lid, and the radiance of the stone stole her breath for a second time.

A picture of Martin flashed in her mind. Stable. Reliable. Loyal. Qualities any woman would admire in a man. So why couldn't Tanya get excited about spending the rest of her life with him? He adored her, treated her well, and wanted to commit himself to a wife and children.

What is your problem, girl? I know you're not still waiting for someone to ride in on that white horse? You say you want a man that makes your heart flutter and your stomach do somersaults? Well, take a memory test. You had that once. And where did it get you? A one-way ticket to Broken-heartville. You ended up hurt, alone, bitter, and ten pounds heavier. Martin is a good man. He'll do right by you . . . and you'll never have to question his love or commitment. Just say yes.

Snapping the box shut, she thought of Martin's words to her. Maybe her expectations *were* in the realm of fairy tales. A life with Martin would be comfortable, stable, and maybe she would find contentment. Her decision made, she pulled out her cell phone. Instead of calling a cab, she started to dial Martin.

"Excuse me, miss."

Looking up, Tanya noticed the woman in a nurse's uniform walking toward her.

"You can't use your cell phone in the hospital. Interferes with the machines."

Gathering her belongings, Tanya headed for the exit. Now that she had decided to accept his proposal, there was no reason to prolong giving her answer.

Punching in the last two digits, she walked briskly through the automatic doors as his phone began to ring. Closing her eyes briefly, she murmured a silent prayer that she was doing the right thing.

Not paying attention to her surroundings, she opened her

eyes and found herself inches from another person. Unable
to stop her forward momentum, she ran smack into the solid
chest of a man. Momentarily startled, she moved her eyes
from his chest to his neck, finally resting on his face.

As her eyes drank him in, she heard the faint voice of another man saying hello. Realizing Martin had answered, she
unconsciously disconnected the call as every hair on her
body stood at attention. His lips curled into a seductive grin
and the crisp air swirling around them defied the warmth radiating from his body. Deserted as this area of the hospital
was at this time of night, they were the only two people here.
Which, to Tanya, was a good thing, because before she could
stop herself, she raised her hand and, with all the brute force
she possessed, slapped him squarely across his cheek. Satisfied, she turned on her heels and headed back inside.

Three

Momentarily stunned, Brandon Ware touched the lingering sting on his cheek. Without access to a mirror, he instinctively knew that his normally café au lait skin had turned a deep shade of red. A year had passed since they had last laid eyes on each other, and he had held out hope that some of her hostility would have died down by now. But he now fully understood that while time might heal all wounds, it definitely didn't do anything for anger. As indicated by her actions, Tanya Kennedy remained just as angry today as she was the day their relationship ended.

Contemplating his next move, he watched her head back inside the hospital. Though she was dressed for the weather in a long cashmere coat complemented with a matching scarf and hat, no amount of clothing could hide the alluring curves of her body. The sway of her hips, her nice round behind, and a slim waist enticed and teased as she retreated.

Following her down the hallway, he wasn't unnerved by her initial reaction. In fact, it encouraged him. There had to be something still there if his presence warranted such a strong, emotional response. Granted, not quite the "hello" he would have hoped for, but he figured something was better than nothing.

He found her sitting in the corner of the waiting room, her head tilted back against the wall with her eyes closed. Ignoring the television mounted on the wall tuned to CNN and

the young man with a toddler sitting in chairs against the opposite wall, Brandon strolled toward her with his head held
high and an air of confidence. Without saying a word, he
took a seat beside her and waited for her to speak. He knew
it wouldn't be long.

"You must have a death wish," she said dryly, without
opening her eyes.

"And you must have an arrest wish," he shot back lightly.
"I think it's called assault."

"No court would convict me if they knew all the facts."

"Which facts?" he challenged. "The ones you think you
know—or the truth?"

As she exhaled deeply, exhaustion settled in. With the
party, Christine's going into labor, Martin's proposal, and
Brandon's appearance, Tanya's energy level dropped to near
empty. "I thought you weren't coming back for two weeks."

With an infectious grin, he said, "Keeping up with my
comings and goings?"

"Actually," she said, turning to face him for the first time
since he had walked into the room, "I'd rather just keep up
with your goings . . . like now. Why don't you just go?"

When he failed to move, Tanya rose. "Fine. I'll leave."

Stopping at the nurse's station, she tapped her foot impatiently while waiting for the nurse to get off the phone. The
faster she could leave a message for Christine and Damian
that she would be back in the morning, the faster she could
get away from him. Casually dressed in blue jeans, sweater,
and black leather jacket, he looked amazing. With a year
since she'd laid eyes on him, one thing didn't change: he was
still gorgeous.

"I hope you're not leaving on my account."

The hairs on her neck tingled as the warmth of his breath
in her ear sent a shiver up her spine. She knew he had approached before he said a word, the same way she knew he
sat beside her in the waiting room. Belaggio. A fragrance

only available in Paris. She had bought it for him when she visited years ago. The only man she'd ever smelled it on; the woodsy, masculine scent became his signature. Turning away from him, she headed for Christine's room. She would tell them herself she was leaving.

Just as she reached the door to their room, he reached out to her, stopping her dead in her tracks.

Her eyes darkened with annoyance and her shoulders squared for a battle. Wanting to scream, but remembering where she was, Tanya said in a low but lethal, voice, "Leave me alone."

At that moment, his eyes locked on hers and every emotion inside her reflected back to him. Anger. Bitterness. Betrayal. Rage. Nothing he hadn't seen before. But this time, he searched deeper, and found two things he had obviously refused to acknowledge ever since he confessed to sleeping with another woman when they were a couple. Hurt and pain.

It had become excruciatingly clear how much he had screwed things up between them. He thought his year away would have allowed time for some of her anger to subside, clearing the way for him to have the chance to show her how much he still cared for her . . . still loved her. But now he understood what "wishful thinking" really meant. If he wanted Tanya back in his life, he would first have to convince her to let him prove himself to her. Judging from the look in her eyes, he was in for the fight of his life.

Releasing her, he stepped back, and neither said a word. After several seconds, he relaxed his stance and reached into his coat pocket. Her eyes followed his movements as he pulled out a horizontal box wrapped in gold paper. Gently, he placed it in her hand. "Happy birthday."

Totally bewildered by the acknowledgment, Tanya stared at the present. *He remembered.* One of the traits that had attracted her to him years ago was his ability to surprise her—to catch her off guard when she least expected it. Every time she thought she had him figured out, he would do or say something that resulted in intensifying her attraction. Something just like this.

Placing the small box in her hand, he covered his fingers around hers. It had been so long since she let him touch her that he reveled in the minute gesture. A vague, sensuous light passed between them and he wondered if she felt it, and, if so, what she would do about it.

Tanya remained motionless as tenderness washed over her fingers, to her hand, and up her arm. A memory of this day five years ago eased into her thoughts. Cold and snowing, Brandon had convinced her to turn thirty with him—on the sunny beaches of Jamaica. Renting a private villa on an isolated section of Ochos Rios, they spent the long weekend skinny-dipping, making love on the beach, and sharing intimate thoughts and dreams. Everything that little girl had wanted when she made those birthday wishes seemed to be right at her fingertips.

Having shared the twenty-ninth year of her life with a man who possessed all that she could want in a man, she knew it was just a matter of time before the wedding bells would ring and they would be talking about starting a family. To this day, "magical" remained the only adjective Tanya could use to describe that time in her life.

The shrill ringing of her cell phone caused her to jump back and break contact. *Get a grip, girl. He's a liar and a cheat.*

Digging in her purse while awkwardly trying to balance the gift in her hand, Tanya dropped the bag, causing several things to fall out. Both she and Brandon quickly dropped to the floor to retrieve the rolling items. Grabbing the phone, Tanya glanced at the number and stood. Martin.

Answering the call, she watched Brandon pick up her wallet, a tube of lipstick, two ink pens, and the small velvet box. Raising questioning eyes from the box to Tanya and back to the box, he slowly rose and put all the items back in her purse. All except the ring box. With steady hands, he opened the lid and stared at the ring.

"Tanya, are you there?"

Searching Brandon's face for any reaction, Tanya hesitantly responded, "Yes . . . yes . . . I'm here."

"Did you call a few minutes ago? I saw your number on the caller ID, but when I picked up, no one was there. Is everything all right? Is Christine all right?"

Gently closing the box, he dropped it in her bag, his expression indecipherable. Walking past her, he disappeared through the door that led to the room of his brother and sister-in-law.

"Tanya?"

Staring at the closed door, Tanya struggled to make sense of the flurry of emotions running rampant through her entire body. Especially the stab of guilt. *Where did that come from?* "Umm, yes, Martin. I'm here, but I'm going to need to call you back. Everything's fine, but I can't use my phone in the hospital."

Disconnecting the call, she attempted to digest all the wild events of the night. Concluding that she had reached her emotional limit, Tanya no longer wanted to talk to Martin, Christine, or Damian. All she wanted to do was go home, climb into her bed, and pretend that Brandon Ware had not just weaseled his way back into her life. Stopping at the nurse's station, she used their phone to call a cab. One minute later, she headed for the exit.

Brandon stood just inside the hospital room, hidden from the occupants by a green curtain. Instead of immediately making his presence known, he took several deep breaths and analyzed what the last few seconds had revealed.

Was that an engagement ring? Did it belong to her? Was she getting married? Searching for a plausible explanation, he felt the room grow warm, and sweat formed on the tip of his brow. Taking off his coat, he hoped to relieve some of the heat that had risen up in him.

Though Damian had never betrayed his friendship with Tanya to Brandon, Brandon had gotten enough out of his brother to know that she was dating someone, but he didn't think it was serious. Well, if an engagement ring didn't say "serious," he didn't know what did.

"Did I hear someone come in?"

Hearing his brother's voice pushed his thoughts back to the present, and a relaxed smile replaced the worry and apprehension evident just a few seconds ago. "You sure did."

The curtain jerked back and Brandon felt some of the stress immediately dissipate as he embraced his older brother in a hug.

"What are you doing here?" Damian asked, stepping back to get a good look at his younger brother. "I thought you weren't coming back to DC for another two weeks."

"The LA office is up and running with a managing partner in place. I saw no need to stay the extra time. I changed my flight and got back in town earlier today. I got your voice-mail message . . . so here I am."

"For good?" Damian asked.

"We'll see."

Damian's disapproving look didn't escape Brandon, but he chose to ignore it. When Brandon announced that he had decided to head up the opening of his law firm's office in LA, Damian knew he was taking the coward's way out of dealing with his feelings for Tanya, and told his brother those exact words. But Brandon insisted that he had to get away. Seeing Tanya with Martin at Damian's wedding reception proved to be more than he could bear. He couldn't face the fact that Tanya wanted nothing to do with him.

"Damian," Christine said from behind the curtain, "who is it?"

"Hope you're decent?" Brandon asked, walking around

the partition. Moving to her bed, he leaned over and kissed her on the cheek. "You're starting this party a little early, aren't you?"

She laughed with him, touching her belly. "This little person is anxious to come out and see the world."

Suddenly, Christine's smile faltered and her face contorted into an expression too horrendous to describe.

Rushing to her side, Damian, stroking her cheek, offered encouraging words. "Breathe, honey, remember your breathing."

As she fervently panted, it was obvious by the sounds coming from deep in her gut that "just breathing" wasn't doing much for the pain.

Grabbing her husband by the arm, she sat forward and her eyes turned ice-cold, her stare burning right through him. Seething with pain, she almost shouted, "That stupid Lamaze class was a bunch of bull and a waste of good money."

"Sweetheart—" Damian started.

"Don't you dare 'sweetheart' me!"

"Listen, baby—"

"No, you shut up and listen," she hissed through clenched teeth. "I'm running this show and I want you to take you and your stupid breathing advice through that door and find me a nurse and get me some drugs."

"Christine—" Damian started, attempting to calm her.

"Now!"

Damian couldn't move fast enough and Brandon tried unsuccessfully to hide his amusement. Stories of women becoming a completely different person during labor were famous. But to witness it firsthand could only be described as priceless.

Following his brother to the nurse's station, Brandon waited patiently while Damian spoke in a quiet but stern voice to the head nurse. After patiently listening, she gave them both a sympathetic look and left to attend to Christine.

"Look, Damian, I'm going to head out. I just wanted to stop by and make sure you guys didn't need anything."

Knowing that his wife was in good hands with the nurse, Damian took a moment with his younger brother. "Did you see her?"

"Excuse me?" Brandon asked, feigning confusion.

Not buying his innocent act, Damian folded his arms across his chest and chastised his brother with his eyes. "I left you a message that said Tanya was bringing Christine to the hospital. Even a commitment-phobic guy like yourself knows it would be hours before she actually had the baby."

Putting his hands in his pockets, Brandon shrugged. "First of all, I resent your description of me, and secondly, what's your point?"

"My point is, you're not fooling anyone—especially me. You've obviously been on a plane most of the day, yet instead of going home you come straight here. I know you love Christine and me, but we weren't the reason you came to the hospital tonight. You only came because you were hoping to see her."

Brandon started to protest, but Damian cut him off.

"A word of warning, little brother—I don't know if that was such a smart idea. I don't think she's forgiven you yet . . . and I can't say that I blame her."

Brandon's facial expression stayed unchanged. The last thing he needed was a lecture from his brother on his treatment of women. "Don't you think you should get back to your wife?"

Peeking down the hall, he saw the nurse leaving her room and Damian relented. "Fortunately for you, you're right. But this conversation isn't over."

"Yippee!" he sarcastically answered. Putting his coat on, he retrieved his cell phone from his pocket. "I'm going home. I'll call you tomorrow."

"Who are you calling?"

"I caught a cab from the airport."

Reaching into his pants pocket, Damian gave him a set of keys. "Take my car. I'm not going anywhere, and besides, we have the truck here if I absolutely have to leave."

"Thanks, Damian. I'll call you tomorrow."

As he stepped through the automatic doors, Damian's assessment of him turned over in his mind. Commitment-phobic? It was true that Brandon's reputation as a young up-and-coming attorney could put any confirmed bachelor to shame. When he had begun his career almost ten years ago, his daily routine consisted of spending his days in the court-room and his nights on the town. Brandon's partying had been described as legendary.

Whenever he had stepped out, a beautiful woman always graced his arm. Models, business owners, and even a princess had enjoyed his company. But all that changed the moment he met her. A match made in heaven. Tanya Kennedy caused a one-hundred-and-eighty-degree turn in just about every area of his life. The problem in their courtship only surfaced when he let fear rule him. With his twisted logic, he cowered to the pressure of being in a committed relationship and confessed to a crime he didn't commit.

Arriving in DC a few hours ago, he had checked his messages in LA while waiting for his luggage. The last voice he expected to hear was Damian's, informing him that Christine had gone into labor early and Tanya had taken her to the hospital. Intending to take a cab straight home after such a long flight, Brandon, without hesitation, changed his plans, stored his bags, and headed straight for the hospital.

His brother's accusation hit the target dead center. Brandon only came because he hoped to see her. A hospital didn't strike him as the best meeting place, but he couldn't pass up the opportunity to see her.

Crossing the parking lot, he spotted a lone figure sitting on a bench under a streetlight near the emergency entrance.

Checking his watch, he wondered why she was sitting by herself this late at night. Didn't she know this wasn't the safest thing for her to do?

Tanya spotted him the moment he left the building and refused to acknowledge him, although ignoring the presence of Brandon Ware could be extremely challenging. With his well-groomed appearance, his air of authority, and the confidence of someone great, Brandon managed to be magnetic and captivating without crossing into arrogance. Tanya had once found every one of those characteristics attractive. Now, they were simply qualities she blocked out of her mind . . . just like him.

Peering down the street, she hoped to see headlights coming into view. The cab company said that they would be there in less than ten minutes. It had already been twenty.

Hearing his approach, Tanya adjusted herself on the bench so her back faced him. If she ignored him, maybe he would just evaporate into thin air.

"Cold out here tonight. Quite a change from the weather in LA."

No response.

"Need a ride?"

Silence.

Blowing on his hands, he tried again. "I pass your house on the way home."

Nothing.

Since chivalry wasn't working, he decided to change his strategy and lure her into speaking to him by doing the one thing that always got her talking—a challenging statement. "Whoever gave you that ring shouldn't let you sit on a bench outside a hospital, in January, at eleven o'clock at night, all by yourself. Anything could happen."

Her jaw clenched and Brandon knew she battled with her will to hold back a reply.

"What's his name again? Melvin, Marcus, Mitchell . . ."

Rising, she still refused to face him. "His name is Martin and my standing out here has nothing to do with him. I know a cab will be here shortly."

Snapping his finger, he sarcastically answered, "Ah, that's right . . . Martin. Well, if I were old Marty, I wouldn't care what you knew. There would be no way my woman would be sitting by herself, on a wooden bench, in forty-degree weather, waiting on a cab."

Refusing to be baited by his words, she answered with silence, the only sound being the sirens of a distant ambulance.

"You know, Tee, all the engaged women I know don't keep their ring in the box. Especially when it's a rock like that."

When she failed to answer, he stepped in front of her, raising her chin with his fingers. Forcing her eyes to meet his, he continued. "Unless they haven't said yes."

She cast her eyes downward, and that move told him all he needed to know. She wasn't lost to him yet. As long as that ring remained in that box, they still had a chance.

Inhaling his smell, she felt her emotions betray her, and she slapped his hand away.

Not intimidated by her response, he shrugged. "Of course, a diamond is so ordinary—so common. Any man who really knew you would think twice—maybe three times—before getting you that type of stone. Me? I would never have gotten you a diamond."

Stuffing her hands deep in her pockets, she remained nonchalant, giving no indication that his statement actually piqued her interest.

"No, you're definitely not a diamond kind of woman," he stated thoughtfully. Taking a step back, he perused her, without hurry, from head to toe. "You strike me more as a woman deserving of a ruby. With its deep red coloring—it's full of passion. Full of intense fire. Just like you."

Giving further thought to his analysis, he moved in closer. "But maybe he hasn't seen that side of you. Maybe you've kept things cool with him—almost aloof—like a diamond. I, on the other hand, have experienced your intense fire. Your unbridled passion—firsthand."

Unable to deny that truth rang in his statements, Tanya gave no credence to his words by responding. If she honestly compared the two relationships with Martin and Brandon, there would be no contest.

Intense. Passionate. Powerful. Potent. Intoxicating. Lethal. Explosive. Those were the adjectives describing her and Brandon's time as a couple. But in a relationship that intense, the breakup has the potential to be devastating. And it was.

Of course, when times had been good between them, Tanya thought they would be together forever. In the end, however, the only thing she could claim when he snatched their future away was a third-degree burn of the heart. That experience, with him or anyone else, she had no intention of reliving.

Focusing on the oncoming headlights, she hoped they were attached to her cab. Flippantly, she finally answered, "It's irrelevant what you think."

Seeing the headlights himself, he knew he only had a few seconds. Stroking her cheek, he reveled in the fact that she didn't push his touch away. "It's not about what I think, it's about what you feel."

Slowly, he ran the back of his fingers down her face. His voice, purposely low and seductive, grazed her ear as he whispered, "When he touches you like this, does your heart skip a beat? Does your mind lose its train of thought? Do you wonder how you could survive without him? Because all those things describe how I feel about you."

Closing her eyes, she inhaled deeply and allowed his soft touch, signature scent, and mellow voice to caress her senses. Then the flash of betrayal ignited in her mind and, once again, she pushed him away, moving completely out of his reach.

"You know," he started with a slight curve of his lips, "you keep this up and I really will be able to bring you up on assault charges."

Relieved that her cab had finally arrived, she stepped around him and opened the door. "What I feel is no longer your concern. Have a nice night."

As the cab pulled off, Brandon headed for Damian's car with a confident smile. There was still something there. For a quick moment, he had seen the anger subside when he touched her. It wasn't much, but it was enough to encourage him. Battling some of the greatest legal minds in the country paled in comparison to the challenge that lay ahead of him. He recalled poring over laws, statutes, and cases, searching for the one thing that would turn his entire case around and give his client the victory. When it came to winning Tanya back, he would have to be just as tenacious, just as focused, and just as determined. He had no choice. Trying to live without her had proved fruitless. He wanted her back. The only thing he had to do was convince her to give their relationship another chance.

Four

Tanya glanced at the clock beside the bed and moaned. It had been almost midnight when she arrived home last night; she wanted to get a few more hours of rest before tackling another day. Unfortunately, whoever was calling ruined any plans she had of sleeping in.

"Hello," she answered in a throaty voice.

"Hey, baby, I hope I didn't wake you."

Sitting up, she propped her pillows and rubbed the sleep out of her eyes. "No, Mommy, it's OK. It's almost eight o'clock and I need to get up anyway."

"I hope you're saying that because you were planning to go to church. I know you haven't been in a month of Sundays. It would do your mama so proud if you found a church that you could call home."

Mabel Kennedy had raised her children to believe that Sunday was made for church and rest. Rarely seeing the interior of one since she had moved out on her own, Tanya heard that same line every time her mother called on a Sunday morning. At least she always went to church when Mabel came to visit . . . and she reasoned that something was better than nothing. If it were up to her mother, Tanya would be in service on Sunday, Bible study on Tuesday, choir rehearsal on Thursday, and visiting the sick and the shut-in on Saturday.

Skirting around the entire topic of church, Tanya asked, "Mom, did you want something?"

"Your father and I were going to call you yesterday, but I knew you'd be out celebrating your birthday. Did you enjoy the party?"

Tanya wasn't surprised that her mom knew about the party. Her parents had known Damian for years and visited with the newlyweds every time they came to the area.

"It was nice," Tanya answered dryly.

Hearing her tone of voice, Mabel's concern rose. "Just nice? Didn't you have a good time?"

Tanya and her mom shared a good relationship and the basics of everything that happened in her life. Knowing that if she didn't tell her, either Damian or Christine would, she rehashed the events of the night before.

Mabel listened carefully and let Tanya finish the complete story before she spoke. "Sounds like you had a busy day. Turned thirty-five, got proposed to, rushed your friend to the hospital, and ran into your ex-boyfriend. So, did you say yes to the marriage proposal?"

"I haven't given him an answer yet."

"Um-um," her mother said thoughtfully.

Feeling the need to defend herself, Tanya offered more. "So much was happening, we didn't really have a chance to talk."

"If you say so, dear."

Hearing her condescending tone, Tanya decided to let her mother get it out—whatever "it" was. "OK, Mom . . . go ahead, get it over with. Just say it."

Hearing the extreme sarcasm in her daughter's voice didn't discourage Mabel from speaking her mind. When it came to her two daughters, she believed she always knew what was best. "OK, you asked for it, so here it is. When your father asked me to marry him, nothing would have prevented me from saying yes on the spot—because I knew he was the one. It wouldn't have mattered how many people were around, who went into labor, or who else may have shown up that night. The answer still would have been yes. Thirty-eight years later, we're still together."

"Anything else?" Tanya asked, pretending that her mother's words didn't register with her. What her mother just described was how Tanya had always thought it would be when she was growing up. When the love of your life popped the question, there would no hesitation . . . no question as to what the answer would be. *I guess times have changed.*

"How was Brandon?"

Tanya could have sworn she heard her mother smiling through the phone. "Annoying." *And still good-looking,* she added silently. No matter what she thought of his personality and selfish ways, that was always one thing she could never deny. The man, without a doubt, remained absolutely the most handsome man she'd ever known. Their years apart had been good to him.

"Well? . . ." Mabel asked.

"Well what?" Tanya responded.

"What did he have to say?"

Tanya didn't want to discuss her relationship with Martin with her mother and she definitely didn't want to discuss her lack of a relationship with Brandon. Hoping to change the subject, she asked, "How's Daddy?"

Not fooled by her lame attempt to ignore her questions about Brandon, Mabel decided to make one more point before changing the subject. "Tanya, if I ended all my relationships because the other person made one mistake, I wouldn't have anyone in my life. And that includes you."

To any sane person, that would have made complete sense, but to a scorned woman dealing with an unfaithful boyfriend, those words meant absolutely nothing. "Is that it?"

"That's it."

"Good, because I know it's time for you to get ready for church."

Hoping her words would eventually sink in, Mabel decided to let Tanya off the hook . . . for now. After her daughter broke up with Brandon five years ago, Mabel had witnessed her work her way through a broken heart. It was torment watching her go through the tears, the bitterness, and the regrets. If she could have, Mabel would have taken on the pain herself. Depressed and angry, Tanya had come home for two weeks to try and pull herself back together.

Having visited with Tanya several times during her courtship with Brandon, and having spent time with them when they came to visit, Mabel had developed a sincere fondness for Brandon. Never excusing or hiding her distaste for him when he hurt her little girl, Mabel's initial reaction was to make the man pay for what he did to Tanya.

But last year, Brandon had called Mabel right after he begged for Tanya's forgiveness. Knowing how close Tanya and Mabel were, he had wanted to clear the air with her too. While Tanya didn't believe a word he said, Mabel reacted differently. She'd heard the sincerity and truth in his words, and believed that he still loved her daughter dearly. But she made a promise to Brandon not to interfere. To give Tanya a chance to cool off and hopefully make the decision on her own to give him another chance.

That promise had not been easy to keep, especially when Tanya's relationship with Martin became serious. Having nothing against the young congressman, Mabel just thought that he didn't appear to be the right person for her daughter. And a mother always knows.

When Tanya had dated Brandon, she was happy, alive, and enjoying life. With Martin, she seemed to just be going through the motions. Now that Martin had proposed, Mabel seriously considered breaking her promise and butting into her daughter's life. But on hearing the hesitation in Tanya's voice about accepting, Mabel thought her interference might not be necessary after all. Hopefully, Tanya would realize all by herself that Martin was not the man for her.

"Lucky for you, you're right. It's women's day and my white suit is pressed and ready to go. Danielle is going too. She's even going to wear white."

At the mention of her sister's name, Tanya's depressing mood dropped even lower. Once as close as a sister could be, Danielle had destroyed that relationship with her selfish and conniving ways. She would have any conversation with her mother—except one that centered on her younger sister. "Well, I guess you better go."

The sibling love between her two children remained rocky and Mabel frequently attempted to get them to mend their differences. After all, if you didn't have family, what did you have?

It could be argued that Danielle had made it difficult for her family to love her in the past, but she had moved back home a year ago, and Mabel had witnessed a definite and sincere change in her younger daughter. Unfortunately, trying to convince Tanya that her sister had turned over a new leaf proved unproductive. Tanya wasn't interested in hearing anything that had to do with Danielle Olivia Kennedy.

"I also wanted to know if you were coming home for your father's birthday. You haven't been home in over two years."

Tanya, long overdue for a trip to Dankerville, Georgia, population seventeen thousand, had provided many excuses for not flying down as often as she should. Then, when Danielle had moved in with their parents, all desire of visiting disappeared. Arranging for her parents to come to DC several times to see her, Tanya decided it might be time to reciprocate the gesture. Maybe a little time in Dankerville was just what she needed to get herself together. Her father's birthday, in a couple of weeks, presented the perfect time to do so. "Go ahead and put me down for the potato salad."

Her mother sighed in relief, and her happiness could be

heard through the phone lines. "We can't wait to see you, including Danielle."

"Mom . . ." Tanya warned.

Usually, Mabel let Tanya's desire not to talk about her sister slide, but this morning she'd hoped to make a little headway in getting her daughters to bury the hatchet once and for all. "I'm not sure of everything that happened between you two, but I do know that since Danielle has been back home, she's changed. It didn't happen right away, but it did happen. If you two would just talk, I'm sure you could work everything out. It would please your mama greatly to see you two patch things up."

Not wanting to agree to anything when it came to Danielle, Tanya pulled back the covers and stepped out of bed. "I'll see you soon, Mom."

Mabel heard Tanya's attempt to end the conversation, but continued anyway. "She's in the next room. I know she wants to talk to you. The least you could do is say hello . . . or happy New Year."

"Not now, Mom."

Mabel exhaled heavily; her oldest was one stubborn woman when she wanted to be. Mabel had seen Tanya dig her heels in so deep on an issue that a team of wild horses couldn't move her. Got it from her father. "Tanya, must you be so hard on everyone? It's really not an attractive characteristic."

"I'm not hard on everyone, Mother. Just her."

Mabel paused when she heard the word "mother." Tanya only pulled that formal word out when her patience ran extremely thin. It was a good thing Mabel couldn't care less about her patience level. "Just Danielle?"

"What's that supposed to mean?"

"What about Brandon? The boy said he was sorry."

"First of all, Mother, it will take much more than a tired old 'I'm sorry' from Brandon Ware to make me forgive him, and second of all, Danielle made her own bed. It's not my fault that she now has to lie in it."

"So what *will* it take, Tanya?"

"What are you talking about?"

"You just said it would take more than 'I'm sorry' for you to forgive Brandon. I just want to know what it will take."

Frustrated at her mother's play on her words, Tanya thought the time to end this call had come, before the conversation turned ugly. "Mother, you know what I meant, but if you don't, let me spell it out for you. Are you listening?"

"Yes, dear, I'm listening."

Hearing the humor in her voice infuriated Tanya even more. Her mother obviously thought the entire situation with Brandon was funny. "There is nothing Brandon could do or say to make me forgive him for what he did."

"If you say so, Tanya."

"I say so," she declared emphatically, preparing herself for whatever smart reply Mabel would counter with.

"Fine. See you in a few weeks. Love you."

Tanya paused and waited for her to say something else. But she only heard silence. It always made Tanya uncomfortable when her mother seemed to accept her statements too easily. It was as if she knew a secret that Tanya was too stupid to figure out. But Tanya decided it would be much more beneficial to her state of mind to get off the subject of Brandon Ware than to continue speaking with her mother to figure out why she was willing to drop the subject so quickly. "Love you too, Ma."

"Then go to church," she quipped.

Laughing, Tanya blew her mom a kiss and said, "Bye, Mom."

Giving one right back to her, her mother joined in the laughter and said, "Bye, baby—and tell that superfine ex-boyfriend of yours I said hi."

Before Tanya could answer, her mother hung up.

"Is there a conspiracy against me?" Tanya yelled to the empty room. First Christine. Now her mother. The last thing she needed was advice from either of them on her relationship—or lack of a relationship—with Brandon Ware. Grabbing her robe, she headed downstairs for a cup of her favorite coffee.

Danielle Kennedy stepped into the kitchen as her mother finished her conversation with Tanya. She'd been hoping that this would be the day her older sister would finally talk to her. "What did she say?"

Mabel shook her head in the negative, delivering the news that once again her older sister had declined to talk to her. Not wanting to diminish all hope of reconciliation, Mabel said, "I'm sure she'll come around real soon."

Reaching in the pantry for an English muffin, Danielle split it and popped it in the toaster without responding. It had been over a year since Tanya had said anything beyond "hello" and "can I speak to Mom?" but Danielle couldn't blame her. If the roles were reversed, she would be acting the same way.

Two years ago, if anyone had told Danielle that she would be sitting in the kitchen of Mabel and Adam Kennedy in Dankerville, Georgia, she would have doubled over in complete hysteria. But here she sat, in her parents' home, trying to rebuild her professional career and her personal relationships.

Pouring herself a cup of coffee, she half smiled as she scooped out two servings of the instant mix. There was a time not so long ago that her gourmet coffee, at sixteen dollars a pound, was delivered to the door of her Park Avenue apartment every week. What a difference a year could make.

Taking a seat across from her mom, she added some milk and began to stir. Up since six o'clock, Danielle had already completed her daily workout routine, showered, and dressed in jeans and a long-sleeved shirt. With her black hair pulled back into a ponytail, her face, devoid of any makeup, portrayed smooth chestnut brown skin. Years ago, when Danielle was at the height of her modeling career, she wouldn't be caught dead without her hair, face, and nails perfect. But since she had left the Big Apple, her long lashes and high cheekbones were the only things she wore on a daily basis that held some semblance to the life she used to lead.

"Face it, Mom, her refusal to talk to me will not go away any time soon."

"Danielle, she's still hurt and angry. You'll just have to give her more time."

Prior to her moving back home, Danielle's response to a statement like that would have been filled with snide remarks and sarcastic words about the immaturity of her older sister. Her superior attitude indicated whatever problem Tanya had with her, she just needed to get over it. But that was then. For the first time in her life, Danielle understood the impact her actions, both past and present, had on others around her. "Did you tell her I've changed? That I've learned some hard lessons?" she asked hopefully.

Mabel's heart went out to her daughter when she heard the genuineness in her voice. The day she had moved back home, everyone in the family told Mabel not to let her. Aunts, uncles, cousins, sisters, and brothers wondered how Mabel welcomed back a child who had grown up to lie, cheat, and disrespect her family and friends. Not listening to any of their reasoning, Mabel responded with a question of her own. How could a mother not take in a child in need?

There was no way Mabel would turn her back on her own child. Danielle had managed to alienate all of her friends and frustrate all of her family. If Mabel had not opened her home to her, she might very well have ended up on the street. So last year, Danielle had moved in—attitude in tow.

One would think that after experiencing incredible career success in the entertainment field, and then losing it all, the person would be humbled—ready to accept that maybe he needed to change something about the way he was living his life. Not true with Danielle. Mabel had picked her up from the airport kicking and screaming. Complaining about everything from having to fly in coach seating, to the one-and-a-half-hour drive from Atlanta International Airport in a 1990 Ford Taurus.

In that one car ride, Danielle had reminded her mother seven times that Mabel should have taken the Mercedes Danielle had offered to buy her five years before. Danielle even had the boldness to complain about the lack of stores offering trendy labels—even though she couldn't afford the smallest item from any famous designer.

Once she had settled into her old room, the complaints intensified. How could the world be so unfair? How could her friends and business associates desert her in her time of need? How could people who begged for a piece of her not too long ago not even bother to return her phone calls?

Danielle spent months in a funk. Then, three months ago, she had flown to New York at the prospect of getting a job as a regular on a cable television show. When she returned, she sadly informed her parents that someone else got the gig. Instead of blaming everyone else for the situation, as she normally did, she just chalked it up to not being a good fit and focused her energy on finding another opportunity.

From that day forward, Danielle was a changed woman. No complaining. No whining. No pouting. No moping. In fact, she began helping her parents out more around the house. Cleaning, grocery shopping, and cooking. Mabel had no idea what had happened in New York, but she thanked God that it did. It was as if she had her old daughter back.

Sighing heavily, Danielle racked her brain to figure out how she could get her sister to talk to her again. How could she prove to Tanya that she'd changed if Tanya wouldn't say more than hello to her?

"Give her time, Danielle. You have to remember, you were pretty much the devil of this family for years, and while I know you're not the same person you were a year ago, it might take some time to convince everyone else."

"I know, Mama. I know."

Reaching out and squeezing her hand, Mabel smiled. "She'll come around, baby. You'll see. She'll come around."

Sitting at her kitchen table, Tanya sipped her favorite brand of Irish mocha coffee, reading the Sunday paper. With a roomy town house located in a quiet neighborhood of Maryland, right outside the Washington, DC, line, Tanya spent most of her time in her favorite room in the house . . . the kitchen. Not because she loved to cook, but because the morning sunlight beamed through the blind-free window, and the walls, done in shades of yellow, radiated an overall ambience that never failed to relax her. And relaxation was exactly what she needed to free her mind from thoughts of Martin or Brandon.

Hearing the doorbell, she glanced at the clock and wondered who would be knocking at eight-thirty in the morning. Walking down the hallway and tightening the belt on her robe, she passed the living room, the formal dining room on the right, and her home office on the left. She tucked her hair behind her ears and leaned into the peephole. With a low moan, she banged her head against the wood door several times in frustration. *This cannot be happening!*

Wanting to choose the place and time to deal with him—if she decided to deal with him—she headed back to the kitchen. A few minutes later, she heard the door open and footsteps on her hardwood floors in the hallway. The footsteps grew louder, and suddenly he appeared.

"Coffee smells good, mind if I have a cup?"

Appalled at his audacity, she stretched out her hand, palm up. "Give me my key."

Going straight to the cabinet where she kept the mugs, he pulled down the black mug with the picture of Dunn's River Falls on it . . . one of the souvenirs he had brought back from their birthday trip to Jamaica. Adding a little sugar before pouring the steaming stimulant, he took a sip and smiled, indicating it was just perfect. "I find it quite interesting that you never asked for your key back."

"My bad," she said, flashing a sadistic grin. "I must have been too preoccupied with throwing you out of my life."

"You didn't do such a good job," he said, stretching his arms out and spinning around. "I'm standing right here."

"What do you want, Brandon?"

Noticing the gift he had given her on the table—unopened—he walked in front of her and kneeled to meet her eye-to-eye. His stare was bold and confident. "You."

Rolling her eyes, she sucked her teeth. "Good thing you're old enough not to expect to get everything you think you want."

Ignoring her gibe, he averted his eyes to stare at her left hand. "I see you're still unattached."

"And I see you're still determined to work my last nerve."

Touching her bare knee, he squeezed gently and said, "This would work much better for both of us if you give up the tit-for-tat comments."

Shocked at the impact of his gentle touch, she ignored the spark of attraction, and not too politely moved his hand, scolding him in the process. "Fortunately for me, I'm not interested in making *anything* work better for us."

Slipping into the chair beside her, he sipped his coffee. "You haven't opened my present."

"That's because I'm not interested in receiving anything you have to give me."

Sliding the box across the table until it rested directly in front of her, he smiled.

"Go ahead, open it. I'm sure you'll like it."

"If I do, will you leave me alone?" Tanya bargained.

"Why would you want the person who came to give you a ride to the hospital to meet the newest addition our family to leave you alone?"

Forgetting the fact that he had let himself into her house uninvited, that he had the nerve to touch her, and disregarding that he said "our family," Tanya leaped up with genuine excitement, oblivious that her robe came undone in the process. "You spoke to Damian?"

Studying her, Brandon scrutinized her body from head to toe. She looked the same, yet different. Her hair, a little longer and a little darker, hung unruly down to her shoulders. The silk shorts and camisole she wore highlighted her best assets, including full breasts, a slim waist, and beautiful bronze legs. Judging by the fit of her clothes, she had gained about ten pounds, but she had done that in all the right places. Seeing her like this at this time of morning reminded him of how it used to be. Making love all night and sharing breakfast in the morning.

Realizing where his eyes were focused, Tanya quickly closed her robe, but not before her body felt him. Dressed casually as he was in all black, the corduroy pants and turtleneck enticed her as the material fit his body just right, highlighting broad shoulders, a solid chest, and a very nice butt.

When they had been dating, it would take nothing more than a look, a touch, or a sweet word in her ear to get all her juices flowing. Judging from the warmth seeping to the core of her body, some things never changed. With that revelation came infuriation. How could she still want him?

Regaining her composure, she moved to the counter to add more coffee to her cup. "What did they have?"

Brandon's eyes sparkled. She wasn't quick enough. The physical attraction was still there. "A baby."

Reaching for the phone, she dialed Information. "In case you haven't figured it out yet, I don't need you. I'll call Damian myself."

Walking to her, he put his finger on the phone and disconnected the call. "First of all, Damian called me less than an hour ago. He and Christine were completely exhausted and planned to get some sleep. I'm sure you wouldn't want to disturb them."

Grudgingly, Tanya admitted that what he said made sense.

"Second of all," he added, leaning in just inches from her lips and seductively lowering his voice, "needing me and wanting me are two different things."

"How's this for clarity?" she said smartly, stepping away from him, avoiding the heat that had settled in her from his nearness. "I don't need you and I don't want you."

"I don't believe you." The statement, said factually and not arrogantly, hung in the air.

The doorbell rang again, and this time Tanya instinctively knew who it was. She hadn't called him back last night and she was sure he came for his answer. Hesitating, she wondered how she would explain to Martin why another man stood in her house at this time of morning with her still in her nightclothes.

"Are you going to get that or should I?"

"You think this is a joke?" Tanya started, her voice rising in irritation. "You pop back into my life after being in California for a year and expect me to welcome you with open arms?" Pointing at him, she made sure he understood everything she was about to say. "News flash! You cheated on me, Brandon. You slept with another woman while you claimed to love me."

Every sign of playfulness left Brandon's expression. "Tanya, I told you—"

"I know what you told me," she said, almost screaming. "First, you told me you slept with another woman. Then you told me you didn't. Either way, you lied."

Not wanting to waste time with any further games, he decided to lay all his cards on the table. "I want another chance."

Surprised at his candidness, Tanya only hesitated a moment before answering quietly but definitively, "No."

"Let me rephrase the question."

"Too late, counselor. You asked, I answered."

Hearing the chimes again, Brandon secretly smiled as the revelation hit him. The person on the other side of the door didn't have a key.

Walking down the hallway, Tanya tried to stay calm as she thought of a way to explain Brandon's presence.

When she opened the door, Martin stepped in and gave her a chaste kiss on the cheek. "Hey, honey, I figured you would want to go to the hospital, so I thought we could . . ." His words trailed off as he noticed a man standing at the end of the hall. "Excuse me, I didn't realize you had company."

Opening the door wider, Tanya stepped aside to allow Martin to enter. "He was just leaving."

"Aren't you going to introduce us?" Martin asked, staring the stranger in the eye. With primitive awareness, Martin acknowledged the comfort level of the man. Casually leaning against the wall, he looked at ease . . . content . . . as if he belonged there.

"Martin Carter, I'd like you to meet Brandon Ware."

Stretching out his hand, Martin said, "As in Damian?"

"Brandon is Damian's brother," Tanya answered.

"I see," he answered slowly.

I bet you do. Accepting his hand, Brandon said, "I understand congratulations are in order. Your first term in Congress? Must be exciting for you."

"Thank you, and it is."

Tanya tried to hide her agitation at both men. Testosterone had kicked into high gear the moment Martin made eye contact with Brandon. Standing a little taller and resting his hand on the small of her back, he made his message come across loud and clear. *This woman belongs to me!*

"Are you in town visiting? I don't recall Tanya mentioning you before."

Brandon stole a glance at Tanya and gave a slight smile. Martin meant that comment to demonstrate how unimportant he must have been in Tanya's life. But Brandon knew different. "I've been in LA for the past year opening up our new law firm location."

"And you'll be returning . . ." Martin paused, waiting for Brandon to fill in the blank.

"Actually, I'm not." Removing his coat from the coatrack, he walked past them and out the door. "It was nice seeing you again, Tanya. Take care."

Tanya inwardly simmered. But irritation wasn't the only feeling creeping through her. Once again she felt guilt.

Closing the door behind him, Martin followed Tanya into the kitchen. Eyeing the extra cup of coffee, and the unwrapped gift, he made no comment but instead retrieved a mug from the cabinet and filled it. "I came by to see if you wanted to ride to the hospital together. Maybe after we visit with Christine and Damian, we could grab brunch."

Tanya heard the polite words, but curiosity, and possibly jealousy, hovered just below the surface. The fact that she had had a man in her home early in the morning with her still in her nightgown did not go unnoticed by Martin. Figuring the offensive was the best route to take, she answered his unasked questions.

"Brandon got back in town last night and I ran into him at the hospital. He stopped by this morning to offer me a ride to see the baby."

"Is something wrong with your car?"

The question sounded innocent, but the meaning behind it was anything but. She opted for the simple answer. "No."

Martin took a sip from his cup and stared intently at Tanya. "It would be obvious to anyone why I would come by, at this time of morning, to see you. Should it be obvious why this man came by?"

"You're making too much of this." Pouring the remainder of her coffee in the sink, she headed for the back stairs. "I'm going to get dressed."

"Do you have a decision yet?"

Tanya froze but didn't turn around. Brandon hadn't been back in town for twenty-four hours, yet he had managed to upset everything in her life.

Martin stepped in front of her and cupped her chin, searching her face for answers. In that moment, he admired her natural beauty. With no makeup and disheveled hair, she was breathtaking. Forcing her to look him in the eye, he asked, "Is the decision really that hard to make?"

"Can we talk about this later?"

"Sure," he answered, dropping his hands and hiding his disappointment. "On second thought, I've got some errands to run." Giving her a peck on the lips, he headed for the front door. "I'll call you later."

Tanya stood stoically as she listened to the front door close.

A couple of hours later, she stepped off the elevator on the third floor and followed the signs for room 384. She had yet to talk to anyone, and anxiously awaited the news of whether she would be the godparent to a beautiful baby girl or a bouncing baby boy. Finding the right room, she knocked and entered.

Christine lay in bed, with Damian by her side. In the corner by the window stood Brandon, holding the baby and talking softly. The sunlight peeked through the blinds, setting off a soft glow around him, and suddenly something intense flared through her accompanied by an intangible sensation in the pit of her stomach. Drawn by the aura created by the scene, she realized she had never considered Brandon in the role of father, but at that moment she knew he would be a great father—even if the husband part remained suspect.

"Tanya?"

Snapping back to reality, she reeled from embarrassment that she had been caught staring. Trying to invoke damage control, she said, "I'm sorry, Damian. I was so taken with seeing something so small."

Brandon winked and she knew she was busted.

"Well, don't admire from afar," Christine said, "go and meet your godchild face-to-face."

Brandon stretched the baby out to her and placed the child in her arms, covered in a soft purple blanket. She pulled back the hood and gasped. Trying to catch her breath, she gulped hard as a hot tear fell silently down her cheek. "She's perfect."

Damian beamed with pride. "I'd like you to say hello to Brianna Angelique Ware."

Words were inadequate to describe the emotions that swept through Tanya's entire body as she held the tiny child in her arms. Brianna stared up at her with small hazel eyes and Tanya instantly fell in love. Overwhelmed by the unexpected rush of emotions, she inhaled deeply as the tears continued to fall.

Wrapping his arms around her waist, Brandon whispered in her ear, "Are you OK?"

Nodding in the affirmative, she walked to Damian and handed Brianna back to him. "I don't know where all this is coming from. I'm going to run to the rest room. I'll be right back."

Once in the hallway, Tanya steadied herself against the wall. Had she really almost fallen apart in there? In the back of her mind, she always knew her biological clock was ticking, but the moment she held that precious child in her arms,

every motherly sensation came flushing forward and the realization that she might never have one of her own sucked
the air right out of her. At thirty-five, she knew her time continued to slip away.

"What just happened back there?"

"Leave me alone," she answered, resuming her walk to the
ladies' room.

Stopping her, his touch sent a sensation of comfort
through her.

"It seems to me that the only thing you've been since I got
back in town is alone. I see you on your birthday, you're alone.
In the hospital parking lot at eleven o'clock at night, you're
alone. Now, there is obviously something going on with you,
and yet you're going through it alone. Let me help you."

"Go back to your brother, Brandon."

"He doesn't need me now. You do."

"I told you. I don't need—"

Without warning, he turned her to him and his lips descended on hers. Not tentatively, but with purpose and
determination. Wrapping his arms around her waist, he
pulled her close to coax a response.

Stunned by the sudden move, Tanya's first reaction was to
try and pull away. But just as she started to move back, it
swept through her like the eye of a tornado. Fire. Passion.
Butterflies. Excitement. As the events of the last few days
descended on her, she found herself leaning into the kiss as
a complete defiance to her age, her restlessness, and her
childlessness.

Brandon sensed the moment her frigid stance of resistance
melted away and she opened her mouth to allow him to slide
his tongue between her lips and taste all of her. So long since
their tongues had danced together, the passion dormant for
five years overtook him with the force of charging bulls. As
he ran his fingers through her hair, the kiss intensified as
he sucked, stroked, and glided over every part of her mouth.

He molded his body to the contour of hers, and the kiss took on a life of its own and every primitive part of him came alive. Hearing a moan from deep in her throat encouraged him and was quickly followed by moans of his own.

Hearing the erotic sound caused Tanya to jump back. *What am I doing?* "How dare you!"

Breathless, Brandon reached out to her. But it was too late, he saw in her eyes the second her mood went from passion to anger. However, Brandon refused to let her shut him out. "Tell me you didn't feel it."

Wiping remnants of his touch from her mouth, she quickly put her hands down when she realized they were shaking. Trying to slow her pounding heart, she held her head high in defiance and declared, "I don't know what you're talking about."

"The hell you don't." The words were harsher than his intention, but all doubt as to whether she still had feelings for him were erased by that kiss. God, his knees were weak and he felt as if he needed to sit down. He could see her unsteadiness as well. Not wanting this opportunity to slip away, he again reached for her.

"Tee, I know what happened between us was messed-up, but that's in the past. We deserve another chance."

"Don't call me that," she said, angry with herself for responding to his kiss. As his hands caressed her hair, her nipples stretched against her bra and every intimate part of her craved his touch. The kisses with Martin had never been like this and she hated herself for comparing the two. But as her mind fought for control of this situation, there was no denying her body's reaction.

"Have dinner with me tonight."

Emphatically, she answered, "No."

"Yes," he softly coaxed, reaching out for her.

"No." Taking a step back, she desperately needed more space between them.

This time, her answer wasn't as strong as the first one. Knowing he had already pushed her to the limit, he decided to back off and give her a chance to think. "I'll be dining at Lenny's. Seven-thirty. All I'm asking for is one dinner."

Getting no response, he took that as a positive sign. At least she didn't say no again. "You go back and visit with Brianna. I'm going down to the cafeteria."

Tanya watched his retreat and appreciated his gesture. He was allowing her time to get herself together and visit with the baby without him there to make her uncomfortable. Just as he disappeared from sight, she released a slow, deep breath. *What in the world just happened?*

Martin sat at his desk chewing on the edge of his pen. Surrounded as he was by all the traditional trappings of success, anyone who walked into this office would undoubtedly conclude that Martin Carter owned a highly profitable business. Huge desk, beautiful sculptures, original paintings, and a wall of fame dedicated to pictures of him with business and political heavyweights.

Carter Technology Services had been his ticket out of the poverty-stricken community in which he'd grown up with his parents and three sisters. Understanding that applied education could change the direction of anyone's life, he had attacked his studies with a vengeance. And when he started CTS ten years ago, he took that same determination that had gotten him through school and applied it to building the best software development company in the area. Within five years, he had touted major corporations as clients, and several lucrative government contracts.

With his first congressional term starting this month, he knew time spent in this office would be almost nonexistent. But he always found he did his best thinking inside the walls of his office at CTS, and today he needed to think.

Ever since he had left Tanya's house, the events of the morning replayed in his mind. Why was Brandon Ware at his girlfriend's house so early in the morning? Did he spend the night? What would have happened if he hadn't come by? Why did he feel as if he was interrupting something?

Careful not to appear jealous, he had opted to keep his questions to himself. However, that didn't squelch the urge to find out the answers.

Not fooled by the other man's overly friendly demeanor, he recognized attraction when he saw it, and Brandon definitely had a thing for Tanya. But the bigger question to be asked was whether Tanya felt the same way. And if so, what did she plan on doing about it? Or worse, had she already done something about it?

Spending the past year in the public eye, he had found that there were certain things that must be sacrificed. Any hint of scandal could cause severe, sometimes unrepairable, damage to a candidate. With his being young and single, the media kept an especially close eye on Martin and everyone around him. Nothing was off-limits to the press, or his opponent. Not his business, his family, and definitely not his private life.

That's the reason his relationship with Tanya had to be carefully scripted, so as not to impede his ability to get elected. Not wanting to spur a debate between family value proponents and liberal constituents, he kept his relationship with her strictly rated G. While his body screamed relentlessly to move their relationship to an intimate level, he couldn't risk any backlash from the voting population. It might seem old-fashioned, but he refused to let anything—including Tanya Kennedy—stand in his way of winning that seat in Congress.

Elected two months ago, he knew the media would watch him closely, just to see if he changed in any way. But Martin had it all figured out. As soon as Tanya accepted his marriage proposal, their relationship could be whatever he wanted. He just hadn't counted on her hesitating to answer when he popped the question.

"You must have a serious problem to call me in here on a Sunday morning."

Martin turned his attention to the man standing at the door and waved him in. With confidence, Martin answered, "Nothing you can't handle."

Stepping into the office, Gavin Blake took a seat in the leather wingback opposite his boss. "That's what they say."

Martin had met Gavin his freshman year in college. With his six feet three and two hundred and fifty pounds, one might think he would be spending his time on a football field, but that wasn't the case. Highly intelligent, Gavin thrived on politics. Not interested in being the front man, he flourished when running things from the behind the scenes.

Initially, Gavin and Martin hadn't hit it off. Martin's first encounter with Gavin occurred when he ran for freshman class president at the University of Maryland. Gavin acted as his opponent's campaign manager, but Martin didn't pay Gavin any attention.

Easily beating all of his opponents in high school, Martin didn't need anyone telling him how to run for office. On paper, there was no contest. Martin had more experience, focused on the issues, and had forged relationships with the college administration to show that he could achieve results.

But this wasn't high school, and Martin had made the amateur mistake of believing that focusing on the issues, coupled with his previous experience, was enough to win the election. This particular election, however, taught Martin lessons that he would never forget throughout his political career.

Gavin used every means available to him to sway votes his candidate's way. Some would label his tactics unsavory, others would say they were downright unfair, while still others would venture to call his actions illegal. But when it was all said and done, and the votes were tallied, Gavin's candidate rarely came up with the short end of the stick.

During this particular election, Martin's opponent sporadically spoke on the issues, but preferred to spend the majority of his campaign parading pictures of his elderly parents he was trying to make proud, as well as highlighting a fight that Martin had gotten involved in during his eleventh-grade year that resulted in a suspension. The fact that the fight occurred because Martin tried to stop a guy from hitting his girlfriend seemed to make no difference to the voting population. Martin had been labeled a troublemaker.

Refusing to give into the underhanded tricks of the competition, Martin stuck to focusing on the issues. While many of his classmates wanted to talk about the fight, or seemed sympathetic to a candidate with aging parents, Martin believed that the voting population was smart enough to see right through the smoke screen his opponent fanned out. But he grossly misjudged the constituents. On Election Day, Martin lost by a landslide and walked away with the most valuable lesson of his political career.

Very few people voting in an election wanted to actually discuss, dissect, and focus on the most important issues. The majority of the people actually liked the smoke screen strategy. It allowed them to make judgments and decisions without having to spend their own time finding out the truth for themselves. To this day, he would bet his entire company that the majority of voters in his state couldn't tell him the three major pieces of legislation projected to make it to the congressional floor this upcoming session that directly affected their state. A sad but true commentary for the state of the society.

The day after that college election, Martin had approached Gavin, making him an offer he couldn't refuse. Jump on board with him and he would take him all the way to the capital. The team of Gavin and Martin hadn't lost an election since.

Reaching for a piece of paper, Martin wrote two words and passed it on to his new chief of staff.

Glancing at the name, Gavin picked up the paper, ripped it into shreds, and tossed it in the trash. "You want everything?"

"From the nurse that slapped his bottom to what he had for breakfast this morning."

Gavin nodded and headed for the door. "I'll have a full report in a few days."

"Good."

"Who's this guy anyway? An up-and-coming?"

Shaking his head in the negative, Martin picked up a file and began to read. "It's personal."

Watching his boss focus on the information in front of him, Gavin understood their conversation was over. He shut the door on his way out.

Martin closed the file he was only half reading and leaned back in his chair. Closing his eyes, he reflected on his life. Getting into politics and making a difference was the prize on which Martin always kept his eyes. Now that the political dream was a reality, he intended to focus his attention on his next dream—a wife and family.

Tanya represented everything he wanted in a spouse. Intelligent, beautiful, and the perfect hostess. Politically balanced, Martin understood the value to his career of being with someone who wasn't too radical about any issues. Not too conservative, yet nowhere near a fanatical liberal. There was nothing he could see that would set the press against her. She was what he needed to make his life complete, and he refused to let anyone interfere with that.

Five

Brandon sat in the hospital cafeteria having a cup of coffee with his brother. Three years apart in age, they'd always shared a special bond. Damian, at six-three, had a full two inches over his baby brother, but neither suffered when it came to the ladies. Damian's sincere heart and romantic antics served him well, while Brandon's playfulness and zest for life worked best for him. Damian, having had a handful of serious girlfriends over the course of his life, knew he had found his soul mate in Christine, and Brandon, having had more girlfriends than he would ever try to count, prepared to give up his bachelor days once and for all.

"OK, big brother. Out with it. How serious is this thing with Morris?"

Damian raised his eyes at his brother, scolding him without saying a word. "If you have questions about Tanya's relationship with *Martin,* I suggest you ask her."

"She isn't wearing the ring," Brandon countered.

"Leave her alone, Brandon."

Feigning confusion, Brandon scratched his head. "First you tell me to talk to her, now you're telling me to leave her alone. Which is it?"

"You're not amusing."

Leaning forward, Brandon stared his older brother directly in the eye. "Don't tell me you're choosing Mason the congressman over your own flesh and blood."

Refusing to correct him again, Damian said, "I couldn't care less about either of you. The only person I'm concerned about is Tanya. While you may be my brother, she's my best friend."

"You've been with her this past year, do you really think she's moved me completely out of her system?"

Hearing the change in his tone of voice, Damian knew the question wasn't asked with arrogance, but with a genuine desire for an answer. But whether Tanya extinguished Brandon from her life wasn't the only issue. Brandon needed to take responsibility for his own actions, and Damian intended to make him see that. "Five years ago, you claimed to love her, yet your relationship ended because you told her you cheated on her. You broke her heart and I was there when she was trying to put her life back together."

Brandon started to interrupt, but was immediately cut off.

"Last year, you throw some story on her about your fear of commitment, which caused you to lie about sleeping with another woman, believing that just because you cleansed your soul, you could justify your lies and she would automatically forgive you."

"But—" Brandon started.

"You come to my wedding reception, claiming you want a chance to win her back, but two weeks later, you accept an assignment and move to Los Angeles for a year. Now, you show up expecting her not to have moved on with her life? Ready to fall into your arms? I can't believe you're surprised at her behavior toward you."

Hearing the recap, Brandon couldn't offer a denial. Every word spoken was the truth. But there was also another truth that he admitted to his brother. "I still love her."

Picking up his sandwich, Damian shrugged nonchalantly. "It doesn't matter. She's moved on."

Not ready to concede defeat just yet, Brandon said, "You've been around Marlon and Tanya the past year, and you witnessed our relationship years ago. Can you honestly say that he is the one she should spend the rest of her life with?"

Exhaling deeply, Damian placed his food back on his plate. "You're being childish, Brandon. You know his name is Martin."

"Mario, Mervin . . . whatever. The question I'm asking is, do you think he is the one for her?"

As much as Damian hated to admit it, he wasn't sure that Tanya truly loved Martin. But instead of encouraging his brother to confuse Tanya anymore, he opted to remain quiet.

Releasing a slow smile, Brandon leaned back in his chair. "Thanks, bro. Your silence is speaking to me loud and clear."

Tanya sat in a chair opposite Christine as she attempted to breast-feed Brianna. Dressed for the winter weather in black jeans, boots, and a burgundy sweater, Tanya wondered what it would feel like to hold her own child in her arms and nourish her.

"Finally," Christine said in victory, "she latched on. The first two times I tried this, I almost broke down in tears. It seems so easy when you're watching it on television, or reading about it in a book, but I'm here to tell you, breast-feeding is not easy. For a minute, I thought my baby was going to starve to death because I couldn't do it."

"Don't worry, Christine, I know you're going to make a great mom."

"Thanks, Tanya, I just wish my mother were here to see her," Christine said. "She would have been so proud."

Tanya leaned forward and grabbed her hand.

"I miss her so much," Christine continued. "It's so sad that Brianna will never know her grandma."

"Good thing she has a wonderful mother in you."

Reassured by her words, Christine said, "Thanks, Tanya, and I'm sure I'll be able to say the same thing to you one day."

Tanya gave a tentative laugh and sat back in her chair. "I don't know if motherhood is in my future. I'm starting to face facts that it is very possible that I will be spending my years alone."

"Ha!" Christine said, thinking of her conversation with Damian earlier that morning about Tanya and Brandon. "I think you may be speaking too soon. If my brother-in-law has anything to say about that, you'll be barefoot and pregnant in no time."

"Please spare me," Tanya moaned. "I cannot have this conversation again."

"What are you talking about?"

Tanya relayed her earlier conversation with her mother, dramatically relaying her mother's roundabout way of getting her to give Brandon the benefit of the doubt.

"Sounds like your mother is a wise woman," Christine said, raising the baby to gently pat her back.

"No," Tanya answered slowly, "it sounds like my mother has lost her mind."

"I don't know, Tanya. I saw the look on your face when you came into this room and saw Brandon holding Brianna. Your mouth can say what you want but the eyes don't lie."

"And what, please tell, did my eyes say?" Tanya asked with a mocking tone.

"They said, 'I still love you.'"

Tanya refused to dignify that ridiculous statement with a response. Instead, she reached out for Brianna and pulled her close. She smiled down on the baby, who had already fallen asleep. But that was OK with Tanya; she found contentment in just holding her.

"Haven't seen you around in a while. What's been happening?"

Brandon opened his menu and smiled at Ray, the owner of

Lenny's. Naming the restaurant after his wife, Lenore, Ray had created an atmosphere of down-home cooking with an upscale style. The restaurant, a hot spot for everyone—from college students, to up-and-coming professionals, to the over-fifty crowd—always maintained a full reservation book. "Nothing much, Ray. Just got back in town and ready to enjoy one of the things I missed when I was on the West Coast."

"What's that?"

"Your Cajun catfish."

Laughing heartily, Ray pulled out his small notepad and said, "I'll put an order in for you right now."

"Thanks, man. But hold off on that order, I'm waiting for someone."

Putting his pen behind his ear, he winked. "I bet you are. If I remember correctly, I've seen you here with quite a few lookers. I'll start you off with a beer. Be right back."

Checking his watch, Brandon stole a quick look at the door. Seven twenty-one. He took a big risk demanding that she meet him here tonight, knowing she wasn't one to be pushed into anything she didn't want to do. But he had spent the past year wondering . . . hoping . . . believing, that there was still a chance for them. And that kiss earlier had eliminated all doubt.

The physical contact had left them both reeling from the power created from it. But beyond that, he felt the emotion that was tied to that kiss. If either of them tried to deny they had a true connection, they would both be lying. However, her anger and pain could not be ignored. With all the history between them, she would fight tooth and nail to protect herself from him. Checking the time again, he let out a tentative sigh. *Don't stand me up, Tanya. Give us another chance.*

"Brandon?"

Glancing up, Brandon took in the long legs, tight leather pants, bared belly button, and short, cropped jacket. Finally, his eyes rested on her smooth cocoa-beige skin, curly auburn hair, and light green eyes. Without returning her smile, he said, "Hi, Robin."

"I thought that was you sitting over here. Long time, no see. What has it been? Two years?"

"Something like that," Brandon answered, cutting his eyes to the door. The last thing he needed was for Tanya to see him with another woman—no matter how innocent it was.

Not waiting for an invitation, Robin took a seat. Throwing back her hair, she licked her lips suggestively and slowly smiled. "If you're dining alone, I'd be glad to join you. My girlfriend and I were just having a drink at the bar, but I'm sure she would understand."

Back in the day, Brandon wouldn't have hesitated to accept her invitation. His experience with Robin, and women like her, told him that after a scrumptious meal in the restaurant, they would go back to her house and feast on each other. After graduating from law school, that had been the story of his life.

When he had ended his relationship with Tanya five years ago, he tried to convince himself that he was better off and placed himself right back into the lifestyle he thought he missed. But he found there was no satisfaction in dating women he had no interest in committing himself to. Now he focused on one goal—winning Tanya back. Not even something packaged as nicely as Robin Sampson could get him off track.

"Sorry, Robin, I'm expecting someone any minute."

Pretending to pout, Robin exhaled dramatically and poked out her bottom lip. "What a shame. We could've had a great time tonight."

Pulling a card out of her pocket, she wrote her number on the back and stood. Leaning over Brandon, she reached out and ran her hand across the front of his burgundy and black button-down shirt until she reached the pocket on the left, sliding the card inside. "If you change your mind, just call."

Watching her walk away from him, Brandon could not deny that she possessed all the attributes of a beauty queen. Any sane single man wouldn't hesitate to take full advantage of what she was offering. As she rejoined her friend at the bar, she blew Brandon one last kiss before turning around.

Reaching in his pocket, he pulled out the small card with the seven digits. Ripping it up, he dropped the pieces on the waiter's tray as he set Brandon's drink on the table. As beautiful as she was, there was nothing Robin could offer a man who had everything he ever needed and wanted in another. Glancing at the door again, he took a sip of his beer. Seven twenty-eight.

Tanya pulled her Volvo into an empty parking space and cut the engine. Making no attempt to get out of the car, she sat silently, trying to calm her nerves. Did she have the strength to do this? Was this really what she wanted? Was she acting on impulse, only to regret her decision later?

Gathering up her courage, she stepped out of the car and immediately pulled her collar tighter around her neck. She questioned whether the chill that ran through her came from the weather or nerves.

Before she made it up the walkway, the front door opened and Martin stepped out onto the small porch. "I heard you pull up."

With a tentative smile, Tanya stepped into his house.

As she followed him into the living room, the fireplace's heat engulfed her and her favorite bottle of wine rested on the table. His patience over the last couple of days should be rewarded, but she wasn't naive enough to believe that he would let her go one more day without giving him an answer.

Without removing her coat, she said, "Martin, I know you want an answer to your question."

Stepping to her, he kissed her lightly on the lips and unbuttoned her coat. "There's no rush tonight. Why don't you get comfortable? Let me get you a glass a wine."

Tanya started to protest, but realized that she could actually use a glass of the smooth merlot.

When Martin left to hang her coat and retrieve two wineglasses, Tanya took a seat on the sofa. Glancing around the room, she admired the various awards lining the wall. Accolades from the community, the business world, and his political party were a testament to his commitment to the people who had put him in office.

Determined to win this election, Martin had feared any type of negative media coverage and worked hard to maintain his image as an upstanding candidate worthy of everyone's vote. But that only pushed the media to pursue him relentlessly. The incumbent had been in office for twenty-four years, and he refused to let a young newcomer take his seat away. However, the people the incumbent served had a different opinion. Feeling the man was no longer serving his constituents, Martin found his running against him well received.

Having been a member of the city council for three terms, Martin thought he was ready to take his crusade for the people to a higher lever. With his little experience in the political arena, a campaign treasury with significantly less funds than his opponents, and being African-American, young, and single, many political analysts believed, and reported, that he didn't stand a chance.

The incumbent didn't hesitate to use all of those things against him. Especially the part about being young and single. Martin's values and morals were constantly being played out in the papers, as his and Tanya's relationship continued to grow. That's exactly why Martin refused to hint at even the slightest impropriety. Since he had officially thrown his name in the race, all of their dates were in very public places.

Standing by his side while he was on the campaign trail,

she had served as hostess many nights in this house for cocktail parties and fund-raisers. Not wanting to spur any gossip, she never spent the night at his place and he rarely stepped foot into her town house for any length of time. The last thing he wanted to do was cause the real issues of health care, unemployment, and rising taxes to be skirted by issues of marriage, commitment, fornication, and family. Sex scandals were always prime media targets, but Martin refused to let them be an issue.

But he had promised Tanya that all that would change once he won the election. With his mind now on serving as congressman instead of running for office, he was determined to make Tanya his top priority. Hence the ring.

"Here you are," Martin said, handing her a glass.

"Thanks," she answered, "I came by—"

"Sshh. Relax. We have all evening." Taking a seat on the sofa, he motioned for her to move closer. Uncorking the wine, he filled their glasses. Without saying anything, he raised his glass to her and she clinked it.

Taking a sip, she enjoyed the smooth taste as it traveled down her throat.

After several minutes of silence, Tanya started, "Martin, I know you want an answer."

Wrapping his arms around her, he stroked her neck. "Not just any answer," he said pointedly. "I want you to say yes."

Tanya shifted and faced him. This was it. The moment could no longer be avoided. She'd known her answer the moment he asked at the party, but had somehow hoped to avoid having to give it. Having experienced rejection, she understood being hurt by someone you cared about. The last person she wanted to be was the one who caused any other person to feel those same things. But in this case, it was unavoidable. Who would have thought one simple two-letter word would be so hard to say?

Standing, Martin walked over to the fireplace and stared at

the dancing flames. Her silence confirmed what he had feared before she walked through the door. "Is it because of him?"

Startled by his question, Tanya answered, "Who?"

Not turning to face her, Martin tried to camouflage his irritation. "Don't play coy, Tanya. It's not becoming on you. The man was at your house at eight o'clock in the morning, looking like he had every right to be there."

"There is nothing going on between me and Brandon."

"Yet," he mumbled.

Not wanting the conversation to turn into an argument, she retrieved the ring out of her purse and set it on the coffee table.

Seeing the box, he refused to let his emotions take over. He had not made it this far in life by letting his feelings get the best of him. What he needed to do now was think. Think about how he could get her to change her mind and understand the impact of her decision.

Throughout the past year, his only concern had been for the election. Everything and everyone else came after that. In hindsight he wondered, if he had given Tanya half the attention he gave his campaign, would she be saying yes instead of no?

"I'm not one to beg," he started, "but I want you to know that you're making a big mistake. We can make each other happy. I know it's been difficult for me to focus completely on us this past year, but now that the election is over, we can move forward with our relationship."

Tanya struggled to hear any emotion in his voice. It was like his proposal at the birthday party—she couldn't tell whether he was having a personal conversation with her or talking to a group of constituents who teetered on whom to vote for. On the way over to his house tonight, she had questioned whether she was doing the right thing. But Natalie's word rang in her ears. *Just because you want to get married and have a child doesn't mean you have to settle.* By accepting Martin's proposal, she knew she would be doing just that: settling.

"I think this is best for both of us," she said, hoping to help him realize that not only was he not the one for her, but she wasn't the one for him. This breakup would give him the chance to find someone who was truly created just for him.

"Don't tell me what's best for me," he said, his voice distant and harsh.

Tanya cringed at his tone. The space that had already begun to develop between them quadrupled in a matter of seconds. Standing, she placed her wineglass on the coffee table and headed for the foyer. Her coat lay across the banister, instead of in the closet, as if he had known what her answer would be.

Opening the front door, she stepped onto the porch just as the tears began to freely flow. No matter what the circumstances, that song from so long ago rang true. Breaking up is hard to do.

"Come now, Brandon, I prepare that catfish myself and all you do is pick at it?"

Brandon put his fork down, deciding he had pretended to eat long enough. "Believe me, Ray, it has nothing to do with the chef. I guess I just lost my appetite."

As he took the plate off the table, Ray's sympathy could not go unnoticed. "Hey, man, don't let it get you down. Why don't you let me get you another drink . . . or better yet, how about a serving of my world-famous peach cobbler? If that doesn't cure what ails you, I'm not sure what will."

Ray had the best of intentions, but the faster Brandon could get out of this restaurant, the better off he would be. "No, thanks, Ray. I think I'm going to head out. Just bring me the bill."

"Sure thing. Let me know if you need anything else."

At almost nine o'clock, Brandon had abandoned all hope that Tanya would show up. He called her at home and got no answer. Not having her cell number, the only choice he had was to keep waiting. After sharing that kiss earlier in the day, he thought for sure that she would at least want to see if anything could be salvaged from their relationship. It appeared that he was completely wrong.

"Looks as if your friend never showed."

Brandon wasn't surprised she was back at his table. Throughout the evening, she periodically glanced his way from the bar, raising her glass to him, and unleashing an extremely sexy smile.

Handing his credit card over to the waiter, he answered nonchalantly, "Looks that way."

Seeing his look of disappointment, she sat down, reaching across the table to lightly stroke his hand. "If this woman doesn't want to spend her evening with an amazingly sexy man, then that's her loss. I personally don't understand why any woman would choose to stand you up. She must be a fool."

Brandon glanced down at their entwined hands but didn't move. Hearing it put that way, the slight blow to his ego tugged at him.

"Why don't we get out of here? We could go to my place. Catch up. See where the night leads us." With a quick wink of the eye, she continued, "No use in letting your entire evening go to waste."

Hearing the invitation that left nothing to interpretation, Brandon removed his hands. "I don't think so, Robin."

Not deterred, Robin tried one last time. "Look, Brandon, we're both adults. And even if you end up working things out with Miss No Show, that has nothing to do with me. Let's just go back to my place, have a drink, and make each other feel really good. Just like old times. And when the night is over . . . the night is over."

Brandon listened to her proposal and wondered if she had a point. Quickly, he glanced at the door.

Following his gaze, Robin turned back to Brandon and gave him a sympathetic grin. "It's been almost two hours, honey, she ain't coming."

Even at this late hour, he was still hoping that Tanya would walk through that door. He'd begged Tanya to take him back. Laid all his cards on the table. Put his heart on his sleeve. And where had it gotten him? Nowhere. By standing him up tonight, Tanya had made it abundantly clear that she wanted nothing to do with him. The entire situation painted him as pathetic.

"Brandon?" Robin asked, as the waiter brought over his credit card receipt to sign. Watching his lips curve into a relaxed smile, she stood with a look of victory on her face. "I'll get my coat."

Tanya sat in her living room with the phone cradled in her neck and a slice of pizza in her hand. After leaving Martin's, she had done what most women did when they ended a relationship—ordered a large pizza with everything, picked up a pint of Rocky Road ice cream, and called a girlfriend to listen to her cry, whine, and complain.

"You did the right thing, Tanya. You said yourself, you didn't love him."

"I know, Natalie, but it doesn't change the fact that at thirty-five I'm single, childless, and have absolutely no prospect in sight."

Natalie didn't hesitate to respond, "I understand you do have a prospect."

Pausing with her pizza halfway to her lips, Tanya asked, "What's that supposed to mean?"

"I stopped by the hospital today and spoke to Christine.

She told me what happened when you held Brianna, and that Brandon was there."

At the mention of his name, Tanya put down her slice of pizza and began to pace the floor. "What is this, Natalie? Gang up on Tanya week? First Christine, then my mother, now you. Doesn't anybody remember what that man did to me?"

"Look how worked up you're getting just at the mention of his name," Natalie said. "Obviously there are some feelings still there."

"You're right, Nat, there are feelings still there. Would you like me to tell you what they are? How about anger? There's a feeling for you. What about fury? That's a real good feeling. Oh, I know, let's add annoyance, resentment, bitterness."

"You forgot one," Natalie said.

"What?" Tanya said, working herself into a frenzy. "Irritation? Rage?"

"No, love."

Tanya froze and held the phone out as if it had suddenly grown a head. "What did you just say?"

"I said—"

"Never mind, I think I might throw up if I hear you say it again."

"Don't be so melodramatic, Tanya," Natalie answered, laughing at her friend. "Look, I'm not telling you how to live your life, but now that it's over between you and Martin, maybe you should consider giving Brandon another chance."

"Yes. You're absolutely one hundred percent right, Natalie. I will give Brandon another chance," Tanya said with a strong conviction. "Just let me grab my planner. . . . Oh, yeah, I'll pencil that in . . . one day after hell freezes over."

Feeling she'd already put in more than her two cents, Natalie decided to go for a whole dollar. "Why is it so difficult for you to forgive?"

Sitting back down and grabbing her pizza, Tanya said, "What's that supposed to mean?"

"Think about Danielle. You said your mom told you that she's changed; yet you won't even talk to her. And Brandon, well, I think he's sincere, Christine thinks he's sincere, you said your mother thinks he's—"

"OK, OK, Nat. I get the picture. But what's your point?"

Ignoring the sarcasm in her voice, Natalie continued, "You're so tough on people, Tanya. It's like they make one mistake and automatically you cut them off."

"Let me get this straight," Tanya said, finding it hard to believe that no one was taking her side on either of these issues. "I have a sister who lied, cheated, and manipulated me and my friends, and an ex-boyfriend who cheated on me. And I'm the one who has the problem?"

"All I'm saying is nobody's perfect . . . including you."

"Well, thanks for that analysis, Dr. Donovan. How much do I owe you?"

"Ha, ha . . . very funny," Natalie said. "If I'm a doctor, then I've got the perfect prescription. Why don't we continue this conversation over a drink? It's still early, we can dress up and do something out of the ordinary."

"Thanks for the offer, Nat, but I'm just not up to it tonight."

"Ah, come on," Natalie pleaded. "A night out on the town would do us both some good. A nice restaurant, a jazz spot, or maybe one of the new clubs? Who knows? Maybe I'll get lucky and find a man."

Getting out for the night did sound good, but Tanya just didn't think she had the energy after such an emotional day. "I've just scarfed down four slices of a supreme pizza and I have on my slum clothes. Sorry, Nat. Another time."

"I'm going to hold you to that," Natalie promised. "I haven't been out, or had a decent date, in months. I'm actually considering calling that guy Christine tried to hook me up with at your party."

"You mean Nicholas?" she asked hesitantly.

"Yeah, why?" Natalie asked, picking up on her tone.

"After you ducked them at the party, Christine introduced him to my assistant, Alicia. I think he took her home."

"That's just great . . . now I really have no prospects in sight."

Stifling a giggle, Tanya switched ears and said, "Now who's the one being melodramatic?"

"Point taken. Listen, I'm going to go, but call me if you need anything."

After hanging up with Natalie, Tanya started to clean up her mess when she spotted the small box wrapped in gold paper. She'd carried the gift from the kitchen, to her room, and now to the living room. Attempting to throw it in the trash twice, each time she didn't have the guts to follow through.

This is ridiculous. Just open the stupid thing.

Dropping the pizza box back on the coffee table, she sat on the couch and turned the gift from side to side. Before she could stop herself, she tore at the paper and revealed a box that no doubt held a piece of jewelry in it. Raising the lid, she stared at the gold ankle bracelet with the heart charm. The inscription on the heart read: *mine belongs 2 U.* She dropped the box with the gift in it on the table as if it scorched her. The memories flooded her mind as she clearly envisioned their last day on the island five years ago. Spending it in the open market, Tanya had admired this item, but had already spent more than she planned. Brandon must have doubled back and gotten it for her. One week later their relationship was over. He never had the chance to give it to her.

Hearing the doorbell, she grabbed the wrapping paper and the gift and dropped it in a drawer in an end table. The grandfather clock in the corner of the living room read nine forty-five and she wondered if Martin had come by to talk her into changing her mind. In sweats, a T-shirt, and socks, she turned on the outside light and peeped through the hole in the door. For some strange reason, she wasn't completely surprised. But that didn't mean she had to let him in. Turning out the light, she went back into the living room and curled up on the couch.

She heard the click, and it was only a matter of seconds before he strolled into the room.

"You stood me up."

Was she really up to this tonight? "First of all, I never agreed to come. Second of all, please leave your key on your way out."

Glancing at the television screen, he asked lightly, "Whatcha watching?"

"And turn the hall light out on your way out."

After he had left the restaurant, he followed Robin to her complex. In her apartment, everything was exactly as he remembered it. The same black leather couch with the slight tear in the arm. The beige carpet that had seen much better days. The glass coffee table and end tables covered with fashion magazines.

Handing him a glass of wine, she had headed to her bedroom, promising to be back as soon as she changed into something more comfortable. Attempting to make himself comfortable on the couch, he realized he couldn't. Nothing about what he was about to do felt right. Behaving just as Tanya believed he would, he not only couldn't go through with it, he didn't want to. How could he give to Robin what didn't belong to him? His body—his heart—the very essence of who he was belonged to another woman. While that woman wanted nothing to do with him right now, he couldn't give up hope. He would just keep trying until he figured out a way to make her see it. Yelling good night, he had let himself out before Robin had a chance to reenter to the room, and headed straight for Tanya's house.

Brandon flipped open the pizza box and smiled. Still eating them with everything on them. When his eyes moved to the ice cream container, warning bells sounded in his ears. He knew those choices to be her comfort food. As he watched her reach for the remote, the emptiness of her left hand glared back. No ring. Did something happen?

Forcing her to make room for him on the sofa, he heard her irritation grow by the sucking of her teeth.

"Whether you like it or not, Tanya, I know something's going on with you right now. You don't have to tell me what it is if you don't want to, but just in case you need someone to talk to, I'll be right here for you if you change your mind."

Shifting his position to get comfortable, he settled next to her, but she immediately tried to push him away.

He didn't budge.

A few seconds later, she pushed him again. This time, he raised a brow in curiosity. This push differed from the first.

The third push came with double the force and he instinctively knew her purpose to move him out of the way was replaced with another. Her fist balled and she punched him in the arm, followed by a blow to the chest. Next, she hit the side of his arm and then back to his chest. Suddenly, it seemed as if all the emotions she held inside from their stormy relationship and painful breakup came gushing through open gates. Her goal became abundantly clear to hurt him . . . as punishment for hurting her.

Smack!

"Damn you, Brandon."

Bam!

"I hate you for what you did to me."

Whack!

"How dare you come back in my life?"

Wham!

"What do you want from me?"

With each connection, Brandon understood the cleansing taking place and he gladly withstood the pain, making no attempt to block the blows.

When the fear of commitment had become greater than his love for her, he had marched into her office five years ago and made the confession that he had been unfaithful. With professional poise, she had instructed him to walk out her door and never contact her again. The entire scene had played out in less than five minutes, denying her the chance to vent her anger and frustration about what he claimed to have done.

Tonight, the chicken came home to roost. And he would not take this away from her. If this was what she needed, then this was what he would give. He was getting exactly what he deserved.

As her blows began to slow, Tanya grabbed him by the collar, prepared to yell and scream in his face until her voice gave out. But just inches from his face, everything stopped around her as she focused on his luscious, brown lips. With the concentrated rise and fall of her chest, and pure adrenaline pumping through her veins, the inability to control the passion festering just below the surface rose to the forefront. Mightily, her lips descended on his with the same force and intensity that she had thrown her blows.

Emotions swirled around every part of her body as she smothered his lips with demanding mastery. With her hands shaking and her heart pounding, screams of *No!* crept up from the recesses of her mind. But the hint of heaven she received from his taste caused her to ignore all reason.

The moment she saw him at the hospital, she instinctively knew. No matter what their past had been. No matter how long they had been separated, she wanted him. Craved him. Needed him. To fight against these feelings became a losing battle. As pleasure ripped through her body, she justified her behavior by convincing herself that she could satisfy the physical, but not turn over her emotions. She could give him her body, but not her heart . . . and never her soul.

Brandon sat impassively, refusing to move as she continued her assault on all of his senses. His ears rang from the sensual moans coming from her. His eyes drank in the curves of her body. His lips tasted her and his pulsing body felt every touch as her hands caressed his chest, shoulders, and arms. The scent of her had never left him, and now he inhaled the flavor that was distinctively hers.

With his hands at his sides, he scooted away from her, only to have her lean in, adding pressure to his mouth, pleading for complete access. As every male part of him reacted to her sexual advances, he concentrated on maintaining control. Without a shadow of a doubt, it would only take one motion from him to ignite the fire that had burned in him since the day they met, and if he wasn't careful, he would take her right here. Right now.

And to tell the truth, nothing in this world would make him happier than to bury himself deep inside her. But with all their unresolved issues, he didn't want a one-night stand that would end with regrets. Having royally screwed up the first time they were together, he had no intention of making another mistake. Just as he began to push her away, she traced his ear with her tongue and softly blew into it, making his desire to stop this assault next to impossible.

In one fluid motion, she straddled him, pushing him against the back of the sofa. Tanya removed her shirt to expose beautiful bronze skin covered only by a lacy bra.

Rapidly losing his battle for control, a breathless Brandon tried to be the rational one. "Tanya, you're upset. You're not thinking straight. We can't do this."

Between kisses, she denied his statement. "Isn't this what you want? Isn't this why you've placed yourself back in my life?"

Calling on every piece of restraint he could muster, Brandon removed her touch and lifted her off of him. "What about tomorrow?"

Panting, Tanya struggled to focus on his words. "Tomorrow?"

Picking up her shirt, he handed it back to her. "If we do this tonight, what about tomorrow?"

Snatching the cotton tank out of his hands, she felt the fog she had been operating in beginning to lift, and the revelation of her actions became increasingly clear. "You obviously didn't think about tomorrow when you confessed to cheating on me. You didn't think about tomorrow when you left for LA a year ago. Why start now?"

Wanting to diffuse what was fast becoming a volatile situation, Brandon reached out for her hands and purposely lowered his voice. Staring into eyes filled with all the emotions of the night, he hoped she would hear his heart in his next words. "That's just it, Tanya. When I said I wanted you back, I meant all of you—and not just for a moment, but forever. I want your heart—your soul. Not just your body. I won't take one without the others. It's all or nothing."

Tanya fought to regain control herself. What had gotten into her? Had she actually just thrown herself at him? Was she losing her mind—going completely insane? With her birthday, seeing Brianna, and breaking up with Martin, her mind must have been muddied in total confusion. Could this have been the unimaginable result? Taking a few tentative steps back, she ignored Brandon's eyes filled with longing, regret, and hope. Tanya, too angry with herself, refused to acknowledge any of them. Hurrying out of the room, she faced him one last time. "Fine," she said. "It's nothing."

Six

Natalie opened the door to her storefront office, cut off the alarm, and turned on the lights. Just after eight A.M. She had about two hours before her first appointment. Her staff, if you could call a receptionist and a part-time administrative assistant a staff, wouldn't be in until nine.

Stepping into the small kitchenette, Natalie started the coffee machine and headed for her small office in the back of the five-room office suite. Dressed in her corporate attire of skirt, blazer, and pumps, she settled in behind the simple wood desk, booted up her computer, and prepared to review several more résumés.

As a certified public accountant spending the first six years of her career at a major public accounting firm, Natalie had dreamed of being elected partner by the time she turned thirty. But the office politics, the unchecked harassment, and the discrimination soured her taste for that type of success, and she had searched her mind for other career options. When Christine asked her about coming to work at her interior design firm, she jumped at the chance. Working for Christine provided her the job satisfaction she craved with her previous employer, and allowed her the flexibility to focus on another dream she had harbored since beginning her professional career. Business Strategies Inc. Founded a year ago, BSI assisted minority business owners in managing the finances of their business effectively, especially in the areas of taxes.

Having worked for a large accounting firm, Natalie handled clients with enough money to fund small countries, but there was another group of business owners who couldn't afford the expensive hourly rates for the expert advice. Small-business owners.

She'd heard too many horror stories of businesses becoming fairly successful, only to end up in bankruptcy because of the lack of knowledge about the financial side of running a business. Working out a deal with Christine that allowed her flexibility in her working hours, she had jumped into her project with both feet.

Having a core group of volunteers, BSI had helped many companies this past year with everything from finding capital to keep their businesses going, to finding ways of cutting tax liability, to working with the IRS to resolve outstanding tax issues.

Finding complete satisfaction in the work that the organization performed on almost a daily basis, Natalie knew that she couldn't keep up the pace of basically working two jobs. She had toyed for almost three months with the idea of hiring an executive director to run BSI on a day-to-day basis. By creating this new position, her time would be freed up to focus on developing new programs and trainings. Since she had run an advertisement in the paper two weeks ago, the résumés were pouring in. Her first interview, scheduled for this afternoon, would be the first of many.

Hiring a new executive director was the reason she had come in early this morning. She had several interviews scheduled for today, but also needed to review several grant proposals. Applying for grants remained a top priority for Natalie. If she wanted to add a director to her staff, offer her assistant a full-time position, and hire full-time accountants as opposed to depending solely on volunteers, she had to keep searching and applying for any money that they could qualify for. As it stood now, she hadn't gotten paid a dime for her work. Although she didn't mind, a new director probably wouldn't be willing to take that same salary.

The grant application process had been a staple in her life ever since she had opened her doors. She'd hoped to have heard back from at least one of her requests that would infuse a half million dollars into her budget. That would more than take care of a director's salary, as well as allow them to implement several of her training and management programs that had sat unused. This grant, from the Whittington Foundation, the charity arm of a Fortune 100 company, would be awarded sometime in the next few weeks. She was grateful to Martin for steering her to this company for funding. Word had it that BSI was in the forefront. And if that was the case, the timing couldn't have been better. It would be months before she heard from the other two grants she had recently applied for, but this money would arrive by the end of the month.

In the groove of her work, Natalie glanced at the clock when the phone rang. Technically, they didn't open for another twenty minutes, so she opted to let it go to voice mail. A few minutes later, her cell phone rang. Hoping there was nothing wrong, she grabbed the device off her hip and pressed the green button.

"Hello."

"Where are you? I've tried you at home, at the design firm, at BSI."

"Sorry, Tanya," Natalie piped in. "I didn't know I had to check in with you before I started my day." As she remembered the night Tanya had had with Martin, her mood immediately became serious and Natalie continued, "Are you OK? Did something happen with Martin?"

"No," Tanya replied. "However, I thought you should know that I plan to seek immediate psychiatric care because I must be losing my mind."

"Now this I gotta hear."

Tanya relived the events of last night with Brandon and experienced the humiliation all over again. As anger and regret began to rise in her, she finished her story and waited for Natalie to respond.

Hearing absolutely nothing from her friend, Tanya wondered if she had lost the call. "Natalie?"

"I'm here."

"Well . . ."

"Well, what?" Natalie said, offering no reaction to what she just heard.

"What do you mean 'Well, what?' I just finished explaining to you that your best friend may possibly need to be committed for insane actions and you have nothing to say?"

"Tanya, being in love is not the same thing as going insane."

"I will give you partial credit for that statement. I am in something . . . but love is not it. More like misguided lust. Between everything that's been going on in my life the past few weeks, it's no wonder that something like this would happen. Distraught woman. Attractive man. The results were straight out of a bad B movie. But now that a new day has dawned and I've gotten some perspective on the situation, things should return to normal."

"And what's normal, Tanya? Living your life in denial?"

"I have no idea what you're talking about."

"Of course you do, that's why I'm not going to bore either of us by rehashing it. But I will say this. If you are really over Brandon and want nothing to do with him, why does every conversation we have lately revolve around him?"

Shifting uncomfortably in her chair, Tanya said, "I gotta go get ready for work, Nat."

"Yeah," Natalie said knowingly, "I figured you would."

* * *

Brandon stepped off the elevator on the tenth floor at Morgan, Rock, Stanton, Mills and Ware. Each time he saw his name on the sign behind the receptionist's station, his chest swelled with pride. With five hundred attorneys and two hundred and fifty support staff member, there were only a handful of black partners, and only one with his name stenciled on the door.

Representing the epitome of the corporate world, Morgan and Rock's corporate practice raked in hundreds of millions of dollars each year, with a client list consisting of a who's who of the Fortune 100 list. The firm relished the rewards that came with running such a successful law practice. Original artwork on the walls, plush carpeting, handcrafted desks for all partners, and huge annual bonuses for everyone from the managing partner to the receptionist.

Recruited heavily by a number of top law firms around the country while attending Georgetown Law, Brandon had come to Morgan and Rock with high expectations put upon him. Not a disappointment, he rose to the occasion. In his ascent to partner, he'd billed more hours, brought in more clients, and earned more money than most people would see in a lifetime.

Early in his career, his social life had fully embraced his rising status. He worked hard and played harder. Initially, competition among the associates was fierce. Not just for the best cases, but for the best everything. Cars. Houses. Women. And Brandon worked overtime to come out on top in every category. But several years into the game, he had met Tanya. Just one rejection from her and Brandon knew it was time to change.

Best friends with Damian since college, Tanya had gone months before she would even entertain the thought of going on a date with him. Well aware of his womanizing ways, she made it perfectly clear that the last intention she had was to become another notch on his bedpost. Another feather in his cap. Another spoke on his wheel.

Thinking her refusals would deter him from pursuing her any further, she always seemed surprised when he'd show up and ask her out again. The more she turned him down, the more intrigued he became. For the first time in his life, the opinion of a woman began to matter to Brandon. The more she said no, the more attractive she became to him.

As the party scene and his fly-by-night lifestyle became less appealing, Brandon found himself staying home more nights instead of hitting the latest club or accepting one of the many social invitations he received almost daily. His friends thought he was sick, and his coworkers wondered if his caseload was too heavy. But it was neither of those things. Brandon found that if he couldn't be with her, he didn't want to be with anyone. And finally, with persistence and charm, he convinced her to give him a chance.

But as their relationship developed, he found himself in new territory. No longer about having fun or hanging out, it became about wanting to see her, needing to be with her. For the first time in his life, Brandon Ware fell in love. And that revelation scared the hell out of him.

Extremely uncomfortable in his new role as a committed boyfriend in a serious relationship, he found panic beginning to set in. Could he possibly live up to the expectations of that role? His track record for being faithful was nothing to be proud of up to that point, and his biggest fear remained that he would somehow, some way find a way to hurt the woman he had grown to love. Figuring it was best to end things before he really screwed it up—he broke it off.

Ignoring the glare of hatred in her eyes when he told her, and pushing down his feelings of guilt over what he'd done, he embraced his return to bachelorhood with a vengeance. No longer living under the pressure of measuring up to his perception of Tanya's expectations, he reverted to his philandering ways.

Attending work functions, social parties, and sometimes

just hanging out at the club, Brandon rarely spent a night in. The fellas he used to hang out with welcomed him back with champagne toasts. But not everyone was fooled by his partying ways.

Damian diagnosed Brandon's frenzied schedule as an attempt to extinguish Tanya from his thoughts, his life, and his heart. Calling that analysis utterly ridiculous, Brandon continued to live footloose and fancy-free. But as time went by, Brandon realized that every woman he dated, he compared to her. And just as he expected—no one measured up. No woman even came close.

When Damian had gotten married last year, Brandon took advantage of that occasion to confess his lie to Tanya and beg for another chance. But there was no forgiveness to be had.

Heeding the warning of his brother that she needed time, Brandon knew he wouldn't be able to take seeing her with another man—namely Martin Carter. Troubled and confused, Brandon had returned to work the Monday after Damian's wedding reception and convinced the managing partner to send him to Los Angeles to head up the opening of that office. Two weeks later, he was packed and on a plane.

"Welcome back, Brandon."

The greeting drew Brandon back from his trip down memory lane. Glad for the unexpected welcome, Brandon shook hands with Thomas Stanton as they continued down the hall. In his late fifties, Thomas had been with the firm for over thirty years. Definitely a member of the old school, Thomas rarely stepped into the office without his bow tie and circular-rimmed glasses. His naturally blond hair, thin from age and genetics, lay flat off his facc, highlighting green eyes filled with wisdom.

Thomas's incredible work in corporate law had been celebrated before Brandon was out of law school. With a razor-sharp mind and a passion for the law, Thomas had his opponents quaking in their five-hundred-dollar shoes whenever they had to go up against him. His strong work ethic and reputation had impressed Brandon enough to accept their job offer two months before graduation. Serving as mentor, and eventually becoming a good friend, Thomas had taken Brandon under his wing the moment he walked through the double glass doors of the firm. Guiding Brandon through high-profile cases, firm politics, and challenges with internal discrimination, Thomas could single-handedly be credited with building Brandon's stellar career in such a short amount of time.

"Heard you came back early," Thomas said, following Brandon down the hall to his office.

"LA is up and running. Saw no reason to delay my return."

Nodding in approval, Thomas answered, "I understand you did a great job."

Entering his office, Brandon set his briefcase on his desk and took a quick look around. Not used in a year, one wouldn't know it by the fresh flowers, vacuumed floor, and dust-free furniture. The office, reflective of his style, consisted of a cherry-wood desk, leather chairs, a floor-to-ceiling bookcase, a conference area, and an entertainment center, complete with television, DVD, stereo, and satellite system. "It's good to be home. I'm looking forward to digging into cases again. I'm better in the courtroom than as an administrator."

Leaning against the edge of a chair, Thomas removed his glasses. "We didn't expect you back this week, so you're without a secretary. If you need one, call Maria and get a temp."

Removing a couple of files from his briefcase, Brandon waved him off. "No problem. I think I can survive a couple of weeks without one."

Nodding, Thomas continued. "Once you get settled in, call Elaine to get on my calendar. I want a full report on LA, including an update of staffing. Plan to set aside some time for me to get you up to speed on three cases I'll be turning over to you. You'll also need to check in with Davis in accounting. He has some questions about some expenses for the phone system in LA. I'm sure you can clear it up. Also, the Lambert case is picking up again. It seems as if Judge Burton is tired of the plaintiff asking for continuances. He's promised to set a court date within the next sixty days."

"Whoa, Thomas," Brandon interjected with a grin. "I've only been back in the office less than ten minutes."

"Then you're already behind," Thomas answered with a knowing smile.

Thomas had a reputation of being a workaholic. Brandon couldn't remember the last time Thomas took a vacation. He barked orders like a pit bull and expected nothing less than perfection from everyone around him. Many associates didn't make it through his rigorous work schedule and requested changes early in their career. No one really knew how much damage those associates may have done to their career, yet none of those associates had yet to make partner.

With Brandon, Thomas had a soft spot. When he had interviewed him almost ten years ago, Thomas saw the determination to succeed in Brandon's eyes. Proud of what Brandon had accomplished in his career, Thomas almost felt his work with him was done. There was just one area that still remained unresolved. Heading for the door, Thomas paused and rubbed his chin.

Brandon knew the gesture well and understood he was seriously contemplating his next statement.

"You know," Thomas started, "I ran into an old friend of yours a few months back."

"Oh, yeah, who?" Brandon asked, opening the blinds to let in the sunlight.

Watching his reaction closely, Thomas paused a moment for ultimate impact. "Tanya Kennedy."

Brandon's hands froze on the rod, and his eyes narrowed slightly at the mention of her name. Yet he remained silent.

"It was a political fund-raiser. She attended as the guest of Congressman Martin Carter."

Brandon's expression remained unchanged and Thomas continued, "Looked absolutely fabulous. Stunning black gown, strapless, I believe. Hair piled up on her head showing off her beautiful face and long neck. She—"

"Is there a point to this story?" Brandon asked, trying to hide his agitation, but curious at the same time.

Thomas shrugged nonchalantly, portraying an air of indifference. "No point. I just remember you two used to . . . Well, in any case, she still works for your brother, right? Have you seen her since you've been back?"

Casually taking a seat in the leather high-back chair behind the desk, Brandon studied his mentor, not deceived by his backdoor tactic. Thomas had called him a fool, an idiot, and a few other choice names to his face when his relationship with Tanya ended. Thomas always believed that that woman was the best thing that ever happened to Brandon. Thomas's last words on the subject were that if Brandon didn't wise up and make things right with her, he would live to regret it.

How right he was.

Not ready to add any fuel to the fire he was fanning, Brandon opted to change the subject. "Speaking of Damian and Ware Construction Company, since I'm back early I'm trying to move up our meeting with them to go over the final plans for our new building. It appears as if the permits will be issued in time to meet our anticipated construction start date."

The evasive tactic sounded weak, but Thomas decided to let it slide. With Brandon back on the East Coast, he would have plenty of time to knock some sense into his hard head. "Good, we're outgrowing this space quickly. As long as everything runs on schedule, we should be ready to move into our new office complex just in time to keep you and me from having to share an office."

"I'll keep you posted."

Alone again, it only took a second for Brandon's thoughts to go back to her. After he had left her house last night, he had no idea what his next move would be. Obviously a physical attraction still existed. But how could he get her to open up her emotions to him again? Getting next to her was going to take a little planning, and until he figured out exactly what that plan would be, he would give her some time and space.

"I heard you were back in the office."

It always amazed him how fast news traveled in an organization this big.

Not waiting for an invitation to enter, she strolled in confidently. "I wish I would have known you were coming in early, I would have met you at the airport. I would have been more than happy to host a very private welcome home party."

The last person Brandon would have called to pick him up from the airport was Lolita Fenton. The old saying leads people to believe that one can't have brains and beauty, but that rule didn't apply to Lolita. She had both—in ample supply.

Graduating six years ago at the top of her class from Stanford Law School, Lolita had won her share of high-profile cases. Looking to make partner in the next year, she had attended all the right social functions and brought in several new clients. That was the brains part of her. Fortunately, the beauty part was just as impressive.

At five feet nine inches, with a short, sexy haircut and a wardrobe that pushed the limits of professional, she destroyed all those beliefs that a woman had to dress like a man to fit into his world. Even today, the burgundy suit would seem innocent and appropriate on any other woman. But on her, it was lethal. The skirt, just tight enough to make a brother wonder if she was wearing any underwear, and a cropped jacket with a single button in the center, showed off two of her best assets. It was a well-known fact that bras were not a part of her daily wardrobe.

Lolita was the last relationship Brandon had had after his breakup with Tanya. And he used the "relationship" term lightly. Now it appeared that she wanted to pick up right where they had left off.

"Thanks for stopping in, Lolita, but I'm just getting settled in. Not much time for anything but work."

Ignoring his distant tone, she walked over to him and leaned over to give him a chaste kiss on the cheek. Brandon wasn't fooled by what appeared to be an innocent peck. Her position gave him a perfect view of her braless breasts, firm and round. Not lingering on the free show, he quickly averted his eyes to look into hers.

With a low whisper, she declared, "When you're ready to take a break from work, call me. Same rules. No strings. Just fun."

Suddenly, Lolita stood and her demeanor instantaneously changed. "Thomas sent me over. He wanted me to brief you on Thornton Textiles. He said you'd be overseeing that case. I have about fourteen depositions taken in the last three months that we'll need to review. Call my secretary when you're ready to get on my calendar."

Brandon used to be surprised at her ability to move from personal to business topics without missing a beat. Now he understood that Lolita took her career very seriously, and when it came to the law, she never messed around. Many opponents had underestimated Lolita's talent because of her looks, and usually started any business discussions with her in kid gloves. However, after a few rounds with her legal mind, they found themselves thoroughly impressed—and sometimes intimated—by her sharp mind and quick wit.

Watching her walk to the door, he knew the extra sway in her hips was just for him. Before walking out, she turned to him one last time and winked. "And call me at home when you're ready to get back into my bed."

Brandon sat for several moments after she left. Lolita of-

fered exactly the type of relationship that he had cherished
years ago. But he once heard that when you become a man,
you put aside childish things. And the moment Tanya
Kennedy came into his life, it was time for Brandon Ware to
grow up. He still found it hard to believe that he had ever
thought life in the fast lane was better than commitment and
love.

Exhaling deeply, Brandon stood and began pacing. How
could he prove to Tanya that they belonged together? What
could he do to convince her to give them another chance?
There had to be a way to get her to see that what they had
was truly special.

Frustration settled in the pit of his stomach. He had tried
everything—even getting on his knees and begging for forgiveness didn't work. Her words said that she had no
intention or desire to give him another chance, but that kiss
at the hospital and last night told him different. He just had
to figure out a way to make her see it.

Hearing his phone, he remembered he had no secretary
and picked it up on the second ring.

"Brandon Ware."

Hearing the voice on the other end, Brandon found himself unconsciously standing up straighter.

"Hello to you too, Mrs. Kennedy. How are you?" *Why
would Tanya's mom be calling me?*

"I'll ask the questions," Mabel responded without a hint
of friendliness.

"Yes, ma'am," Brandon answered, feeling as if he had just
taken a seat on the witness stand.

"What are your intentions with my daughter? She spent
two weeks with me after you broke her heart, crying and sad.
I won't tolerate you hurting my baby again."

Brandon, speechless, searched for an answer.

"If you're wondering how I know you've been chasing my
girl, it's because of Christine. I called to check in on that pre-

cious little Brianna, and she's been the only one to give me a straight answer as to what's going on with you two."

"Actually," Brandon said, finally finding his voice, "nothing's going on between us. She won't have anything to do with me."

"You told me once that you lied about cheating on her. That you were young and dumb and didn't know any better. Now, I'm going to ask you one more time. Did you or did you not cheat on her? And don't lie to me."

He couldn't help cracking a smile. She didn't have to worry about him lying. Even though she was six hundred and fifty miles away, he was too intimidated to tell her anything but the truth. "No, ma'am. I didn't cheat on her."

"Are you still young and dumb?"

Too scared to laugh, he swallowed and answered, "No, ma'am. I'm older and wiser."

Mabel, hearing the disappointment and sadness in his voice, understood that he continued to pay a high price for his deception. The only good thing that may have come out of this entire situation was that Brandon Ware learned his lesson. Starting to laugh, Mabel said, "Loosen up, son. It's OK. I believe you."

Relief flooded through Brandon. Knowing that Mrs. Kennedy knew all about their past, he was glad that she had forgiven him.

"Do you still love her?"

Without skipping a beat, he truthfully answered, "With all my heart."

Brandon held his breath as the phone went silent. If he'd heard a click, he would have sworn she had hung up.

After several seconds, Mabel answered, "She loves you too, but you'll be hard pressed to get her to admit it. Too stubborn."

Hoping to gain valuable insight to help him with his cause, he anxiously asked, "So what should I do?"

"I don't know," Mabel said, almost flippantly. Now that

she knew his intentions were honorable, it was up to him to find a way back into her daughter's heart. "That's your problem. But you just said you're wiser now. You'll figure something out. Now I got to go. Sister Barnes is waiting on me to take her to visit Brother Sadler in the hospital. Poor man, had his appendix taken out at the age of fifty-two. Too bad he's acting like a ten-year-old."

Laughing and enjoying their relaxed conversation, Brandon said, "Thanks for calling, Mrs. Kennedy."

"Don't thank me, just hurry up and get it together. I know Brianna's cute as a button, but I want some grandbabies of my own."

Ending the call, Brandon stared out his window, contemplating her final words. Five years ago, words like marriage, children, and family had caused Brandon to selfishly abandon the one woman who now meant the world to him. Now, he wanted all of those things. But he didn't want them with just anybody. He wanted them with her.

Looking out at the busy downtown streets, he watched a crane steadily lift steel beams to workers building the office center across the street. *If Damian, Christine, Natalie, and Mrs. Kennedy know we belonged together, why can't Tanya see it?*

The workers grabbed the beam and placed it on the frame, and a lightbulb finally clicked on. Smiling broadly, Brandon couldn't believe his answer had been staring him in the face. The plan—so simple, he was surprised it hadn't occured to him before. Without hesitation, Brandon picked up the phone and dialed. It shouldn't be too challenging to get all the information he needed.

Thursday morning, Tanya sat in her office reviewing the contracts for the Morgan and Rock job slated to begin in about two months. The subcontractor and supplier contracts were signed, and she was working on getting the final permits from the county. Winter months for a construction company could be slow, so she was glad she had this contract and a few others to keep her busy.

Hoping work would help make the events of the past week disappear, she pushed back thoughts of an unwanted birthday party, an unwanted marriage proposal, and an unwanted ex-boyfriend. With determination, she focused on the one thing she knew could take her mind off her personal life—work. But her ability to concentrate diminished the longer she sat there. Adding up the same column of numbers for the fourth time, she got yet another total. Closing the file, she opted to take a mental break. Unfortunately, the moment she did, he crept back into her mind.

It had been almost a week since she'd heard from him. Not since that crazy night she had practically thrown herself at him. It appeared he had finally gotten the message and left her alone. Amazingly, Tanya wondered why she wasn't ecstatic.

Ever since he had literally bumped into her, she'd spent every waking moment screaming, yelling, and practically begging for him to leave her alone. With his obviously obeying her wishes, Tanya questioned why she wasn't in the mood to celebrate. As the week progressed, she found herself staring at the phone at work and waiting for the doorbell to ring at home. On a few occasions, she actually thought he would just use his key and be waiting for her when she got home. But it had been almost a week, and she hadn't heard one word from Brandon Ware.

Even when she stopped by Christine's to visit with Brianna, she had been on the verge of asking about him. However, she quickly berated herself. Why should she be concerned about someone who had treated her so badly? How could she waste her brainpower on what he was up to?

It shouldn't make a difference to her whether she ever heard from him again.

"That man is nothing but trouble," she said out loud.

With renewed determination, she reopened her file and began crunching her numbers again. Brandon Ware may have wreaked havoc on her life in the past, but those days were long over. She had lived without him the past five years—and she was determined to live without him for the rest of her life.

After about a half hour had passed, she closed the files and squeezed the bridge of her nose, trying to counter the beginning signs of a headache. Checking her watch, she couldn't believe it was only ten forty-five in the morning. Years ago, she had never watched the clock. So busy with new contracts and growing the business, she had many days when she skipped lunch and got home too late for dinner. But lately, things had been different.

Tanya, a business major in college, hadn't known what direction her life would take until Damian talked of starting his own construction company. With their friendship since her freshman year in college, it was a given that she would work for him. Many people thought that a man and a woman could not be friends and not ever cross the line to something more. Never having contemplated becoming a couple, Damian and she had developed the most enduring friendship she'd ever had.

In the beginning stages of the business, Tanya had worked as a jack-of-all-trades. Answering phones, ordering supplies, hiring workers, and negotiating with the unions. But as the company grew, she found her niche in contract administration and had been there for the past five years. Once categorized as a workaholic, she reveled in the satisfaction she received from completing a job. But lately, that satisfaction hadn't been as fulfilling as it had been in the past. She had wrestled for a solution, but had been unable to come up with one. *How do you change careers when you've devoted your entire adult life to one thing, and you have no idea what you want to do?*

Turning her attention back to work, she once again focused on the files in front of her. The Morgan and Rock project. Promising to finish the building on time and within budget, Damian had gotten word that a meeting with the building committee members at the firm had been moved to this afternoon since Brandon was back in town. Thank God Christine insisted that Damian go. With a new baby, Damian hated to leave her side for a moment, but the meeting, scheduled for only an hour, would have Damian back at home before the next feeding. That meant Tanya wouldn't have to go . . . and she wouldn't have to face *him*.

"You look to be in deep thought."

Not wanting to admit whom she was thinking of, she said, "What are you doing here? I didn't think we'd see you in the office for a few more weeks now that you have beautiful Brianna."

"I just stopped in for a minute to pick up some paperwork before the meeting this afternoon. Moving this meeting up by over a week is actually a gift. After today, I'll be able to devote my time to my lovely wife and beautiful new daughter."

Seeing the joy in his eyes and the happiness on his face, Tanya said with sincerity, "True love looks good on you. I'm glad you've found happiness."

"And what about you?" he asked, taking a seat across from her.

"What about me?" She shrugged, returning to the pile of papers in front of her.

"Are you happy?"

Not looking up, she gave a tentative laugh. "What kind of question is that?"

Leaning over her desk, he placed his hand on top of the

file to block her view of the numbers. "A question I want you to answer."

"Would there be any reason I wouldn't be?" Tanya responded flippantly. Having this type of conversation with someone who knew her so well made it difficult for her to lie.

Damian could tell he touched a nerve, but he really didn't care. One of the reasons they had such a special friendship was that they'd always been honest with each other. He saw no reason to change that part of their friendship now. "You just had a birthday that you didn't want to celebrate—"

"Which your wife made me celebrate anyway with a stupid surprise party," she interrupted.

Ignoring her snide remark, he continued, "You turned down a marriage proposal from someone who loves you."

"I don't think I need a recap of my life from you," she declared, her patience running thin.

Forging ahead, Damian refused to let her off the hook. "My brother is back in town for less than a week and you can't, even though you want to, deny your attraction to him."

"You have no idea what you're talking about," Tanya said, slamming the file shut. "The fact that I once—in a moment of sheer madness—found myself attracted to your brother has no bearing on me today. Your brother is, and always will be, a playa. It's in his blood—no offense—and even though he may wish himself rehabilitated from his need to move from one woman to another, I am not fooled." She paused, catching her breath. "Now, I will admit that I once fell into his trap. Who wouldn't? But now? Uh-uh, no way, not on your life am I once again attracted to your brother."

"He told me about the kiss," Damian challenged, watching her reaction closely.

"Weak moment."

"He told me what happened at your house."

Exasperated at the conversation, Tanya countered, "I think the legal term is temporary insanity."

Having remained silent on Brandon and Tanya's relationship out of respect for their friendship, he decided it was time he broke that rule. "You still have feelings for him, and if you want to know what I think . . ."

Standing, she ran her fingers through her hair in frustration. "Believe it or not, I don't care what you think."

Damian stood as well. "I think you still love him."

Her eyes grew large and she couldn't hold back a cynical laugh. "Did they give *you* some drugs at that hospital? After what he put me through? After what he did to me? How on God's green earth can you sit in my face and tell me I still have feelings for that two-timing man? And I use the man part lightly."

Her defense shield held firmly in place, but it only covered the tremendous pain she felt on the inside.

"Since you guys broke up, the brightness in your eyes has dulled, the glow of your skin has diminished, and you dated Martin. Martin! A man who represented everything my brother wasn't. Safe, conservative, not easily moved by emotions."

"And those are bad qualities in a man?" Tanya questioned in amazement. "I don't think so."

"They are bad qualities for *your* man. And you know it."

Glancing down, she decided not to answer. She already knew Martin wasn't the man for her. But that didn't mean that Brandon was right for her . . . did it?

"And you know how I know it? Because the minute you saw Brandon, everything changed. It may have been a year, but it didn't take long for that sparkle to return to your eyes and your skin to glow."

With a wave of her hand, she dismissed everything he'd just said as nonsense.

Damian wasn't fooled by the gesture. "I hate to be the one

to tell you this, Tanya. But you can't do it . . . no matter how hard you try."

"Do what?" Tanya asked.

"You can't deny love."

Turning away from him, Tanya refused to let him see how much his words affected her. Sarcastically, she replied, "Thank you for that in-depth analysis of my life. You and Natalie should go into business together. Now, listen closely, as I'm only going to say this once. The last thing I need in my life is Brandon Ware. I don't need someone who finds it so easy to cheat."

"He didn't cheat on you," Damian said, defending his brother for the first time to Tanya since their relationship fell apart.

"So he's said."

"Give him the benefit of the doubt. You know you want to."

Regaining some internal control, she turned back toward him and picked up some papers off her desk. "What I want to do is finish reviewing these contracts. So if you'll excuse me."

Not ready to concede, Damian countered, "You broke it off with Martin."

"That would have happened whether your brother came back to town or not."

"Tanya—"

"Don't push it, Damian," she answered, staring with unwavering eyes.

Knowing he was about to cross the line with her, he decided to back off. Heading for the door, he paused and turned back to her.

Confidently, he added, "You know as well as I do that once my brother makes up his mind about something, he's relentless. He doesn't know the meaning of not getting what he wants."

"I think you're wrong this time, Damian. When he left my house last weekend, I made it crystal clear that there would never be another relationship between us. He must have gotten the message because I haven't heard from him since."

"Don't be fooled. He may have been silent this week, but don't take it as a retreat . . . or defeat. If anything, it only means he's coming back stronger than ever before."

With a nervous laugh, she prepared to go back to work. "That's a ridiculous thought."

"I wouldn't be so quick to think that. You see, Tanya, I know you want him, but more importantly, he knows you want him. It's just a matter of time before he figures out a way to get you."

Seven

Natalie stood as her receptionist, Jea, escorted Derrick Carrington into the small conference room. Not sure what to expect, Natalie was taken aback by not only his good looks, but also his commanding presence. The characteristics of people who came for their services were those of small-business owners in need of financial guidance and help. Rarely did they arrive wearing custom-made suits. Especially ones attached to someone whose body screamed words such as *charismatic, compelling,* and *fascinating.* Standing about six feet tall, he wore his hair in short twists. She stared a moment at his clear bronze complexion and his eyes. A cross between brown and gray, they were the most unusual color she'd ever seen. Never being physically attractive to any of her clients, she tried to push out of her mind just what an enticing package he presented.

"Ms. Donovan?"

Natalie heard her name and snapped back to reality. *How many times did he call my name?* Wanting to avoid any further embarrassing behavior, Natalie motioned for Mr. Carrington to take a seat. "You'll have to excuse me. Even though it's only ten o'clock, my mind is on a million things I need to get done."

Hoping the excuse for her behavior sounded legitimate, she took a seat and opened her folder labeled *Carrington Cleaners,* ignoring the expensive smell of his cologne, his manicured fingers, and his alluring smile. "Jea tells me that you need some advice on getting your business back on track."

Derrick had prepared himself for the questioning look he would receive for seeking out an organization such as this. What he hadn't prepared for was the woman he would meet with. He hoped he hid his surprise—and pleasure—at the woman who stood before him. Beautiful wouldn't begin to describe her features. Honey-brown skin, light eyes, and dark hair. He definitely wouldn't have a problem working with her. "Actually, it's not my business I'm here to discuss—it's my parents'."

Graduating at the top of his class from Duke University, Derrick had completed medical school at Stanford. Choosing to stay on the West Coast, he had gone on to build a successful practice. "I've spent the past fifteen years building a career that would reward me with financial stability, respect from my peers, and a ticket into the society of business movers and shakers. And with hard work, I've accomplished all of that.

"Four months ago, I got a call from my mother. My father had become ill and I thought it best if I came back to the East Coast. I flew home the next day and was shocked to see my father in the hospital, hooked up to machines, fighting for his life.

"As it turns out, the dry cleaner's my parents have owned since I was a child wasn't doing so well, and the medical bills were piling up. Taking a look at their books, I realized that their business practices over the years left them with little money, and very few options to get money. I had no idea that their financial situation was in such disarray. And it never occurred to me that they weren't preparing for the future. Over the years, I've given them material things, but never thought to make sure the business was in good shape."

"Have they looked into getting a loan?"

"My mother indicated that she wasn't sure if they would

qualify for one. They still have a loan for the equipment up-grade they did three years ago."

"I see," Natalie said, taking a few notes. She knew of several lenders who made high-risk loans in certain situations. She'd have to see if that would be a good option for Carrington Cleaners.

"I offered to pay whatever was needed . . . for the business . . . to the hospital. But my mother, too proud to accept any money from me, just patted me on the shoulder, trying to reassure me that everything was going to be all right."

Standing, Derrick began to pace. "I was at a loss as to how I could help them. Not to mention the guilt of not knowing the state of their affairs." His voice softened for a moment.

Natalie's heart went out to him. "How did you hear about us?"

"Two weeks ago, I visited an old college friend and he told me that his sister had used your services to help get her business back on track after being hit with a big tax bill. That's why I'm here. My parents may not accept money from me, but they will accept help."

Natalie listened to his story and nodded in understanding. She had heard this same story hundreds of times. People start businesses with the best intentions, most of them reaching some level of success. But most small businesses, especially minority businesses, are only two payrolls away from being wiped out. She'd hoped her organization could teach people how not only to efficiently run their business, but to build wealth in the process.

"I was hoping that if I brought by their tax returns, receipts, and bank statements, you could help prepare a plan to put their business back in the black."

Closing the folder after making some final notes, Natalie stood as well. "Well, Mr. Carrington—"

"Derrick," he interrupted, his lips curving into a relaxed smile.

Natalie controlled her breathing as she tried not to focus on his lips. When he had arrived, he looked tense, no doubt from the situation with his parents. But now that he had found help, the smile he just gave her only increased his good looks. "Well, Derrick, why don't you set an appointment with Jea for next week to drop off the information? I'll review it and try to get back with you in the next two weeks."

He stretched out his hand, and as they shook, Natalie paused at the sensation that started at her fingertips and worked its way throughout her body. Physical attraction she'd experienced, but this attraction touched off something more. Not wanting to seem too desperate, Natalie removed her hand and headed for the door. "Thanks for coming by, Mr. Car . . . I mean Derrick. I hope we can help your parents out of their current situation."

Derrick stepped out of the conference room and acknowledged her words. The jolt of electricity that shot through his body upon making physical contact with her threw him for a loop. Yes, she was attractive, and yes, he had even thought of asking her out, but that was nothing new to Derrick. He met attractive women quite often. However, there was definitely something different about his encounter with Natalie Donovan. Never had he felt such an immediate draw to a woman. Not wanting to overstep professional boundaries, Derrick said good-bye, silently counting down the days until he would see her again.

The conference room buzzed with private conversations as lawyers and members of the administrative staff waited for the meeting to be called to order. Discussing construction costs, building permits, and new office space was not what partners billing out at four hundred fifty dollars an hour wanted to spend their morning doing, but it boiled down to being a necessary evil. That's why Brandon volunteered to head up the project—to make sure the planning phase didn't take up more time than absolutely necessary. With his understanding of costs associated with this project through his experience in opening up the Los Angeles office, and having a brother who owned a construction company, Brandon was the logical choice.

The project had begun almost two years ago when the managing partner realized that with their current growth in staff and business, building their own office complex would be vital, as well as economically sound, to accommodate their growing organization. Scouting out locations and collecting bids from construction companies had lasted most of the first year, and last year, while Brandon was in Los Angeles, Thomas reviewed bids and made the final selection— awarding the coveted project to Ware Construction Company. With the groundbreaking ceremony scheduled for early March, Brandon called this meeting to get an update of the entire project.

Even though he wasn't surprised when Damian entered the conference room without her, his disappointment could not be hidden. Quickly recovering, he remembered that with his plan, it wouldn't be long before Brandon had Tanya's undivided attention.

Brandon almost caved in from not contacting her all week, but he wanted to make sure that the plan he had laid out would go off without a hitch. Not to mention the fact that he wanted to give her time to think about them. He had been in her face so much since he returned, he hoped their time apart would cause her to miss him—if only just a little.

Calling the meeting to order, Brandon spoke a few words about the project in general before turning the floor over to Damian. Damian laid his notes on the podium in the front of the room and began his presentation. Reviewing the architects' plans, as well as laying out time lines, Damian touted his company's record of completing projects on time and within budget. The only item remaining was the issuing of the final building permits. Damian expected those to come through within the next two weeks.

As he listened to his brother speak of subcontractors and suppliers, Brandon's mind floated to Tanya. A million times he had run that scene at her house. The strength to walk away from the night of passion she was offering had drained him. The need for a physical connection caused a primitive ache on every male part of him, but it could not compare with the raw desire to reconnect with her on an emotional level. Tanya had shared her innermost thoughts and dreams with him years ago, and he took that closeness and not only tossed it aside, but stepped on it and smashed it until it would appear to be unrepairable. But even a glass, shattered into a million pieces, could be put back together with patience and faith.

"I think you'll find that at the end of this project, you will be completely satisfied with our work."

Those words bought Brandon's thoughts back to the meeting as applause resonated around the room, acknowledging their satisfaction with his report. After several questions were asked, which Damian expertly answered, the meeting ended just over an hour after it had started.

As the attorneys and staff members began to file out, Brandon remained seated and prepared for battle. What he was about to do challenged every ethical bone in his body. But for her . . . it was worth it.

Filling two cups of coffee, Brandon handed one to Damian and motioned for him to take a seat. "Great presentation, bro. Everything looks to be in order."

"How would you know?" Damian joked. "You spaced out halfway through and I wouldn't need many guesses to figure out who you were thinking about."

Flipping through the pages of the binder provided to all the committee members with projected costs, design information, and time lines, Brandon gave his brother a cynical grin. "You understand how important it is that this project run smoothly . . . without any glitches?"

Hearing his tone caused Damian to pause. Hesitantly he asked, "Brandon, are you questioning my ability to do this job?"

"No," Brandon answered, closing the binder and carelessly tossing it aside.

The motion did not go unnoticed by Damian and he adjusted his posture to reflect the change in the air. A few seconds ago, they were two brothers having a general conversation. Now, Damian got the feeling that the friendly discussion was turning into something else, and he put his mind on alert.

"I'm just saying that as the newest partner at this firm, I need to make a good impression on any project I lead—especially one that's going to cost my company twenty-five million dollars."

Eyeing the binder suspiciously, Damian knew his brother was up to something, and it surely had nothing to do with his concern for this project. Remaining silent, Damian quickly analyzed the cryptic grin and the sparkle in his eyes. A dead giveaway. Growing up, Brandon's reputation had developed from his scheming ways and manipulative talents. Qualities that made him a brilliant attorney.

Because Brandon rarely took himself, or life, too seriously, Damian marveled at his ability to influence people in his life to eventually get what he wanted. The only people who usually saw right through him were his parents and Damian. And it had remained that way until he met her.

Tanya's initial reaction to Brandon's charms years ago had completely baffled Damian's little brother. With his good looks, fancy job, and ever-increasing bank account, Brandon never had to work too hard at getting a date with anyone. But with Tanya, not only could he not get a date, he couldn't even get a conversation.

She had practically laughed in his face the day they met at Damian's office. Already aware of Brandon's reputation from Damian, she used descriptions like "immature," "womanizing," and "not my type" to define what she thought of him. Damian found the situation amusing when he heard her tell Brandon to his face that there was no way she would reduce herself to a relationship with someone who was only interested in the here and now. But the one thing about Brandon that Tanya didn't count on? He never took no for an answer. And his pursuit of Tanya was relentless.

In the beginning, Damian had warned his brother about pursuing a relationship with his best friend, believing that Brandon, once the chase was over, would revert to his typical ways of short-lived relationships that usually ended when the woman got too serious.

However, as time went on, Damian realized that Brandon's attraction to Tanya went beyond the chase. Changes in Brandon's demeanor and attitude convinced Damian that this time, his brother was serious. But in the end, he screwed up, and now he wanted a second chance. Damian just hoped that his plan to win Tanya back had nothing to do with this project. But looking at him now, he wasn't so sure that was the case. Damian had an inkling he was about to be recruited for a plan he had no interest in being a part of.

"I'd like five guaranteed dates with your contract administrator in the next two weeks."

"What?" Damian laughed. "You're kidding, right? You think I have the power to get someone to do something they don't want to do?"

"You're smart, I'm sure you'll figure it out," Brandon answered confidently.

Setting the coffee aside, Damian put files back in his briefcase, preparing to leave. "Wrong, little brother. This is your problem, not mine."

Sitting forward in his chair, Brandon made his expression

serious and he stared directly into his brother's eyes. "This building project rides on whether you *do* figure out a way."

Realization sank in and Damian's blood pressure began to rise. His typically light brown eyes grew dark and he inhaled deeply before speaking. No way was his brother going to put his construction company in between him and Tanya. In a deceivingly calm voice, Damian answered, "If you want to find a way to get next to Tanya, that's your right, but I highly suggest you leave me and my business out of it."

Picking up his briefcase, he headed for the door. "If you'll excuse me, I'm going home to my wife and daughter."

Not moving from his spot, Brandon casually leaned back in his chair and clasped his hands behind his head. "Fine. Have it your way, but the bottom line is, either I get five dates in the next two weeks or we go with another builder."

Damian froze in his tracks. Did he hear him correctly? Understanding that being in love could make you do and say crazy things, Damian counted to ten to calm down instead of cussing his brother out. He remembered what it was like to love someone who had trouble loving back. Christine had come to him with so much family baggage, he didn't know if his love was strong enough to see them through. But he never resorted to using people—however, he wasn't sure he wouldn't have if it had meant getting the woman he loved.

Taking a deep breath, Damian responded in a calm voice that directly contradicted the storm that was brewing on the inside of him. "You just said this project had to come in on schedule and within budget. You get another construction company at this point, and you've set yourself back months—if not a year."

Opening a folder he had brought into the conference room, Brandon threw some papers across the table. "We took several bids for this job, including one from Anderson Builders—your number-one competitor. Their bid came in second. I put them on notice this week that the job might be theirs. All they're waiting for is one phone call from me. They guaranteed the change would only set our schedule back three months."

Damian dropped his briefcase to the floor, his eyes narrowed, his nostrils flared, and he did nothing to hide his complete shock and agitation. Ware Construction Company had been in business for almost ten years and their reputation throughout the business community had always been impeccable. It was that reputation that garnered them more business than they could handle. And Brandon knew it. Losing a twenty-five-million-dollar project was nothing to sneeze at, but both men knew that the loss would be made up quickly.

"You're pushing my limit, little brother. Nothing about what you're saying is ethical—and it's probably illegal."

Unfazed by his assessment of the situation, Brandon shrugged. "I know."

"I don't appreciate you using my company to help your own personal agenda, especially with a friend."

"I know that too."

"I don't appreciate you taking advantage of this situation to force someone to spend time with you."

Stepping to the credenza against the wall, Brandon placed his hand on the phone. "We could stand here all day and listen to you rattle off all the things you don't appreciate about me—as I'm sure you have many more. But, time is money. So, tell me, do I make the call or not?"

Damian glanced at the phone and decided to challenge Brandon. "The other partners would probably never agree to a company switch at this point."

"This project has been my baby from the start," he countered with confidence. "If I say new company . . . we get a new company."

Damian shoved his hands in his pockets to keep from putting them around his brother's neck. Actively participating in a conversation such as this was absolutely ludicrous.

"I should call your bluff and see for myself what the partners would think of you using your position at this firm for personal gain."

"Call it."

Damian inhaled a deep breath and slowly let it out. "Is she worth this to you? Putting your relationship with me and your position here at the firm in jeopardy?"

Squaring his shoulders, Brandon made his position clear. "Whatever it takes."

Silence hung in the air as Damian contemplated his next move. Neither spoke and Brandon wasn't bothered. The first rule of negotiation—the first one who talks at a stalemate loses ground. He was prepared to spend the rest of the day standing in this conference room not saying a word.

Finally, Damian shook his head in the negative. "Can't do it. Too many jobs riding on the integrity of the way I run my business. If you want to go with another company, then so be it."

Brandon was not surprised, or deterred, by his brother's initial response; Damian's integrity level had always been high. However, any attorney worth his salt always prepared a rebuttal. "You just said it yourself. Too many jobs riding on this project. You hired new laborers, a foreman—do you really want to go and tell those people they are out of a job?"

Thinking of his current and future contracts, Damian answered, "There'll be other projects, Brandon. No one would lose their job."

"Surely your clients, both present and future, would question how, and why, you lost such a lucrative deal."

"We didn't lose this deal," Damian countered, his patience expanding to maximum capacity.

"Whatever the reason you give them, the result will be the same. You once had a contract with Morgan and Rock, and now you don't. Will people really care about the reason?"

That point caused Damian to pause. The PR on losing this

deal would be brutal, especially after last year's fiasco where one of his foremen took bribes from a supplier, causing inadequate wiring to be placed in a building that later caught on fire. Damien knew that even though Ware Construction Company was cleared of any wrongdoing, the business community might begin to wonder about his leadership abilities if this deal fell through.

When he thought he had lost Christine, he had fought tooth and nail to get her back, showing her the true definition of love and devotion. Brandon seemed bent on doing the same thing, even though his tactics were suspect.

While what Brandon suggested went against everything he believed in, Damian wanted Tanya to have a chance at happiness . . . with Brandon. "Are you going to do right by her this time?"

Relief flooded through Brandon. "Yes."

"When you screwed up last time, I didn't take sides. If you mess up this time, I'm not only taking sides, I'm going to kick your—"

"Don't worry, big brother. This time, I'm not screwing up."

Picking up his coat and briefcase, Damian swung open the door. "Fine. I'll break the news to her—but I'll still give her a choice. If she asks me to let the contract go . . . I will."

Brandon nodded in agreement. "I understand."

Pausing just before he walked through the door, Damian turned to his brother with unwavering, stoic, and serious eyes. "Don't ever play this game with me or my business again. Next time, not only will you lose, but I won't be so forgiving of your behavior." He slammed the door behind him.

The next morning, Brandon leaned over his desk reviewing depositions for Thornton Textiles. Lolita had dropped off the files late yesterday afternoon, along with an invitation to join her for a drink . . . at her place. After politely declining her request, Brandon had focused his attention on the case. But Lolita hadn't been quite ready to let him off the hook.

"Word has it that you aren't seeing anyone right now," she stated, tilting her head to the side and slowly licking her lips.

"You shouldn't always believe what you hear through the office grapevine."

"Then let me get it straight from the man himself."

When Brandon didn't respond, she continued, "Are you seeing anyone?"

Brandon stopped reading the deposition and focused his attention on her. Dressed as she was for casual Friday in dark green fitted pants and a tight knit sweater, Brandon had no trouble remembering what it was about her that attracted him. But that attraction didn't move beyond body parts, and his life of dealing in physical relationships had ended long ago. "I don't think it's a good idea if we discuss each other's personal lives. We are business associates. Nothing more, nothing less. I suggest we keep our topics of conversation within those parameters."

Brandon watched Lolita's jaw tighten and for a few seconds she remained silent. Believing that the conversation was over, Brandon returned his attention to the file.

"It wasn't business when you caressed my body from head to toe. It wasn't business when you crawled into my bed and we spent little time sleeping. It wasn't business when—"

"Lolita, that's enough," Brandon warned.

Pushing away from the table, she jumped up, nearly knocking over her chair in the process. "No, Brandon, it's not enough. You men are all the same. You take what you want, and when you've had your fill, you move on."

Brandon sensed the situation spiraling out of control and realized the part he played. While he never made promises with any woman, she may have expected more out of their

continue her rampage when he leaned forward, just inches from her lips.

Softly, he said, "You could make this so much easier if you just agree to the terms of the deal."

The moment of intense attraction faded with his words. Crossing her arms across her chest in defiance, she answered, "Sorry, but I don't make deals with the devil."

"But you'll kiss him?" he teased.

It was a statement more than a question and his cocky attitude grated on her last nerve. "We are over, Brandon. O-v-e-r. Is there some part of that word you don't understand? Should I say it in Spanish? French? Portuguese?"

Twisting a few strands of her hair, he didn't seem the least bit put out by her obvious displeasure. "Are you sure you want to fight with me again? The last time we argued, we ended up in each other's arms."

Inhaling the scent of the fragrance that was distinctly his, Tanya fought for not only control of her body's reaction to his sensuous touch, but also control over her mind. Adjusting the collar of her suit jacket did nothing to relieve the warming sensation that traveled from the tip of her head to the bottom of her soles. The thought of his lips caressing hers, his tongue exploring the recesses of her mouth, the feel of his arms enclosed around her, caused a slight tremor. Trying to ignore his closeness, she responded with a throaty whisper. "A grave mistake. A mistake I guarantee will not be repeated."

Taking one step closer, he leaned to her ear. "How can you be so sure?"

Tanya's head felt light and she called on every piece of strength inside her to thwart his sexual advances. Her words could barely be heard. "Trust me. I'm sure."

Dropping his eyes to her lips, he whispered, "Prove it."

The knock at the door caused Tanya to jump back, temporarily flustered. Thomas entered and failed to hide his surprise, and pleasure, at seeing the two of them together again. When he had gotten the call from Tanya to meet with her on a critical issue concerning the construction project, he'd referred her to Brandon. With Brandon insisting that he take part in this meeting, he had reluctantly agreed. Now that he was here, he had a feeling that this meeting was more than just about contracts and permits.

Regaining her composure, Tanya turned away from Brandon and in her most professional voice said, "Mr. Stanton, thank you for coming on such short notice. I'm not going to take much of your time, but there are a few things I'd like to make you aware of."

She spoke in a considerate and professional manner, but her eyes gave her away. Thomas noted they toggled between anger and longing. He wondered if she knew it was the eyes that always gave you away.

His protégé, on the other hand, wore his courtroom face. Unreadable expression, raised chin, and steady eyes. That look had won many cases for him. The question Thomas asked himself: what—or who—was on trial?

Motioning for Thomas to take a seat at the conference table, Tanya all but ignored Brandon. "Are you aware that Mr. Ware is considering voiding his contract with Ware Construction Company and using another builder at this stage in the process?"

"No, I can't say that I am aware of such discussions," he said cautiously, feeling as if he were walking right into a trap. Stealing a quick glance at Brandon, he paused as he noticed that his expression had changed from earlier. The eyes. Staring at Tanya. Love had replaced the look of indifference. The discovery pleased the older man immensely. So, he wasn't a complete idiot after all. Now, what was Brandon going to do about it?

"The discovery was a shock to us as well," Tanya said. "I'm sure you'll be able to straighten this out."

"I've discussed my concerns with Damian," Brandon calmly interjected, "and we've reached an agreement. I actually think this meeting was unnecessary, as we found common ground on our outstanding points yesterday."

"And I actually think that the agreement that you have reached is not reasonable," Tanya argued, staring at him with contempt.

"The deal has already been made," Brandon countered.

"Not if I have anything to say about it," she hissed.

Thomas cleared his throat dramatically, and the childish bickering came to a halt. Not sure what he had been dragged into the middle of, he hesitated before he spoke. It was obvious that there was an underlying issue that neither had mentioned yet, and somehow he got the feeling that it had to do more with their personal lives than a business deal.

However, Thomas's intellectual mind confirmed one thing. Tanya and Brandon still had feelings for each other. Far be it from him to jeopardize their chances of getting back together. His gut told him that that's what this little meeting was all about. Rising, he headed for the door.

Shock at his impending departure caused Tanya to stand. "Where are you going? We haven't finished our discussion."

With a slight smile and wink to Brandon, Thomas opened the door. "Whatever Brandon thinks is best, we'll go with. I trust him." After a brief moment of silence, his face grew serious and he placed his complete attention on her. "And I think you should do the same."

Alone again, Tanya failed to keep her boiling anger intact. Was the whole world against her? It had to be a conspiracy. Were they just going to let him get away with this outrageous demand?

Facing her nemesis, she felt his confident smile ripping her to the core. "I wouldn't look so smug if I were you. Blackmailing your own flesh and blood is nothing to be proud of . . . not to mention that it's a federal offense."

"Blackmail?" he said innocently. "Such harsh words from such an amazingly beautiful woman."

With her hands on her hips, she bucked for a fight. "Compliments will get you absolutely nothing, and neither will these five dates."

Casually walking behind his desk, he said, "Then you have nothing to worry about."

Hoping to sound convincing, she huffed and said, "I'm not worried."

"Then why are you here?"

"To warn you."

"About?"

"This game of yours will only end in your grave disappointment."

He took a seat and casually leaned back in his chair as if he hadn't a care in the world. "According to our passionate kisses at the hospital and at your house, that's a lie."

Shifting uncomfortably from left foot to right, Tanya answered, "You caught me at a vulnerable moment, it was purely a physical response."

"I don't believe you."

Grabbing her coat, she shoved her arms through the sleeves and said, "I don't care what you believe."

"Well, we'll have five dates to decide which one of us is telling the truth."

As the reality of the situation settled in her mind, she considered it next to impossible to spend any significant amount of time with him, and decided to put an end to this fiasco. "No one makes me do anything. Ware Construction Company will thrive whether we have your contract or not. Damian gave me the option of saying no."

"But you won't," he said with quiet assurance.

"How can you be so sure?"

Taking a calculator out of his desk drawer, he carelessly tossed it across the desk to her. "You do the math. Your company has spent a significant amount of time preparing for the proposal for the bid, and you've already spent a large amount of money on suppliers and contractors. If I pull the plug on this now, Ware Construction Company stands to lose a great deal of money. You wouldn't do that to your best friend. Would you?"

Refusing to acknowledge the truth in that statement, she grabbed her gloves and hat and put them on. "We'll sue you."

"And spend even more money."

"Not when we win."

"*If* you win."

Reaching for the door, she said, "I can't believe you would screw your own brother."

"Think what you like, but you have a decision to make. Is it five dates or do I call Anderson Builders?"

Eight

Tanya stepped off the elevator and barreled down the hall of Ware Construction Company, speaking to no one. Ignoring her assistant, Alicia Jones, she stepped into her office and slammed the door with enough force to rattle the paintings on the wall. Like a lion scouting its prey, Tanya paced the floor, willing the anger to subside enough so that she could think clearly.

Did she really believe that, in this day and age, a woman could be forced into spending time with a man she despised? Hadn't women made enough progress over the years that they always had a choice?

"I do have a choice," Tanya said to the empty room. "If that man thinks he can steamroll me into five anythings, he just doesn't know me very well. If he wants to pull this contract, then so be it. I know Damian would understand."

Her confidence renewed, Tanya hurried to her desk to call Brandon and tell him precisely where to stick those five dates.

"Tanya," Alicia buzzed over the intercom, "you have a call on line three."

Not wanting her mission to be delayed, she said, "Who is it? I'm right in the middle of something."

"It's Frank Anderson."

Pausing, Tanya eyed the phone suspiciously. Why would the president of Anderson Builders be contacting her—on today of all days? Ware Construction Company and Anderson were competitors on several high-profile projects, and there was no love lost between them. They came out one and two on just about every bid where they battled head to head, though Ware prevailed more times than not.

While healthy competition was good for any company, this rivalry went one step further. Damian had started his career at Anderson, and when he decided to step out on his own, Frank tried feverishly to get him to stay. First by offering him part ownership, then by telling Damian that he'd never make it on his own. But Damian ventured out anyway, and his business flourished.

Since Ware Construction Company had won its first contract, Damian's reputation as an astute businessman and a more than fair boss garnered him public recognition. It was this commitment to his business and his employees that made Ware Construction Company an attractive employer. Over the years, several Anderson employees were now working for Ware. Because of this success, Frank took great pride in every bid his company won over Damian. Frank always considered it a personal victory. "I'll take it. Thanks, Alicia."

"Mr. Anderson, what can I do for you?"

"Hello, Ms. Kennedy. So nice to hear your lovely voice."

Having never received a social call from Frank before, Tanya wasn't fooled into believing that this would be one. "Get to the point, Frank."

"Just what I like in a woman—aggressiveness."

"You've got about three seconds to start talking business or I'm hanging up."

Laughing, Frank knew she meant every word. "I know this call is out of the ordinary, but I understand we are in a very strange predicament."

"I'm not sure what you're talking about," Tanya answered, even though she'd already concluded that this call and her conversation with Brandon earlier were related.

Quiet for a moment, Frank cleared his throat. "I was under the impression that Brandon Ware spoke with you about his firm's building project."

Taking a seat, Tanya tapped her pen against the desk impatiently. "I've spoken with Mr. Ware briefly, but I must say I am not aware of why you would be contacting me."

"I'm sorry, Tanya," Frank said, feigning confusion with his tone. "I thought that Mr. Ware clearly stated to me that you were aware that his firm was close to making a decision to change contractors, once again having Anderson Builders beat you out of yet another deal."

Tanya's resentment at his arrogance hovered just below the surface and she fought hard to maintain her professionalism as he continued to speak.

"While a decision to change companies hasn't been finalized, for a firm to consider something like this at this stage of a project usually means a change will more than likely take place. I just thought we could get a jump on things if we could arrange a time for you to turn over the blueprints and architectural designs."

Tanya silently counted to ten, steam threatening to rise out of her ears. How dare Brandon contact Anderson Builders and insinuate that this deal would be awarded to them! Doing a complete one-eighty in her decision to let this contract go, Tanya burst with energy and determination as she prepared to take on Brandon and his harebrained scheme. Not only would she accept Brandon's outrageous deal, she'd take great pleasure in showing him how fruitless this little plan of his would be. After five dates, the only thing he'd have would be a lonely life, while her company would have its contract, and she would have had the satisfaction of watching Brandon take a gamble only to finally realize that there could never be anything between them again . . . once and for all.

"Mr. Anderson, I'm sorry you've wasted your time with

this matter, but I can assure you that Ware Construction will be building the office complex. Have a good day."

Without waiting for his reply, Tanya slammed the phone in the cradle.

Frank Anderson jumped as the sound of the hang-up resonated in his ear. Handing the receiver to the gentleman sitting behind the desk, he watched him place it on the base. Letting out a slow grin, he said, "You are not playing fair."

"I know. But all is fair in love and war, and this, my comrade, is both."

"She's not going to like being manipulated. I've had enough business run-ins with her to know that when you push her around, she pushes back."

Brandon stood and confidently smiled. "I know, but I also knew that the moment she left my office, she would talk herself into calling my bluff. That's where you come in. One phone call from you would push all her competitive buttons. Right now she's probably planning how this arrangement will put us both in our place. Preventing you from having this project awarded to you, and showing me that she is completely over me."

"Looks like you got it all figured out," Frank said. "Are you ever going to tell her the truth about that call?"

"Don't worry, I'll tell her all about it when we're playing with our grandchildren."

"And what about your brother? Do you plan to tell him that you never had any intention of switching companies?"

"I will . . . on my wedding day."

Frank considered why he had agreed to make that phone call. "When you helped my son out of that messy situation last year and I told you I owed you one, I never thought this would be how you would collect."

Walking him to the door, Brandon patted him on the back. "Believe me, I got the better end of this deal. I may have kept your son out of jail, but you have given me the chance to win back the love of my life."

Before he left, Frank turned to Brandon and said with gratitude, "I appreciate what you did for Eric. He's turned his life around and started college this past fall."

"Tell him I meant what I said—if he gets a degree, I'll find him a job."

Nodding, Frank added, "I hope everything works out for you and Tanya."

"You and me both, my brother. You and me both."

"Tanya, Natalie's on line one."

"Thanks, Alicia." Pushing the line, Tanya sat forward in her chair and prepared to unleash her fury. "Natalie, you won't believe what that two-timing, no good—"

"Tanya, slow down," Natalie interrupted. "I can't understand a word you're saying."

Taking a deep breath, Tanya started over and explained the latest development in the "Brandon is getting on my nerves" saga.

The only thing that kept Natalie from hanging up on her friend was the hope that she could talk some sense into that hard head. "So go on your five dates, you know you want to."

"What I want to do is call my lawyer and sue his butt for breach of contract."

"Tanya, listen to yourself. You claim you don't want to have anything to do with him, but every time we talk, he's the topic of your conversation. Brandon this, Brandon that. If you really don't want to renew your relationship with him, why does every conversation about him garner such an emotional response? Personally, I'm tiring of talking to you about this."

"If that's how you feel, you'll be glad to know that this story actually has an ending in the very foreseeable future.

In two weeks, the dating game will be over and Brandon Ware will not only be out of my life . . . he'll be out of our conversations."

How long did Tanya plan to fight her attraction to Brandon? Inwardly admitting that his tactics seemed a bit extreme, Natalie had to give credit where credit was due. After fighting with Tanya from the moment he had stepped onto East Coast soil, he'd finally found a way to get the two of them together. Now the question remained if they would survive their five dates—or would Brandon end up needing emergency medical attention?

Hearing silence, Tanya suddenly remembered that it was she whom Natalie had called, not the other way around. "I know it was you that called me and I just took over the conversation. I apologize. So tell me, what's up?"

Natalie unconsciously smiled. "Now that you've asked, I've got two words for you. Derrick Carrington."

Searching her memory, Tanya had no idea whom Natalie referred to. "Derrick who?"

"Carrington. My appointment from yesterday. Girlfriend, let me tell you, that man had it going on!"

Relaxing for the first time that morning, Tanya laughed. "Now, this I got to hear . . . and don't leave out any details."

"When he walked into the conference room, I swear the temperature went up at least twenty degrees. I'm telling you, Tanya, this man put the *f* in fine, the *h* in hot, the—"

"OK, OK, Nat, I get the picture," Tanya interrupted, her laughter growing louder.

"Oh, no, you don't," Natalie said, her voice laced with animation. "That was just talking about the face. Let me tell you about the body. Does the description Greek god mean anything to you?"

"Now I think you're exaggerating."

"Uh-uh," Natalie countered. "I may not be a fitness guru, but I know a great body when I see one—even when it's tucked away in a custom-made gray four-button suit. Let's just say his body put the *h* in hard, the *s* in sexy, the—"

"Enough," Tanya yelled playfully into the phone. "Did he put the *d* in date . . . as in did he ask you out?"

"Are you kidding?" Natalie asked. "Weren't you listening, we're business associates now. Nothing can be done until we take care of his parents' dry cleaner's."

"How long will that be? It sounds to me you won't make it another day without Mr. Carrington."

Hearing the mocking tone, Natalie smiled. "Let me tell you something—after the last three disastrous dates Christine set me up on, I'm just excited to find a man who has all his teeth, can speak in coherent sentences, and doesn't reek of a strange odor very similar to curry."

Tanya wiped the tears of laughter from her eyes. "I wish you the best on this one. But didn't you say he has a life on the West Coast? What if he changes his mind and decides to go back? Where will that leave you?"

"Hadn't looked at it that way," Natalie answered thoughtfully. Hearing the knock on her door, she stood. "But if he does decide to leave, I wouldn't mind giving him a going-away present he would not soon forget!"

"Girl, you are too bad."

"I'll take that as a compliment. I got to go, Tanya, my next appointment is here."

"Maybe this one will put the *h* in handsome, the *g* in gorgeous . . ." Tanya couldn't help but tease her friend.

"Let's hope not," Natalie added. "I don't want Carol Stanfield to put the *a* in anything!"

Tanya hung up the phone still laughing. Over the past year, Natalie's dating stories had been something out of a situation comedy. She actually had gone out with a guy that was missing at least half his teeth. She could have gotten past that slight imperfection, except that he also still wore a Geri curl and insisted on replenishing his activator every hour on the hour. Natalie still had a small stain on her couch from his first and only visit.

Then there was Antoine. No matter what he said, no one could understand one word. It was as if he were speaking a foreign language. Halfway through dinner, Natalie stopped trying and just began nodding every ten or so seconds. Natalie called it the longest night of her life.

Finally, there was curry man. Natalie had actually gone out with him three times, and each time he smelled like curry. He wasn't a chef, and he claimed not to eat Indian food. To this day, they couldn't figure out where that smell came from.

Derrick Carrington was the first man in a long time to warrant a phone call like that. Attraction could always be measured by how fast you told a friend about him. And Natalie didn't wait twenty-four hours before calling Tanya. Hopefully, when they finally went out, he'd put the *n* in normal.

"Tanya, you have a call on line two. It's her . . . again."

Tanya dropped her pen on the desk and threw her hands up. How much worse could this day get? Danielle had left two messages on her home phone this week, but Tanya never returned the calls. She would see her soon enough when she went home for her father's birthday celebration. This was her third call today, not counting the two messages she had on her home answering machine last night. "Take a message."

"Again?"

"Yes, again, Alicia. Just ignore the serious attitude she'll probably give you for not putting the call through. I'm sure she's already given you a taste of her nastiness."

"Actually," Alicia said thoughtfully, "she hasn't said one word I would consider to be rude in all the times that she's called this week."

"Really?" Tanya asked, surprise evident in her voice. One thing that you could count on from Danielle Kennedy when she didn't get her way: instant attitude. Her temper tantrums were legendary and Tanya refused to give in to any of them.

"I'm serious, Tanya. I've known your sister to be rude, ignorant, and downright nasty. But today, she seems . . ." Alicia hesitated as she searched for the right word. "Calm."

That was the last word Tanya expected to hear out of her assistant's mouth. When Danielle wanted something that didn't immediately come to her, calm was the last thing that would be used to describe her.

"What do you think?" Tanya asked, at a loss as to what to do. She didn't want to talk to her, but she couldn't avoid her forever.

"I think if you don't take this call, she'll only keep calling until you do."

Realizing that Alicia's point had validity, she grabbed the phone and pushed the line. "Hello, Danielle. I don't have a lot of time, so make this quick."

"I won't take much of your time. I'm calling because I really need your help, Tanya."

Something in her voice caused Tanya to sit up. It wasn't what she said, for she had heard those words from her many times, but it was how she said it. A level of sincerity reigned in her voice that Tanya had never heard before.

Younger than Tanya by two years, Danielle had spent most of her adult life stepping over people and making enemies of her friends, family members, and business associates as she built a successful career as a model and actress. Measuring only material wealth, Danielle had had it all. A highly sought-after runway model, Danielle commanded upwards of twenty-five thousand per show. Her wealth had continued to significantly increase with endorsements from Cover Girl and Guess.

Danielle had coveted life on the fast track and enjoyed every solitary second on her rise to the top. Everything about the entertainment industry fascinated her and drove her to become an intricate part of all it had to offer. The money. The power. The parties. People around her catered to her every need and she reveled in the attention.

After years of living the lifestyle of the rich and famous, Danielle had made the ultimate mistake. She started believing her own hype. Taking on all the negative connotations associated with the word *diva,* her brass, rude, and bossy behavior began to overshadow the person she had used to be, as well as her God-given talent. She began demanding special attention and accommodations for every show, and the hospitality riders on her contracts became just as long and detailed as the contracts themselves.

A private dressing room, fresh seasonal fruit, imported water, rare flowers, German chocolates, personal hairstylists, makeup artists, and masseuses were staple requests for each appearance. But even her demanding ways in her profession didn't compare to the heartache, pain, and pure hell she caused to the people closest to her.

Engaged to Damian before he met Christine, Danielle had openly received his devotion and love, only to smash it into a thousand pieces. Damian believed Danielle when she promised to slow her career down to start a family. Making plans for an extravagant wedding, Damian believed he had found in Danielle everything he could ever want in a woman. But when business opportunities presented themselves, Danielle threw away Damian's love like an old piece of furniture, accepted the new business ventures, and never looked back.

Years later, Danielle began to reap all the drama, pain, and heartache she had sown. Finding out her business manager not only made bad investments with her money, but siphoned off millions of dollars from her, Danielle awoke one day with no money, no professional jobs, and a pack of creditors chasing her down. Left with nothing, she attempted to repair the damaged personal relationships she had created on her rise to the top. However, instead of reaching out to her family and friends with sincerity, she opted for manipulation and using people. She pretended to want to atone for her mischievous ways, though Tanya learned she only wanted to scam her friends out of money. Her plans to deceive back-fired and in the end she lost everything. Broke and alone, she got exactly what many would say she deserved. And Tanya openly admitted that she was one of those people.

Tanya wondered how Danielle was adjusting at home with their parents for the past year, hundreds of miles away from the glamour and glitz of the entertainment industry. Except for the brief, polite conversations the two of them had had when Tanya called home, there hadn't been one conversation of substance. For Danielle to call several times at work proved that she deemed whatever she wanted extremely im-portant, but Tanya didn't want to jump the gun, thinking she heard sincerity in her voice. Danielle had fooled them all before with her apologies and sincere tones. Tanya wasn't in-terested in being duped again.

"What do you need, Danielle?" she asked.

Glad that her sister didn't hang up on her, Danielle breathed a sigh of relief as she collected her thoughts. Hav-ing practiced several times what she would say, she bit her lip nervously, realizing the prepared words of her speech wouldn't come out. The only thing she could do called for her simply to speak from her heart. Softly, she started. "I'm sorry."

Tanya heard the words, and goose bumps formed on her arms. As children, they had often gotten on each other's nerves and argued frequently. When it was time to make apologies, each would always know whether the other meant it or not. This was one of those times Tanya believed the words were true. In those two simple words, Tanya heard the remorse and regret for the past.

Danielle closed her eyes and said a silent prayer. No one knew her better than her sister, and when she had chosen fame and fortune over family, she paid the price by losing the one relationship she cherished. When Danielle dialed this number for the third time today, she worried that the bond only two sisters could share had been permanently severed, but hoped her words might move Tanya's heart and spirit—might convince Tanya that this time she meant it.

"I'm sorry for everything. The lies, the arrogance, the screaming matches, the name calling. I'm sure there are plenty of negative words to describe my behavior over the past years, but let's just say I know now that I was a genuine jerk and probably got everything I deserved."

Hearing silence on the other end, Danielle hurriedly continued. She didn't want to give Tanya a chance to change her mind about talking to her and hang up. "I destroyed my relationship with you and I ruined my chances with Damian. I can't go back in the past, but I can control the future. I know I have no right to ask for your forgiveness, but I was hoping that we could begin to rebuild what I tore down."

Tanya remained quiet, waiting for Danielle to continue. It was true, she had been one evil woman ever since she became a supermodel. Was it possible for her words to be a reflection of her heartfelt desire to mend their broken bond? Tanya wasn't quite ready to give in completely, but she had to admit that this was the first time she actually considered that her sister was telling the truth.

"Tanya?"

"I'm still here."

Tanya had always been tough and Danielle admired her ability to stand strong for what she believed. But that quality was the very thing that could prevent Tanya from accepting her apology. When it came to forgiveness, Tanya rarely gave in. During their school days, Danielle had witnessed Tanya carrying a grudge for years.

"There is something else."

Here it comes. She'd never known Danielle to do anything without an agenda. What was it that she wanted this time?

"I've gotten a job opportunity to host a syndicated television show on fashion and style. The viewing market will be small to start with. It will only broadcast in a few major cities and the production will be done out of their Washington, DC, studio. Filming in DC instead of New York will keep the costs down. This would be the first real chance I've had to get my career on track in over a year."

Those words couldn't have rung more true. Turning thirty could be considered the death of a career in the modeling industry, but Danielle had compounded her problems by treating other industry professionals as if they were beneath her. Yelling at photographers, showing up late for shoots, and refusing to wear particular outfits in the middle of her New York and Paris shows had models, designers, and agents talking of her long after the shows ended. Halston, DKNY, Tommy Hilfiger, and Phat Farm had banned her from their fashion shows, and many other design houses thought of doing the same.

Working to shift her career from the runway to the small screen, Danielle found that her reputation had preceded her, and the few television shows that allowed her to audition either didn't get picked up by the networks, or the production staff decided they didn't want to work with her. The only person Danielle managed not to alienate was her agent, Michelle Ford.

"Sounds like things are looking up for you, Danielle. I'm really happy for you."

Tanya spoke the words, and after they were out she realized she truly meant them. Once Danielle hit the big time, it had taken years for Tanya to have a civilized conversation with her younger sister. Dealing with someone who had become self-centered, arrogant, and as conceited as Danielle had emotionally drained Tanya. Trying to talk sense into

Danielle about her alienating actions had proved useless, and all the conversations had ended with Danielle accusing Tanya of being jealous of her fame, fortune, and success.

When Tanya had severed all ties with her, she did so without regrets. But over the past year, their mother had been trying unsuccessfully to get the two of them to make amends. Talking with Danielle today, Tanya could honestly say that while she wasn't interested in being Danielle's bosom buddy, she was glad that her career appeared to be on the upswing. Maybe her baby sister had finally grown up.

Danielle allowed herself to relax just a little. Tanya sounded genuine in her words, and she hoped that her next question would garner that same sincere response. "I have to go through quite an audition process. The director wasn't exactly thrilled that he has to consider me." Pausing, Danielle sighed as she remembered the conversation with her agent about this job.

Michelle had told Danielle she'd had to call in every favor to get her in the running. Years ago, this same director had been hired to direct a special for *Fashion Week* and Danielle was the featured model. As usual, her personal requests far exceeded those of the other models, but faced with the option of not having her, the director conceded.

Live on a major network in prime time, there was room for zero errors. Everyone involved worked the show on edge, knowing that the slightest mistake would cause major damage to the show, the sponsors, the network, and the ratings. Halfway through the show, Danielle became infuriated when her final two outfits were switched with another model at the last minute. When the designer quickly explained that the coloring on the dresses with the current lighting onstage would make her skin look flushed, Danielle refused to give in. She argued for several minutes, claiming that if the designer couldn't properly put a show together, that was his problem—not hers. She would either wear the original dresses assigned to her or not go back onstage.

By this time, the director had appeared in a panic. He had gotten word in the booth that he'd better get backstage immediately. Not sure what he would find, he definitely didn't think it would be a spoiled model arguing with a French designer. "What the hell is going on? We're back on live in two minutes."

The designer's heavy French accent had only incensed the director more as he struggled to understand what he said.

Danielle, losing patience with the entire scene, had stepped between the director and the designer, staring the director squarely in the eyes. "The bottom line? I either wear my original assigned pieces or I don't walk back on that stage."

"Forty-five seconds!" someone yelled.

Glancing from the designer to Danielle, the director quickly made his decision. "Put on the original assigned clothes and get your butt onstage."

Danielle gave the designer a victorious smile, grabbed the first dress, and quickly changed. Months later, when she caught the show on a rerun, she watched herself strut in those final scenes with both dresses and realized the designer was right. She looked completely flushed out.

Jumping back to the conversation, Danielle secretly prayed the director wouldn't continue to hold that one encounter against her. "With the screen tests, meeting with writers, and talking with producers and the director, the process will last almost two weeks."

Hearing the hesitation in her voice, Tanya knew she wanted something and braced herself. "Just spit it out, Danielle."

Being a person in need was new for Danielle. Up until a few years ago, she hadn't wanted for anything. Now, everything in her life seemed to be out of her hands. Her career, her money situation, even her living arrangements were at the mercy of others.

Humbled seemed too soft a word to describe Danielle's new

personality. Had it not been for her parents' support, she could have ended up on the street. Taking the time to get to know herself, Danielle had reviewed her life's choices and realized months ago that every person who enjoyed her demise had every right to do so. Chances were, she wouldn't be able to go back and apologize for all the wrong she'd done, but she hoped to make amends with at least one person . . . her sister.

"Typically, my expenses would be covered, but in this particular situation, the director refused. The DC area is quite pricey when you're talking about a two-week stay in a hotel. Is it possible that I could stay with you?"

Mabel Kennedy had told Tanya a few months ago that Danielle was different now, but Tanya had refused to believe it without solid proof. Mabel explained that after a trip to New York a few months back where Danielle didn't get a small part on a television drama she'd auditioned for, she returned to Georgia with an entirely different demeanor. Telling Tanya that only a visit from the almighty God himself could have caused such a drastic and immediate change in her daughter, she had tried to cajole Tanya into giving her sister another chance. Tanya had refused, not ready to believe that Danielle deserved it.

Asking to elaborate on what caused this great transformation in her sister had failed to render any further information. Mabel insisted that if she had more questions about her sister, Tanya would have to ask Danielle. Remaining skeptical, Tanya hadn't contacted her sister, but listening to her today, she thought her mother may have been right. Yet, she'd been fooled by Danielle's sympathy tactics before. "I'll think about it. When do you have to know?"

Shrieking with excitement, Danielle practically dropped the phone. At least she hadn't flat-out refused. "Thank you, Tanya. Thank you so much. The auditions begin the Monday after Dad's birthday weekend."

"I'll call you back."

After hanging up with Danielle, Tanya stared at the phone for several minutes. Could she really stand to be around her sister for two whole weeks?

Her message light began blinking and Tanya dialed the access code and punched in her pass code. "Tanya, Brandon. I'm ready to get this deal of ours started. I believe we have a date to set. Call me."

Slamming the phone did nothing to relieve her agitation, so she picked it up and slammed it down again. The audacity of that man! Was she expected to put her entire life on hold for him? Jump through hoops on this deal? He must be out of his mind.

This had been one of the wildest mornings of her life. First Brandon's outrageous deal, then Natalie's new attraction, and now Danielle's request. Feeling the walls closing in on her, Tanya decided to take the afternoon off and do some shopping. She would deal with Brandon Ware and his stupid dates when she was good and ready—and not one second sooner.

An hour later, Tanya stood inside Cherished Cherubs, a store with everything you could ever want or need for a baby. Amazed at all the cute outfits available for little girls, she took her time browsing through the boutique, careful not to miss any item. Only intending to buy a few things for Brianna, she found her arms growing heavy as she filled them with a variety of onesies, jumpers, and adorable dresses in beautiful soft shades of pinks, purples, oranges, and yellows. Once Tanya added the socks, hair bows, and soft shoes that matched every one of the dresses she picked, Brianna wouldn't have to wear the same outfit twice for months.

Working through the various racks of clothes, she approached the area that housed the baby furniture and abruptly stopped. Almost instantly, overwhelming feelings that had arisen at the hospital returned. Eyeing the baby cribs, strollers, and basinets, she pictured all those items in her second bedroom—the perfect size for a nursery.

Growing up, never would she have imagined that at thirty-five she would be husbandless and childless. As a little girl playing with dolls, she had looked forward to the day she'd have a family of her own. Her baby's room would be done in shades of purple and the theme would be Noah's Ark, no doubt making her mother beam with pride at the biblical decor. But life has a way of throwing curve balls, and sometimes things just don't turn out the way you plan them.

"Is there something I can help you with, miss? All of our baby furniture is twenty percent off this week."

"Um, no, thank you," Tanya told the saleslady whose name tag read Dottie. "I'm just looking."

"Just take your time," the older woman said, walking over to a mahogany crib. "But for my money, I think this is you. A custom-made, hand-carved, imported sleigh crib from Italy with a matching, hand-painted dresser and changing table."

Stepping to the other side, Dottie motioned to the chair. "And of course, no nursery is complete without the sleigh glider with the ottoman, a must-have for any new mother. Ordering today will have it here by spring."

Realizing the assumption she made, Tanya opted not to correct her. Instead, she motioned to the items she held in her arms. "I think I'll just take these for now."

As she watched Dottie carefully fold the items in tissue paper and place them in pink gift bags, Tanya suddenly felt the weight of the world on her shoulders. Turning thirty-five. Breaking up with Martin. Dealing with Brandon. Talking with Danielle. Holding Brianna. Her entire life suddenly felt too overwhelming. Fighting the tears in the corner of her eyes, she wasn't sure how much more she could take.

Gavin sat across from Martin briefing him on the upcoming activities, meetings, and press appointments scheduled for next week. Becoming a member of Congress was similar to joining a fraternity. There were certain initiation processes, both public and very private, that new members were subjected to. Staying on top of all the information became more important, as everything from delegating office space to making committee assignments was being done. Having finished speaking on the last item on his list, Gavin realized his boss was paying very little attention to what he was saying.

"What's on your mind, Martin? I have a feeling you haven't heard anything I've said in the last ten minutes."

Standing, Martin walked to a window and stared out. "How long before you have my special report?"

Reaching into his briefcase, he pulled out a manila envelope and placed it on Martin's desk.

Having already read the information provided by the investigator, Gavin had a gut feeling that Martin would not be pleased. Boy Scout, high school basketball player, honor student, academic scholarship to college, top law school, and heavily recruited by one of the largest law firms in the country. Not even a parking ticket. If he had been any cleaner, he'd be eligible for sainthood.

Reading through the information quickly, Martin closed the folder and threw the envelope back to Gavin across the desk. "And what do you expect me to do with this?"

"I know it's not much—"

"Not much?" Martin interrupted. "There's nothing. How am I supposed to convince Tanya that this man is no good for her if this is all you have?"

"So this is about her?" Gavin asked, slightly irritated. He didn't mind poking around on people if it meant furthering his and Martin's political careers. But for a woman? They could ill afford to expend their energy, and resources, on anything not related to moving them to the next level.

Gavin watched closely as his boss paced the floor and thought of the minute Martin had laid eyes on her at that construction symposium. Intending on getting to know her, Martin had turned on the charm and wooed her.

It could be a tricky situation running for public office and beginning a personal relationship with someone, and it was no different for Martin. But he had forged full steam ahead, convinced that he could balance them both. Now, things seemed to be getting a little complicated and Gavin needed to make sure that Martin kept this situation in perspective. He could not afford to have Martin lose his patience over this. Both of them had worked too hard to get where they were to have a woman cause anxiety and friction. Their run in the political scene, just beginning, needed no setbacks.

Gavin tried to understand why he was getting so worked up over her anyway. Even though they'd been a couple for a year, their courtship could in no way be considered ordinary. Media attention, campaign appearances, and fund-raising events had composed most of their dates. The last thing Gavin needed was a love-struck congressman on his hands.

"There's got to be more on Brandon Ware than that," Martin said.

"Is she worth all of this? No one knows about the proposal, why not cut your losses? There's so much going on now. You're just beginning your career."

Martin shook his head in disagreement. He'd worked too hard to shape her into the woman he needed by his side. "She's exactly what I want. Besides, how will I explain this breakup to the press? With so many people at her party, I wouldn't be surprised if it has already leaked. The PR on this must be handled with extreme care."

Now, that statement Gavin agreed with. The saying "bad publicity is better than no publicity" didn't apply to any person in the political scene. Regardless of what information Gavin put out, some members of the press would assume there was more to the story. They would dig to find something negative to print about Martin or Tanya, forcing them to defend themselves and their actions. They could not afford any negative publicity from anywhere.

Thinking that it might be better to work it Martin's way, Gavin said, "This is just the preliminaries. We'll have more when we hear from the investigator next week. He's been tailing him since day one."

"There better be more, because there's nothing in this information that's of use to me."

Pointing to the folder, Martin said, "Destroy it and bring me something I can use. You know as well as I do that everybody has something. If he doesn't have a skeleton in his closet, find me a bone. But I want something on him . . . fast." Pausing a moment, he added thoughtfully, "I have a strange feeling my time is running out."

Tanya pulled into the driveway behind a red rental car. Reaching into the backseat, she grabbed all the bags with her gifts for Brianna.

Damian answered the door and Tanya walked past him without saying a word.

It didn't take a rocket scientist to figure out why she gave him the evil eye. "I told you that you had a choice," he said.

Handing him her coat to hang up, she grunted. "Some choice, hand over a prime contract to our biggest competitor or share five excruciatingly long dates with your brother. Either way, it's a hell of a choice."

Closing the closet door, he motioned her to the study. His brother's deal had upset Tanya, but this foul mood she'd been marinating in had started weeks before his brother came back to town. What was really going with her? Shutting the door behind him, he motioned for her to take a seat and waited.

Sitting, Tanya crossed her arms over her chest. "I feel a lecture about to take place."

Damian took a seat next to her and searched her eyes for any indication of what she was feeling. Happiness, laughter, enthusiasm for life used to be staples in Tanya's life. Now, he wasn't sure if when he saw her she would be angry, upset, or just in a bad mood. "Then make it easy on me. Instead of my going through how well I know you, that I can feel something is wrong, and then proceeding to beg, plead, and pull it out of you, why don't we just skip the preliminaries and go straight to the main topic? Tell me what the problem is—the real problem."

There was no other friend in the world that meant more to her than Damian. When her relationship with Brandon had ruptured apart like a volcano, instead of taking sides, making judgments, or offering unsolicited advice, Damian had guided her through the fog of a broken heart and helped her heal her soul. Resting her head on the back of the sofa, she rubbed her temples and boldly declared, "I'm thirty-five."

"And?" Damian asked, trying not to show his confusion.

"And I'm thirty-five," she repeated forcibly.

With a grin, Damian responded, "You gotta give me something more than that."

Raising her head, she said, "OK, how about this? I'm thirty-five and not married. I'm thirty-five, childless, and my biological clock ticks at breakneck speed. I'm thirty-five with a job I could do with my eyes closed—it's a good job, but do I really want to do this for the rest of my life? I'm thirty-five—"

Reaching out to her, Damian grabbed her arms and interrupted. "OK, OK, I get the picture."

Her expression turned sad and there wasn't a trace of enthusiasm in her next words. "No, Damian, I don't think you do."

"Then tell me, Tanya. Make me understand," he answered with complete sincerity.

"I stood in the middle of Cherished Cherubs today staring

at baby furniture. The saleswoman, Dottie, thinking I was expecting, pointed out a beautiful Italian handcrafted mahogany sleigh crib." Swallowing hard to keep the lump in her throat from growing, she continued. "She said it looked like me. And you know what? She was right. That would be the exact type of furniture I would choose."

"Tanya . . ." Damian said, pulling her close and offering a shoulder for her to cry on. "I don't know what to say."

"Did I mention I'm thirty-five?"

Watching her crack a smile at that last comment, Damian relaxed. "I wish I could make it all better. I really do."

"I know you do, Damian," Tanya said with appreciation. Taking his hand in hers, she squeezed tightly. "Just talking it out helps."

Damian had witnessed Tanya move through many phases of her life. From a carefree college student to a woman building a career and making her own way in the world. Now that she faced an obvious crossroad in her life, he wanted to do all he could to help. "Well, I know one thing I can do. As of this moment, you are on vacation. I don't want to see you in the office for at least two weeks . . . longer if you need it."

Sitting back from him, Tanya raised her brow in surprise. "You've got to be kidding. I can't take off now!"

"Of course you can. I just said so . . . and I'm the boss."

Tanya leaned back and tried to remember the last time she had taken a real vacation. Then it hit her, five years ago . . . Jamaica. Shaking those thoughts out of her mind, she said, "We're still waiting on the permits from Morgan and Rock, the Metropolitan Plaza project should be awarded shortly, and we have two bids we're working to complete now."

"Alicia can handle the work, and if she has questions you're but a phone call away. Otherwise, I don't want you anywhere near Ware Construction Company."

Tanya tried to think of other excuses, but couldn't come up with any. "What am I supposed to do for two weeks?"

Damian shrugged and gave a devilish grin. "Find a husband, get pregnant, and decide if you want a new career."

"Ha, ha," Tanya replied. "Very funny."

"Funny or not, as of this moment you are officially off the clock."

Tanya let his orders sink in. Maybe time off was just what she needed. "You know, you might be on to something."

"I see you're warming up to my idea." Standing, Damian headed for the door. "Now that that's settled, let's go see my beautiful baby girl."

Brandon quietly slipped down the hall into the kitchen. Eavesdropping on such a private conversation was not his style, nor his intention. When he had arrived a few minutes ago and saw Tanya's gray Volvo, he prepared to corner her and find out exactly when they could begin their dates, but following the voices to the study, he wasn't prepared for the vulnerability he heard in her voice.

The night he had literally run into her at the hospital, he felt there was something different about her. Physically, she looked the same, but her zest for life that had been a part of her personality from the day he met her had seemed to diminish. At first, he thought it was related to the long night she'd had, but the more he thought about it, the more he realized that her normal walk and talk, usually filled with excitement, had seemingly disappeared. Listening to her conversation with Damian shed some light. Hopefully, she would let him be the one to give her everything she ever wanted.

Tanya stepped into the nursery and greeted Christine and Stephanie Hollister, the owner of the rental car in the driveway. Stephanie and Christine, friends since college, had been with each other through thick and thin. Tanya remembered

Christine telling her that Stephanie, living in Atlanta now, would be visiting soon after the birth.

Dressed comfortably in sweatpants and a T-shirt, Christine sat in the glider holding the sleeping Brianna in her arms. With her extremely short hair lying flat against her scalp, tired eyes, and no makeup, contentment showed all over her face. Envy had never reared its head in Tanya's life, but watching the scene playing out before her, she fought hard to keep her jealous thoughts at bay.

Rising, Christine placed the baby in the crib and signaled for Stephanie and Tanya to follow her through the double doors that connected the master suite with the baby's room.

Stretching out on the bed, Christine yawned and pulled the covers over her. "Thank you guys so much for coming by to help out. Sleep has been at a premium and I'm seriously re-thinking Damian's offer to hire a full-time housekeeper. Can you believe I actually told his parents to wait a month before they came to visit? How stupid was that? The books you read never prepare you for the full reality of life with a newborn. I have no idea what to do half the time and the other half— well, I still have no idea what to do."

"Why don't you call them and tell them to come earlier? I'm sure they wouldn't mind," Stephanie said. "If not, I'll be glad to stay as long as you want. I told Nathan this would be good practice for me, as we're thinking of starting a family soon."

Once working with Christine at her interior design firm, Stephanie had moved to Atlanta last year to marry the love of her life, Nathan Hollister. Tanya thought back to last February when Nathan and Stephanie had tied the knot in a beautiful ceremony held in a large, historical church in Atlanta. Commemorating the official day of love, the church and the reception room gleamed in a sea of red and white. With the processional starting at dusk, one hundred candles illuminated the sanctuary in a soft glow and created the most romantic picture Tanya had ever set eyes on.

When Nathan read his own vows to Stephanie, there was not a dry eye in the house. Declaring to love, cherish, and honor her, he ended by stating that he promised to make every day of their lives together just as special as this day. Remembering the wedding had Tanya once again pushing down thoughts of jealousy.

"That's wonderful, Stephanie," Christine said, snuggling deeper under the covers. "You'd be a great mom. And, Tanya, you know I have to hear what's been happening with you and Brandon. I heard about 'the deal.' Can't say that I'm upset about his tactics."

"I'm sure you're not," Tanya replied sarcastically. "But enough talking. Brianna is asleep, so this is the perfect time for you to get some sleep."

"She's right," Stephanie said. "I've bought groceries, so while you sleep, we're going to cook enough food to last you the week."

Yawning, Christine didn't put up much of a fight. "Thanks, guys, I really appreciate it."

Turning out the light before heading downstairs, both women smiled at each other. They swore they heard her snoring before the door completely closed.

Entering the kitchen, Stephanie headed for the refrigerator while Tanya went to retrieve pots and pans. Stopping abruptly, Tanya didn't realize the kitchen was already occupied. Brandon and Damian sat at the table eating a sandwich.

"We didn't know anyone was in here," Tanya said, trying not to stare. Brandon must have come over straight from work, because his custom-fitted dark blue three-button suit looked absolutely fabulous across his broad shoulders. If there was ever a time when a man left Tanya speechless, this was it.

"Don't mind us, we'll be out of your way in a few minutes," Damian answered.

"What you could do is offer to help," Stephanie answered. "I'm sure your mama didn't raise you without teaching you how to make your way around a kitchen."

Thirty minutes later, Damian found himself chopping vegetables for beef stew, Brandon stood at the center island peeling potatoes, and Stephanie and Tanya were in various stages of cooking several chicken dishes. Talking nonstop about the baby and the perils of parenthood, Stephanie and Damian kept up a steady stream of conversation. However, Brandon and Tanya failed to contribute more than a few words. They cut their eyes at each other when each thought the other wasn't looking, the tension between them remaining thick and uncomfortable. The only reason Tanya didn't leave was her stubbornness. She had just as much right to be here as he did.

Wanting to settle their issues once and for all, Brandon set his food aside. "Tanya, can I see you for a moment in the family room?"

"I'm in the middle of washing this chicken," she answered without looking his way.

Taking the pieces of meat out of her hand, Stephanie said, "I've got it. You two go ahead and talk."

Stephanie stared at Tanya for a moment, and Tanya picked up her silent message loud and clear. *Talk to him. Give him a chance.*

Glaring right back with unwavering eyes, Tanya relayed a message of her own. *I'm going to get you for this.*

"Go on, Tanya," Stephanie encouraged, obviously ignoring her expression. "Damian and I can handle this."

"Thanks a lot, Stephanie."

"Any time, sweetie."

Tanya heard the sugary tone and realized at that moment that Stephanie had become one of them. Joining her mother, Christine, Natalie, and Damian in conspiring against her and rooting for Brandon. Tanya slowly dried her hands on a paper towel before following Brandon to the other room.

The door had barely closed behind them before he got the conversation started. "You didn't return my phone call."

"Returning a phone call and a date are two different things," she snapped back, trying to extinguish the spark of attraction that threatened to explode. His having removed his jacket and loosened his tie, she finally relented that her physical attraction had never wavered. But that revelation only agitated her further. "I believe my requirement is five dates. No more. No less. So let's get this over with as quickly as possible. As a matter of fact, since we're together now, we can count this as date one."

"Oh, no," Brandon answered emphatically. "This is my deal. I make the rules. And rule number one is that a date is defined as you and me—alone. So tonight definitely does not count."

Placing her hands on her hips, she shook her head in the negative. "No, *we* make the rules. And here's rule number two: absolutely no touching."

"Agreed," Brandon said easily.

Tanya raised a curious brow at his quick agreement to her rule. Why did she feel disappointed when he was giving her exactly what she asked for?

Leaning in closer, he added, "Not unless you ask me to."

"Don't hold your breath."

Not deterred, Brandon continued, "Rule number three: I choose the place and the time."

"Fine . . . but nothing at your house." She waited for his agreement before she continued. "Rule number four: We meet wherever we go. We arrive separately and leave separately."

Shaking his head in the negative, he wouldn't agree. "I'm an old-fashioned kind of guy. When I take a woman out, I pick her up and I take her home. Nonnegotiable."

Hesitating, Tanya finally relented. "Rule number five—"

Throwing his hands up, Brandon jokingly said, "Enough with the rules Tanya. You're going to *rule* all the fun out of this."

"Oh, I'm sorry," Tanya said sarcastically, placing her hands dramatically over her heart. "Was this supposed to be fun for me? Dating a man who claimed to love me only to rip out my heart, stomp on it, and then hand it back to me? Is that what we're calling fun these days?"

Exhausted at fighting the same battle over and over, Brandon exhaled deeply and folded his hands in front of him, carefully scripting his next words. "Tee, for years I've been dealing with the results of my actions. I lied to you, I destroyed our bond of trust, and I made it *almost* impossible for us to have a future together. But the thing that's kept me going all this time? The 'almost.'"

Reaching for her hands, he remembered the rule of no touching he had just agreed to and reluctantly dropped them. "Last year, I watched you drive away from me after I got on my knees and begged you to take me back. At that moment, I fully comprehended the magnitude of what I had done. Then, seeing you with Mor . . . Martin . . . was more than I could bear. So I left."

Stepping away from her, he moved to the other side of the room, knowing he wouldn't be able to keep from reaching out to her. "I hoped our year apart would flush you out of my system. I had made my bed, so to speak, and I was prepared to lie in it. But it didn't work. I can't get you out of my heart, my mind, my spirit, my soul."

Tanya fought the feelings swelling inside as his words seeped in. All of a sudden, what had appeared to be so obvious to her weeks ago was now clouded by confessions of regrets, mistakes, second chances, and words of love.

Before his return, Tanya had pegged Brandon as the enemy. His lack of respect and his inability to commit to a relationship made the line drawn in the sand a clear indication that they were on opposite sides. But over the past week, all of what she thought she knew had become muddied and murky. She wasn't sure who or what she should be directing her anger toward . . . if she even had the right to still be angry. Struggling to determine if the enemy stood before her or lived inside her, she had no idea what to do.

"Everything all right in here?" Damian peered into the room, with Stephanie close behind. They had heard the screaming and yelling from the kitchen and neither of them dared to step into the room. But when the yelling stopped, they both crept down the hallway—just in case there was bloodshed and they needed to call 911.

"Everything's just fine," Tanya answered. "But I've got to go." Without a backward glance, she headed for the entryway and out the door.

"Tanya, wait . . ." Brandon said, following her.

But it was too late. Not even stopping to get her coat, she jumped in her car and drove off.

Pulling out of the driveway, Tanya dialed on her cell phone. Getting the answering machine, she left explicit instructions. For one night, she decided to let it all hang out and forget about her confused feelings for Brandon. If she was officially on vacation, she decided to start things off with a bang.

Nine

For the first time in her life, Tanya Kennedy was drunk.

And every person at the nightclub knew it. The dance floor in front of the bar vibrated as the lights flashed in an array of colors and the music resounded loudly against the wall. Her slim body gyrated from side to side while she danced with several men at the same time. With her hands raised high above her head, she twirled around and around, taking extreme care not to spill her drink.

When the song ended, she smiled seductively at her dancing partners and sashayed off the dance floor. Mingling in and around the crowd, Tanya laughed at silly jokes and batted eyes at unavailable men, while making her way to the bar to continue her attempt to clean out the house supply of Absolut vodka. Having arrived almost three hours ago, she had taken just half that amount of time to flirt with just about every man in the club, while simultaneously upsetting the women they were with.

As she was not a drinker, the alcohol took effect immediately, and six drinks into the night Tanya was feeling pretty good. Determined to take charge of her own destiny, she put Martin, Brandon, babies, her stagnant career, and Danielle out of her mind and decided to jump off the path of the straight and narrow and just enjoy the moment. After all, isn't that what taking a vacation is all about?

As she stepped to the bar, several men took pleasure in the

short, black leather skirt that fit the curves of her bottom like a glove and the red silk top that dipped suggestively in the front. The sassy outfit highlighted her five-foot-seven-inch frame without making her look cheap and tawdry. The clothes, which strayed far from her normal attire, should have made her uncomfortable at revealing so much of her, but she strutted with the confidence of a runway model. Slamming her glass on the oak top, Tanya loudly demanded another drink.

Having kept a close watch on Tanya all evening, the bartender leaned forward and pasted on a polite smile. "I think you've had enough for one evening, miss."

"Don't youse dare tellz mez when I've had enuff," Tanya answered, her words slurred and difficult to understand. "Now, youse just turnz yoself around, grab oneses of those bottles, and refillz this glass."

From the opposite side of the club, Natalie shook her head in utter amazement.

"I wouldn't believe it if I hadn't seen it with my own eyes," Natalie mumbled to no one in particular. "Never in a million years could I have imagined her acting this way."

For the past several weeks, one would have thought a death sentence had been declared on Tanya. First, there was the issue of her birthday. She had moaned and groaned for weeks about turning thirty-five. Next, the broken engagement. While Natalie had the inkling that Martin wasn't the man for her, she still understood that breaking up with someone whom you'd been with for a year could be depressing. And finally, there was Brandon. God only knew when Tanya would stop fighting against her attraction to him.

When Natalie had gotten the message that Tanya was ready for that night out on the town they had talked about last weekend, Natalie hoped a nice dinner out would bring Tanya out of her funk. But when she entered the dimly lit club called the Basement, shock was a mild word to describe the scene before her. Upon her finding Tanya sitting on a bar stool inhaling her second drink, something told Natalie that she was in for a long and wild night.

Efforts to convince Tanya to move to a table in the far corner had failed miserably. In fact, the only thing that got Tanya off that seat was the sounds of the latest number-one hip-hop song blaring through the speakers. Prodding Natalie to join her on the dance floor rendered no results, but that didn't deter Tanya. Natalie sat in awe, witnessing Tanya's attempt at demonstrating the latest dance grooves. With Tanya's hips swaying, her feet stepping from side to side, and her arms pumping in the air, Natalie wondered if she had just entered the twilight zone.

It wasn't that Tanya didn't like to have fun, but her naturally reserved nature didn't lend itself to this type of public display. And what a display it was turning out to be. An hour ago, Natalie's eyes had widened in shock when the DJ yelled, "How low can you go?" and Tanya proceeded to show everyone that with a tight skirt and high heels, a person could, in fact, go quite low.

"Now that is quite a sight."

Turning toward the speaker, Natalie sighed in relief. Tanya would curse her for calling him, but she didn't know what else to do.

"Brandon," she said, relief etched across her face, "I've never been so happy to see anyone in my life."

As he pointed his fingers to his ears, indicating he could barely hear her above the loud music, she leaned in closer, repeated her phrase, and pointed to the other side of the club.

Brandon followed his sister-in-law's gaze and blinked several times to confirm that his eyes weren't playing a trick on him. As he watched the exchange between Tanya and the bartender, the corners of his mouth curved into an unconscious smile.

Seeing the look, Natalie lightly punched him in the arm. "Brandon, this is not funny. She won't listen to reason. I've never seen her like this before."

Seeing the lines of concern on her face, Brandon grew serious and asked, "What's going on with her?"

Putting on her cashmere coat, Natalie shrugged. "Pick one. Turning thirty-five, breaking it off with Martin, and"— she hesitated a moment before she continued—"you."

Brandon had stopped listening after the Martin part. So she told him no!

"When I arrived, she wasn't in the mood to converse. She just ordered another drink and headed back out on the dance floor. That was almost two hours ago."

Dressed casually in black jeans and a pullover shirt, a far cry from the dress slacks and silk shirts worn by most men in the club, Brandon asked. "Does she know you called me?"

Seeing the hope reflected in his eyes, Natalie searched for her car keys, hoping to find the right words to spare his feelings.

Her delay tactic, coupled with her inability to look him in the eye, provided the answer. Sighing heavily, Brandon reached out to her. "It's OK, Nat. We saw each other earlier and, of course, we argued. I didn't think I would be the first person on her call list."

Feeling empathy, she tried to explain. "She threatened to leave and find another hot spot if I called anyone."

Laughing, he answered sarcastically, "I didn't know Tanya knew any hot spots."

"After tonight, I wouldn't put anything past her," Natalie said.

Brandon peered across the room at Tanya and felt a stirring deep inside. Natalie, with her chin-length bob cut and deep-set eyes, was quite attractive. But no one could hold a candle to Tanya's beauty. How would she react when he made his presence known?

Natalie knew from firsthand experience that Brandon could make Tanya spit nails, but he also remained the only person she trusted to leave her with. Martin was out of the question and Damian and Christine were busy with Brianna. Pushing aside the fear of the repercussions for calling him, she said, "I appreciate this, Brandon. It's almost midnight and I'm beat. I'm not sure I could handle her by myself."

Laying a comforting hand on her shoulder, he said, "No problem, Natalie. I'll take care of her."

Natalie stood and gathered her gloves and hat.

"Let me walk you to your car."

Not wanting Tanya to be out of their sight for even a minute, Natalie gave an assuring smile and replied, "Believe it or not, I got to park less than half a block from here. I'll be fine."

Seeing that he still wasn't convinced, Natalie pointed to the huge man standing at the entrance. "If it'll make you feel better, I'll ask the bouncer to watch me. He can see my car from the door."

Waving good-bye, Natalie disappeared into the night, partly hoping that forcing Tanya and Brandon together would restore their torn relationship.

Brandon refocused his attention to the far end of the bar where Tanya remained engaged in an animated discussion with the bartender. Walking toward her, he had a feeling he was walking out of the frying pan and into the fire.

"I'mes not giving youse my car keyz. I drove misself here, I can drive misself home."

With the patience of Job, the man behind the counter spoke calmly. "Look, miss, I would be more than happy to call you a cab."

Rising on her tiptoes, Tanya leaned across the bar top, squinting her eyes in the semidarkness. Attempting to make out the words on the bartender's name tag, she mumbled, "Keith . . . Kenney . . . Karl . . ."

Frustrated at her inability to read the fuzzy white letters, she stepped back. Just as she stood straight, the heel of her four-inch sling-backs caught the brass pole stretched across the bottom of the bar. She quickly lost her balance and, unable to catch herself, her eyes widened in surprise as her arms flailed wildly in front of her. Both feet left the floor and she was unable to prevent the inevitable. In a split second, her butt hit the floor with a definitive thud.

The music continued pounding through the speakers, but the snickers and laughs from several women somehow made it to her ears. The men, who moments ago were trying to get her number, now stood still, amazed. Taking in their reactions, Tanya needed several seconds before realizing that no one was going to come to her rescue. Attempting to get her bearings, she rested her head in her hands.

"May I?"

Glancing up at the familiar voice, she knew the outstretched hand offered her the assistance she desperately needed, but raising her head a little higher, she confirmed her worst fear. Of all who could have offered a helping hand, why him? What was he doing here?

Making no effort to acknowledge his offer, she closed her eyes, hoping the man that stood before her would magically disappear. However, when she opened them, the hand was still there, and instantly, her embarrassment turned to anger.

Purposely ignoring the chivalrous gesture, she awkwardly stumbled to her feet, using the edge of the bar for support. After several shaky attempts, she finally managed to stand on her own, pushing stray strands of hair out of her face. Continuing to ignore him, she turned her attention back to the bartender. Opening her small evening bag, she dropped a twenty-dollar bill on the bar and demanded to be served another drink.

Squeezing into the small space between her and the bar,

Brandon stared into her eyes and calmly said, "I think you've had enough, Tanya. It's time to go home."

"Youse don't tellz me what to do," she said, sticking out her chin defiantly.

Brandon watched with slight amusement at her attempt to sound bold and confident, when in reality she only sounded drunk. The people around them, who moments ago were engaged in their own conversations, began to focus their attention on the scene playing out before them.

Standing so close, he inhaled her scent and immediately felt his body react. Relishing in their closeness, he noticed her glossy eyes, flaring nostrils, and pouty lips. She was every bit alluring and attractive as the day he had met her, and he wanted nothing more than the chance to once again experience her touch, her feel, and her love. Not wanting her to become another form of entertainment for the spectators who had started to gather, he leaned close to her ear and whispered, "You know the old saying, Tee: You can walk out or I can carry you out. Your choice."

She was still fuming over their deal and the confused feelings generated from their last conversation; determination to get away from him coursed through her. "Well, herze's anover old saying for yous—you can kizz my—"

Before she could finish her phrase, her feet left the floor again. This time, instead of falling down, she was lifted up and swung over his shoulders. As if a participant in an old Tarzan movie, she automatically took on the role of Jane, pounding her fists against his back, demanding to be put down. But her efforts delivered no results. As he maneuvered his way through the crowd, the patrons, having a cross between shock and laughter on their faces, began to clap and cheer as they parted to let them pass.

"Put me down," she yelled, wiggling unsuccessfully to break free.

Ignoring her pleas, he nodded at the bouncer, who chuckled out loud as he held open the door for their dramatic exit.

Once Brandon was on the street, the crowd waiting to get inside stared openly at the couple as he made his way to his car, parked almost two blocks away. The cold January air, a welcome relief from the sweat and body heat radiating inside, touched his face. Glancing upward, he noticed light snow flurries swirling around with the wind.

Stopping in front of his black Jaguar, he set her down between himself and the car, keeping one arm around her to block any attempt at an escape. If given the chance, he knew she would bolt right back to the club.

Unsteadily swaying from side to side, Tanya mustered all the confidence her intoxicated body could and jabbed her finger into his chest and boldly declared, "I refuse to love youse."

One second later, she passed out, right into his arms.

Holding her limp body, he cringed at her words. Brandon felt the sting of her statement pierce his heart. He knew that wasn't the alcohol talking. Gazing at her flawless face, he mumbled under his breath. "I know you do."

Setting her in the seat, he gazed at her blouse, noticing her body's natural reaction to the cold air against the flimsy material. She had obviously opted to go braless for her night on the town—another action he knew to be out of character for her—and her nipples pierced through, causing a slight groan from Brandon. Swallowing deliberately, he inserted the buckle, shut her door, and quickly trotted to the driver's side.

Starting the car, he turned the heat on high and warmed the leather seats. The skimpy outfit offered little, if any, protection against the bitter cold. The black leather miniskirt and silky red blouse left little to the imagination. If provocative and enticing was the look she was going for, she had certainly accomplished it. The revealing clothes, the high heels, and the makeup—all came together to create a picture of pure sexiness that caused his reaction to be hard and strong. Shifting gears, he forced his attention back on the road and pulled out of the parking space.

Weaving his way through the streets of Washington, DC, he headed for his town house in Georgetown. The last couple of weeks had been trying for Tanya, but was it enough to make her resort to this?

Pulling into the garage, he cut the engine. The stray strands of hair falling over her eyes served as a friendly reminder of the wild and crazy night she had had. Moving it away from her face, he let his fingers linger along her cheek. With her smooth skin, long lashes, and luscious lips, she never failed to turn him on, even in her sleep. Feeling memories about to overtake him, he cleared his throat and shook her lightly.

"Tanya, wake up."

Getting no response, he got out and moved to the passenger side and opened the door. Shaking her again, he waited a few seconds, but still . . . nothing. Sliding his arms under her body, he carried her into the house.

As he made his way up the stairs to the second floor, her head bobbed against his chest and a few seconds later, he felt her body begin to stir.

Trying to gauge her surroundings, she glanced up at him with half-opened eyes and declared, "What are you doing? Put me down!"

"Please, Tanya, don't talk," he said, a slow grimace growing on his face. "Your breath will knock us both out."

Not finding any amusement in his statement, she demanded, "Put me down."

Reaching the top of the steps, he honored her request.

As soon as her feet touched the carpet, she stared at Brandon with questioning eyes.

Concern coursed through his body. "Tanya, what is it?"

Wrapping her arms around his waist, she stammered,

"I . . . I . . . don't feel . . ." Her words died on her lips as her body convulsed. Reacting a few seconds too late, he lost the battle to get her to the bathroom, and in the middle of his hallway, everything that was in her stomach was now on her hands and clothes and his carpet. Finishing her release, she groaned and fell to her knees. Tears stung the corners of her eyes and she willed herself to hold them at bay. There was no way she was going to let Brandon Ware witness her complete demise. All she needed to do was hang on to what little strength she had left until she was safely away from him.

Emotions swirled around Brandon as he read the pain etched across her face. Noticing the wet corners of her glazed eyes, he knew she was calling on every fiber of strength she possessed to prevent herself from breaking down in front of him. Gathering her in his arms, he helped her to the bathroom in the master suite.

Sitting her unceremoniously on the toilet, Brandon started the shower. Leaving her for a moment, he went back into the bedroom and pulled out one of her nightgowns. Returning to the bathroom, he stopped short when he realized she had fallen asleep.

"Tanya, wake up," he said, gently shaking her. "We have to get you cleaned up."

Her only response came in the form of deep, even breathing. He knew he couldn't leave her sitting on the commode, and he definitely couldn't let her sleep in those clothes. The room had already begun to reek of a foul odor. Realizing he would have to be the one to shower and change her, he said a silent prayer for inner strength.

Slowly he removed her blouse and inhaled deeply as he gazed at her golden bronze skin. Gazing heavenward, he pleaded again for strength. Her breasts, firm and full, cried out to be touched. But he never touched a woman sexually unless she wanted him to, and while the craving on the inside of him tempted to wear down his resolve, he remained strong and kneeled to remove her shoes. Reaching for the strap, he paused and stared at the gold object wrapped around her ankle. Why would a woman who claimed to hate him wear a gift from him?

Standing her up, he waited for her to come to, but by now her deep breathing had turned into a soft snore. Unzipping her skirt, he pulled it down, along with her panty hose. His eyes grew wide with surprise at the black thong underwear. As he perused her body from head to toe, his eyes confirmed what his spirit already knew. Exquisite—inside and out.

Hearing his own breathing become labored, he realized he wasn't going to get any help from the man upstairs, so he concentrated on ignoring his own growing desire, and refocused his attention on getting her showered and in the bed. Putting himself on autopilot, he removed the final piece of clothing.

With the shower big enough for two people, he knew the only way to make this work would be to get in with her. Weighing his options, he removed his shirt and pants, but opted to keep on the rest. A few more pieces of ruined clothes wouldn't make a difference at this point.

Moving them both under the spray of warm water, he made quick work of lathering her body. Willing himself to ignore the soft curves and mounds that his hands touched, he tried to think of things to take his mind off the woman who was naked before him. But no thought could ever be that strong and he found himself remembering when they had shared showers as a couple.

Losing the battle to remain objective, he decided she was clean enough. With soapsuds still on various parts of her body, he turned off the water and wrapped her in a thick, terry cloth towel. Carrying her to the bed, he mumbled, "You must have really tied one on to be able to sleep through this."

Putting the silk nightgown over her head and through her arms, he removed the towel and laid her down. There were two other bedrooms he could put her in, but it had been years since she had lain in his bed, and he had to admit that he liked seeing her there.

Ignoring the wet spots he was leaving on his carpet and the chills forming on his body from his clinging T-shirt and underwear, he covered her with a blanket, and stared. Who would have thought that there would ever come a day when Tanya Kennedy would be back in his bed?

Stepping back into the bathroom, he peeled off the remainder of his clothes and walked stark naked back into the room. Pulling a pair of pajama bottoms out of his drawer and heading for the door, he paused one last moment and said, "Sweet dreams, Tanya."

A few hours later, Brandon returned to his room, clicked on the small lamp beside the bed, and stared down at the sleeping figure. Knowing Tanya wasn't a drinker, he found it hard to rest comfortably without confirming that she was fine. Her deep breathing let him know that all she needed to do was sleep it off.

As she had kicked off the covers at some point during the night, he admired her body from head to toe. No part of that body could be classified as a mystery to him. He knew every intimate detail. The small birthmark behind her left ear, her sexy belly button, and the two-inch scar from a sixth-grade fight on her right knee. Resting his eyes on her ankle, he once again stared at the gold. Not wanting to read anything into it and getting his hopes up that somehow she wanted to reconnect with him, he leaned over and kissed her sweetly on the lips. Turning off the lamp, he left the room just as quietly as he had come.

Ten

The jackhammer pounded endlessly and Tanya wondered why someone would be doing construction inside her town house. Attempting to raise her hands to cover her ears, she gradually realized that the pounding sounds blazing in her ears were coming from inside her head and there was nothing she could do to stop them. Trying to sit up, she groaned as a flurry of darts hit their bull's-eye in the center of her brain. Shots of pain coursed through her body, and as she tried to adjust, she realized everything hurt. Her head, her stomach—even her butt. *What happened to me?*

Resting on her elbows, she slowly opened her eyes and wondered how her lids could weigh so heavily. The semidark room made it difficult to gauge the time or the day. Panning the room, she inventoried the oak armoire, the sitting area with the burgundy fabric, and the dark cherry-wood entertainment center. Glancing down at her nightgown, she fingered the lace before running her hands along the smooth sheets on the king-size bed. Recognizing everything, she grimaced from the revelation. *Please let this be a bad dream.*

As if on cue, the subject of her nightmare walked into the room.

"Look who has returned to the land of the living," Brandon said, carrying a tray of hangover remedies.

Attempting to tell him not to talk so loud, Tanya found her words swallowed by the balls of cotton that had taken up residence in her mouth. Unable to form one coherent word, she thought death would be preferred to what she was feeling now.

"Come on, Tanya, I need you to sit up. I brought you some toast, aspirin, and a glass of my special cure-all drink."

Lying back, she pulled the covers completely over her head. Finally finding her voice, she moaned, "Go away."

Sitting on the edge of the bed, he forced her to scoot over while he set the tray on the nightstand.

"Ow!" she exclaimed, feeling every aching muscle in her body while he attempted to make room for himself. "Go sit somewhere else and leave me alone."

"As I recall, you were the one who made a drunken spectacle of yourself. Falling down on your butt in front of a huge crowd of people, and ultimately being carried out over my shoulder. Not to mention that you threw up on my carpet."

"I don't recall asking for your help last night," she said, lowering the covers to her neck.

Taking a good look at her face, he inventoried the bloodshot eyes, the remnants of makeup that lingered around her eyes and lips, and they still hadn't done anything about that breath. Giving a slight smile, he said, "You look like hell."

"As usual, your unsolicited comments are not appreciated," she said, ignoring the piercing pain that pounded in her head. "Just like your interference in my life last night."

"Let me remind you that you were the one arguing with the bartender, flirting with men you didn't know—making the women look like they wanted to rip your eyes out. I would hate to see what would have become of you if I hadn't come to your rescue," he answered lightheartedly.

"If you're waiting for my gratitude, you can forget it," she said, not completely believing everything he said. Was she really flirting with men who were there with other women? "Just give me my clothes and I'm out of here," she answered.

Trying to solidify her statement, she sat up . . . and immediately regretted the sudden move. A swarm of butterflies made a sudden appearance in her stomach.

Recognizing that look in her eyes, Brandon picked her up in one fell swoop and rushed her to the bathroom. This time, they made it. After several minutes, his concern for her health battled with the amusement of the situation, and the humor side won. Watching her hug the bowl, he chuckled loudly as she heaved one final time and leaned her head against the cool rim.

"I'm glad one of us finds this amusing," she said, feeling her stomach returning to normal. How had she gotten herself into this situation? Her head was pounding, her stomach was cramping, and to top it all off, this entire episode was being witnessed by the one person who made her skin crawl, but whom she couldn't stop thinking about.

Struggling to stand, Brandon reached out to help her. Feeling the pain of his betrayal invade her memory, she jerked away and yelled, "I don't need your help."

Raising his hands in defeat, he remained silent and stepped out of her way, watching her move to the sink and wash her face. She reached aimlessly for a towel as water dripped into her eyes.

After a few moments of watching her frustration grow, he handed her a face towel and said smugly, "Do you *need* me to hand you one of these?"

Snatching it, she dried her face, threw it back at him, and marched back into the bedroom. With her entire body pulsating from the abuse it had suffered the past twenty-four hours, she refused to let him see how much pain she was in. It was bad enough that she had to pay for her partying last night, but to end up in Brandon Ware's house was more than she could bear. Sitting on the bed, she said, "Give me my clothes so I can go home."

Heading for the tray he brought in with him, he answered, "Number one, you ruined your clothes last night; number two, your car is still downtown at the club; number three, gauging by the fact that you still haven't fully opened your eyes, you may want to take some aspirin and rest; and number four—"

Exhaling loudly, she declared, "I'm not interested in number four or your stupid counting game." Leaning back against the pillows, she massaged her temples. Grabbing the aspirin and the purple concoction, she popped the two small pills in her mouth before downing the gooey liquid. "Ugh, what is in this drink?"

"Believe me, you're bettor off not knowing," he answered, taking the glass and placing it back on the tray.

Tanya took a deep breath and stretched out on the bed. "My head is killing me. I'm just going to rest for a few minutes, and then I want you to take me home."

Standing, he covered her with a blanket and watched her body relax. It only took a few seconds for her lids to close. Picking up the tray, he headed for the door. He would let her sleep, and then he would get some answers to the many questions swirling around in his head.

When Tanya awoke for the second time, the sun had set and the room was clothed in complete darkness. Amazingly, her head felt better, and when she sat up the expected dizziness failed to appear. Clicking the switch on the lamp beside the bed, she adjusted her eyes to the light and took another look around. Everything was different, yet familiar. Suddenly, she remembered her nightgown—dark green silk with lace trim. Definitely one of hers. Where had this come from? Could it be possible that he kept things that she had left over here when they were together?

Pulling the covers back and stepping out of the bed, she stood still for a moment, making sure her legs were steady and her stomach remained calm. Staring at the double doors that led to the walk-in closet, she let curiosity get the best of her and, nervously biting her bottom lip, placed her hand on the knob.

As she stepped inside, her eyes focused on the far left corner and her breath caught. Various articles of clothing that had accumulated over their year as a couple hung across the top bar. She pressed her hand against her chest, her heart rate accelerating as the unexpected flood of emotions coursed through her. Walking into the wide space, she ran her fingers across his suits, shirts, and jeans before she came upon a few of her suits, a couple pairs of jeans, casual shirts, and several dresses. On the shoe rack, besides lace-ups, tennis shoes, and Timberland boots, were several pairs of her pumps and her running shoes and sandals. She closed her eyes, and her mind flashed backed to five years ago, when everything was right with them.

With both of them running late for work, Tanya had attempted to get dressed and out the door in fifteen minutes, but Brandon had other plans. Having spent most of the night making love hadn't deterred Brandon from needing more—or her wanting more. As she stood in the closet buttoning her blouse, Brandon walked up behind her as bare as the day he was born and wrapped her in his arms. She felt electrified as his hardness pressed against her, as he nibbled on her ears and whispered words of endearments. Methodically, Brandon unbuttoned each button the moment she buttoned it.

Stepping out of his embrace, she had playfully pushed him away. "Your brother will fire me if I'm late for one more meeting."

"Let him. I'll take care of you for the rest of your life."

Unzipping her skirt, Brandon had dropped to his knees, taking the material with him.

Even though her body screamed for his touch, she only had twenty minutes to make a thirty-minute drive to her office.

Continuing to argue her case, she lackadaisically pushed him away. "We can't do this, Brandon. I don't have time."

Brandon answered by tugging at her panties with his teeth, cupping her behind in the process.

"Brandon . . ." Tanya sighed, knowing this was one battle she was ready to lose.

As his tongue traced the outline of her center, Tanya felt her knees weaken and her power to refuse him crumble when he tasted the essence of her. Slowly working his way up her body with his tongue, he removed her blouse completely. Gently easing the cup of her satin bra aside, he caressed one breast while his tongue traced the outline of the other. Guiding her to the floor, he lay atop her and the moment he entered her, thoughts of meetings, contracts, and time flew out the window. As they concentrated fully on each other, Tanya caressed his back and matched the urgency of his thrusts, feeling all that was him become an intimate part of her.

The expert touch of his hands skimming her side and thighs sent her to the highest level of ecstasy. The pleasure, pure and explosive, pushed her to the edge of sanity. Just when she thought she couldn't take it any longer, she yelled his name and shattered into a pool of sheer delight.

For several minutes, neither moved, but fought to bring their racing hearts under control. Too emotion-filled for words, they found satisfaction in lying in the middle of the closet floor in each other's arms. Days later, they were still treating each other for the rug burns.

Jumping back to the present, Tanya fanned her face and felt the moisture between her legs as she stood on the very spot where Brandon had had her shouting his name. Snatching a pair of her jeans and a shirt from the rack, she headed for the bathroom, determined to keep her mind from memories like that.

Running her fingers through her hair and turning her head

from side to side, she stared at her reflection in the mirror and unwillingly agreed with Brandon. She looked like hell.

Not one curl could be found in her hair, her eyes were still slightly bloodshot, and cupping her hand in front of her mouth, she realized she was in desperate need of a toothbrush. Opening the drawer under the medicine cabinet, she was glad to find just about everything she needed to make herself presentable. Twenty minutes later, she headed out of the bedroom and went in search of her unwanted host.

Brandon sat in his study with his back to the door. He felt her presence before she spoke. No matter where he was or how many people were in a room, he knew the moment she entered. He had a connection with her that challenged all logic.

"How are you feeling?" he asked without turning around.

Ignoring his question, she said, "I want to go home."

"Can't we talk?"

"No."

Still facing the window, he said, "For the record, this does not count as one of our dates."

"Your sense of humor needs to be adjusted."

Turning to face her, he smiled. "Really? I thought it was quite clever myself."

"How's this for clever? If you won't take me home, I'll call a cab."

Rising, he reached inside the desk drawer and pulled out her evening bag. "I have your purse and the money in it. Unless I give it to you, you're not taking a cab anywhere."

Watching him place the black satin evening bag back in the drawer, she drew in a breath to calm down. Though childish, she couldn't stop herself and declared immaturely, "You make me sick."

Shrugging, Brandon appeared unaffected by her statement. "You've been saying things like that ever since I got back into town. However, actions speak louder than words, and your tongue in my mouth and your hands caressing my body tell me the last thing I do is make you sick."

Her eyes narrowed and she seethed on the inside. "You caught me in a weak moment."

"Rare moment, weak moment—whatever kind of moment you want to call it, the fact remains that it did happen," Brandon said, leaning forward on his desk. "Don't you think it's time you stopped fighting it and just admit that not only can we rebuild our relationship—you want to?"

"Give me one good reason why I should. Would you forgive me if I cheated on you?"

Calmly, Brandon moved from around his desk and stood directly in front of her. Placing his hands in his pockets, he paused a moment before speaking. "I told you—"

Cutting him off by raising her hand, Tanya instinctively knew what his next words would be and refused to hear him say them one more time. "I don't want to hear it."

"Tanya—"

"You know what, Brandon, I don't want to have this conversation right now. In fact, I don't ever want to have this conversation. You should have stayed in California." Tanya saw the flash of hurt in his eyes, but she ignored it. "I don't need you to take me anywhere, I'll call . . ." Tanya struggled for someone she could call. Damian and Christine were definitely out of the question. And Natalie . . . well she was angry with Natalie for calling him in the first place. "I'll call Martin."

At the mention of Martin Carter, Brandon cursed under his breath. Natalie had said their relationship was over, but in desperate times, people did desperate things. Maybe for Tanya this was the most desperate she had ever been. It was plausible that she would call anyone—even Martin—if they could rescue her from her present situation. But Brandon had a feeling not even Martin could save her today. His gut told him that everything they'd been through had led to this moment. The time to settle their relationship had arrived. To prove that to himself, he opted to call her bluff. Lifting the receiver, he held it out to her. "Call him."

Not looking at the phone stretched toward her, she placed her hands on her hips and narrowed her eyes in frustration. "You can't keep me here against my will. That's called kidnapping."

Replacing the receiver, he realized she didn't want to talk to Martin and he failed to suppress his joy. Curving the corner of his lips into a sly grin, he offered no response and walked past her and out the door.

"Don't walk away from me," she yelled to an empty room.

Following him into the kitchen, she hesitated when she saw him pull a plate out of the oven.

"You haven't eaten all day," he said, placing a warm plate of chicken and pasta on the table.

Eyeing the food with an empty stomach, Tanya resisted the urge to accept his offer. Now that she had fully recovered from her hangover, her purpose became clear. Not to spend one more unnecessary moment in his presence. "If I have to walk home, I will."

Brandon continued to ignore her, and his inattention sent her over the edge. Turning on her heels, she retreated from the kitchen, headed down the short hallway to the front door, and swung it open.

Brandon didn't follow, but instead poured a glass of iced tea to go with her dinner. Taking a seat, he patiently awaited her return. It only took a few seconds before the front door slammed shut and her footsteps led her back to him. Trying to suppress his smile, he failed miserably. By the time she reentered the kitchen, his laughter was resonating around the room.

"You think this is a big joke, don't you? Well, I don't think it's funny. You let me make a fool of myself."

"You were doing quite a good job of that all by yourself."

"You couldn't tell me that we were buried in almost a foot of snow?"

Gesturing for her to take a seat, he politely answered, "I tried to tell you earlier, but you cut me off. That was my number four."

Refusing to sit, she leaned against the wall in despair, fighting the emotions that were wreaking havoc on her heart.

"Face it, Tanya, we're stuck together, at least for another night, maybe longer. As soon as the roads clear, I can take you to get your car."

Confused about her feelings for Brandon, she didn't know if she could take being snowed in with him.

Brandon watched the play of emotions across her face. She was upset, frustrated, tired, hungry, and full of anger, but their current situation could not be ignored. "You have to eat."

"Not with you." She left him standing there and headed for the study. He followed.

Stopping just inside the door, she inhaled deeply before turning to face him. Pulling on all of her five feet seven inches, she moved to stand directly in front of him. Ramming her finger in her chest, she spoke with conviction. "I am only going to say this once, so listen closely. Brandon Elliot Ware, I do not want to eat with you, I do not want to make small talk with you; as a matter of fact, I don't even want to be in the same room with you."

"Tanya—" he started.

Emphatically, she continued, "I don't even want to hear you speak my name."

Understanding the seriousness with which she spoke these words, Brandon relented. He had hoped this opportunity would allow them to talk out their problems. But he could see that the pain was still fresh. Until she was ready to let some of the anger go, there was little he could do.

"As you wish." Turning on his heels, he headed back to the kitchen.

Shutting the door behind him, Tanya leaned against the frame and exhaled a deep breath. All the strength she had just exhibited suddenly flushed out of her body. As she leaned her head back, the events of the past couple of weeks consumed her. As much as she willed herself to believe the words she had just spoken, she couldn't ignore the pounding of her heart and the sweaty palms that manifested themselves just from being in the same room with him.

When she had looked up in the club last night and realized that Brandon Ware was the man offering a helping hand, all the anger and hurt swelled in her. But a small part of her had felt the pull of his alluring looks and that devastating smile. The sexy eyes surrounded by thick lashes. The way he filled out those jeans. The lethal combination had sex appeal written all over it.

Walking to the desk and picking up the phone, she started to dial. There may have been nothing she could do about the weather, but being stuck in the home of her ex was not her fault, and she had every intention of placing the blame exactly where it belonged. And with each number she punched, her agitation continued to grow.

Before Natalie could say hello, Tanya lit into her like a fire.

"How could you do this to me? How could you call him when I asked you not to call anyone?"

Natalie adjusted the phone as she heard the rise in Tanya's voice. Not surprised to hear from her, she was surprised that it had taken her this long to call. "You weren't being reasonable. I couldn't leave you alone. I had to call someone."

"You could have just left. I would have been fine," she answered, trying to sound convincing.

Natalie laughed. "I don't think so. By the time I arrived, you were well on your way to having the wildest night of your life. I hardly recognized you in your leather skirt and made-up face." Growing serious, she added, "I know it's tough breaking up with someone."

Hesitating before answering, Tanya wrapped the phone cord around her fingers. "Look, Natalie. You're right, I should have been more considerate of you."

Noticing the change in subject, Natalie refused to let her off the hook. "You said you were fine with the decision with Martin, and felt like going out. When I arrived, you were already well on your way to being drunk. You didn't want to talk and you wouldn't leave. Did something else happen?"

Suddenly tired, Tanya closed her eyes and took a deep breath. "I guess I'm going through a phase."

"A phase?" Natalie asked, not quite understanding. "At your age?"

At your age. Those three words shot straight to the core of Tanya and she fought to maintain her emotions. It had been like that for the past two weeks. Just the mention of being thirty-five reminded her that she was still husbandless and childless.

Hearing the pause, Natalie continued with sincerity, "Talk to me, Tanya, tell me what's going on."

As if the floodgates had been opened, Tanya told Natalie about her loneliness and her desire to have a child.

After she finished, there was complete silence on the other end, as Natalie searched for the right words to help her friend. "It's not easy taking stock of your life. Look at me, at twenty-nine I spend all my time working. Between being the controller for Christine's interior design firm and running a foundation to help small businesses, my social life is nonexistent. However, we're not in the same boat. Brandon deserves another chance."

Hearing that statement reminded Tanya of her predicament: trapped with the one person who made the veins pop out in her neck. Releasing a slow breath, Tanya proceeded to explain the situation to her friend. Her grip on the phone tightened when Natalie started laughing.

"I don't see the humor in this," Tanya said.

"Of course you do," Natalie said, "if you would just loosen up. Stop trying to be a relationship martyr. Sacrificing yourself for some unknown relationship rule."

"In other words, you have no sympathy for my situation?"

"I'm sorry, Tanya, but as a single woman who hasn't had a decent date in six months, I can think of worse things than being snowbound with a hunk of a man like Brandon Ware."

"Yeah, well, the packaging may be enticing, but it's what's on the inside that makes my blood boil," she answered, attempting to relay the message that Brandon Ware was no longer a factor in her life.

Not quite buying her statement, Natalie said, "Remember what I said, girl. Give Brandon a chance."

Tanya ended the call without making any promises.

As soon as Natalie hung up the phone, it immediately rang again.

"Hey, baby."

Recognizing the voice immediately, Natalie rolled her eyes. *I have got to get caller ID.* "Um, who is this?"

"Come on, Natalie, it's only been a week. I know you haven't forgotten my sweet voice. You know who this is."

Natalie childishly pretended to put her finger in her mouth as if she were trying to throw up. That's how much sweetness she heard in his voice. "You're right, Russell. Unfortunately, I do know who this is. My only question is . . . what do you want?"

Talking in a deep, breathy voice, he said, "Aw, come on, Nat, honey. How long you going to give a brother the silent treatment?"

Natalie knew he meant to sound seductive, but the only thing he accomplished was a lot of breathy air in his words.

"You haven't begun to experience my silent treatment. If you think a week is long, try eternity."

As he lowered his voice even more, Natalie covered a laugh as she knew his goal of sounding sultry and sexy was aimed at softening her up to forgive him. He must think she was an idiot to give her that lame story about the underwear she found being his mother's. Thank God she had never slept with him.

"Don't be so mean, girl. You know you want to forgive me. Why don't we just move past that previous slight misunderstanding? Why don't I just jump into my Hummer H-Two and join you on this cold, wintry night? I could bring a bottle of Cristal and we could keep each other warm by the fireplace."

Natalie grew quiet, rolling her eyes. That was the problem with some successful brothers. Get a little money, a fancy car, a black American Express card, and they expect women to put up with their load of bull. If she hadn't had Damian, Nathan, and Brandon in her life to show her differently, she might actually allow herself to get caught up with a jerk like Russell.

"So what's it gonna be, baby?"

Wanting to turn the table, Natalie lowered his voice and whispered in a seductively husky voice, "Russell, you asked to come over and keep me warm. Are you ready for my answer?"

Confidently, he replied, "Yeah, baby. Lay it on me."

"Here it is." With those last words, she hung up the phone.

It amazed Natalie that in today's world, men thought that they could get away with treating a woman any kind of way. The horror dating stories she had heard from her friends would put the fear of dating any man in her if she let them. But watching the relationships of Christine and Damian and Stephanie and Nathan gave her hope. All she had to do was find a man like them.

She thought about Dr. Derrick Carrington. Now that's the type of brother that would make any woman give the dating game another chance. Fine, successful, and he appeared to have all his teeth. Natalie decided she would take matters in her own hands. Regardless of what tradition told her about waiting on the man to make the first move, she planned on asking him out the day he brought in his parents' paperwork.

Glancing out the window, she watched the snow fall and admired the beautiful picture. The perfect scene for romance. Snow on the outside, fire on the inside. Her mind jumped back to Tanya and she smiled. That girl didn't know what she was in for. When you're snowed in with a hunk of a man determined to get his way, it's going to be mighty hard to resist if he turns on all the charm. And knowing how badly Brandon wanted Tanya back, Natalie also knew Tanya's willpower of refusal would most definitely be put to the test.

The shrill of the phone startled Natalie out of her thoughts.

Taking a seat on the sofa, she grabbed the cordless and answered.

"Natalie, it's me."

Taking a deep breath, she mentally prepared herself for the ensuing conversation. If dealing with men was draining, then dealing with Margaret Donovan was downright exhausting. "Hi, Mom."

"I haven't heard from you in a while. I could have been sick, in an accident—anything. And how would you know?"

"Mother, I'm listed on all of your insurance and emergency phone numbers. If something happened to you, I'm sure I would know." Why her mother couldn't help thinking the worst at times, Natalie would never know.

"I guess so," Margaret relented. A little more upbeat, she continued, "I was calling because I heard about the snowstorm. Of course, it's a sunny seventy-eight degrees here."

Natalie heard the teasing in her tone and smiled. With her mother's moving to south Florida a year ago, the sun and water had done a world of good for her attitude. Growing up,

Natalie had never known Margaret to be truly happy, but that had all changed in the past twelve months.

Having had Natalie with a man she later found out was married had caused Margaret Donovan to live most of her adult life in bitterness, anger, and resentment. She hated him for lying to her and then turning his back on his daughter—and her. The man that had bedded Margaret and never looked back? Henry Ware . . . Christine's father.

The entire situation had come to a head last year when Margaret wanted half of Christine's million-dollar inheritance after both Christine's parents passed. Even though Christine agreed to split the money before having to go to court, Margaret never forgave Henry for his betrayal and took it out on the only person she could, Christine.

As time passed, Natalie had hoped that her mother and Christine would make amends, but while Christine was willing, Margaret wasn't. Every time Natalie attempted to get the two of them together, Christine would show, but Margaret refused. While Natalie still held out hope that one day they would become civil, if not friends, Natalie was grateful that her mother had managed to find some happiness in her life when she moved to Florida.

"I'm glad you're enjoying the sun; meanwhile, I'm buried under almost a foot of snow. It's a good thing I went to the grocery store a few days ago. As usual, the weatherman didn't have a clue. He called for a light dusting—maybe an inch. Six inches later, that same weatherman talked of 'change in the storm pattern' and suddenly we're in for a foot of snow."

"I'm sure you'll be fine, Natalie. You're a trooper. Always have been. Always will be." The pride in Margaret's voice could be heard loud and clear. "I always knew you would do something with your life. I may have made the mistake of putting my trust in a man who claimed to love me, but thank God you didn't make the same mistake."

Natalie remained quiet, waiting for the words that always

followed a statement like that. Margaret took full advantage of any conversation that lent itself to reminding Natalie about letting a man get her off track.

"You have a great job and that nonprofit organization. And you did it all without the help of anyone from the male species."

Not a good time to tell her mom about Derrick. Natalie decided to keep him a secret. No use in getting her mother worked up at the prospect of Natalie becoming serious with a man since she'd never had a date with him.

"Trust your mother on this, baby—you'll always be better off without a man."

After promising to call her more often, Natalie finally got her mother off the phone. Needing to unwind from that conversation, she headed to the kitchen to make the perfect snowed-in drink: hot chocolate. Not a fan of anything instant, she opened the pantry door and pulled out cocoa, sugar, and salt. Reaching for a saucepan, she turned the stove top on low and added her ingredients. Getting milk out of the refrigerator, she returned to the stove and slowly began to stir her mix.

Natalie thought about her mother's final words. Accomplishing quite a bit during her lifetime, that's where her agreement with her mother's comments ended. Natalie's views on falling in love were not as cynical as her mother's and she looked forward to finding someone special to share her life with, have children with, and grow old with. The only problem was, every time she thought she had met Mr. Right, he inevitably turned out to be Mr. Wrong. Thinking of Derrick Carrington, she wondered if her luck was about to change.

Natalie stopped stirring when she thought she heard the doorbell. Who would be at her door in this weather? The roads were virtually impassable. Her ranch-style house, located in the suburbs of the city, was not easily seen from the road. Set on a little over two acres as her house was, her closest neighbor was at least a mile away. Hearing the doorbell again, she headed down the hallway, turned on the porch light, and gasped at the sight. If she were living in Alaska, she would have sworn she was looking at an Eskimo.

A thick goose-down white jacket, hood raised over a skull-cap, and a scarf. The only thing Natalie could see staring back at her were coal-gray eyes. "Can I help you?"

"My truck skidded in the snow and got stuck on the side of the road about a quarter mile from here. So much for my sixty-thousand-dollar SUV."

His voice, muffled from the layers of clothes, was barely audible. Not convinced she should open the door to a total stranger—snowstorm or not—she kept the lock on and asked, "Don't you have a cell phone? Can't you call a tow truck?"

"Of course I have a cell phone," he said. "Who would be dumb enough to leave home in this weather without one? But when I called my auto club, they told me they would arrive anytime between now and tomorrow morning. I thought it better to take my chances by finding a *friendly* neighbor."

Natalie heard the sarcasm in his voice, and even though she knew it was twenty degrees outside, she had seen too many horror movies to just open her door. "Why were you out anyway? Only an idiot would drive in the weather—SUV or no SUV."

"I'm a doctor on my way to the hospital. They're very short-staffed and I'd hoped that I could make it even though the streets in this area haven't been plowed."

Natalie hesitated before speaking. Reasoning told her even a serial killer wouldn't come out voluntarily in this weather. Standing in Timberland boots, several layers of clothes, and a heavy jacket, scarf, and gloves didn't stop him from shivering. If he had walked that far, he had to be almost frozen.

"Can I please come in? I think frostbite is settling into my toes."

Debating her next move, Natalie said, "Take off your hood and hat."

"What!" he yelled. "Look, lady, I'm half frozen as it is."

Hearing nothing from the other side, he wondered if she was still there. "Hello . . . are you still there?"

Natalie returned to the door with her digital camera. "Look, Mr. Snowman, I don't know you from the man on the moon. So you'll have to bear with me."

Understanding her need to be cautious didn't make this process any easier. He just hoped that whatever she was going to do, she would hurry up.

"I'm going to let you in, but before I do, I want to take a mug shot of you to e-mail to my friends. That way, if anything happens to me, you won't get away with it."

"You've got to be kidding me," he said, half amused, half annoyed. "How long will that take?"

"The faster you take off your stuff, the sooner it will be."

Cursing under his breath, he pulled back his hood, took off his skullcap, and removed his scarf.

Opening the wood door, Natalie kept the screen door locked as she positioned herself to take his picture. Glancing up, she froze. The dark hair, gray eyes, and mocha skin caught her completely off guard, but she recognized him right away. Dr. Derrick Carrington.

Eleven

Dr. Derrick Carrington filled the woman's foyer with snow, water, and a layer of clothes. Busy shedding his wet clothes and warming his body, he barely looked at his saving grace. "Thank you so much for opening the door—finally."

Stripping off his boots and attempting to get the circulation flowing in his toes again, he continued, "I'm not sure how much longer I would have lasted if you hadn't decided to open that door. I think I was about one minute away from becoming a real live snowman."

Hearing the humor in his voice, Natalie smiled. "Some may call me overly cautious, but Ted Bundy looked like the boy next door."

Setting his outerwear on the bench in the foyer, he paused when he heard her voice. The familiar sound touched a nerve and for the first time since entering her home, he looked at her.

"Natalie Donovan?"

"That's what my driver's license says."

For a brief moment, they both just stared at each other and Derrick felt his bones warming up—not from the heat inside the house, but the reaction his body was having to the woman standing in front of him. Finding his voice, he smiled. "I have to admit, five minutes ago I told myself I had the worst luck in the world, but now it appears as if the tides have turned."

Natalie silently admitted that he didn't have the copyright

on a change of luck. After dealing with Russell and her mother, Dr. Carrington was a welcomed change.

Giving Derrick her sexiest smile, her expression faltered when Derrick sniffed deeply and crinkled his nose.

"What's that smell?"

Drawing a deep breath, Natalie wailed, "Oh, no . . . my hot chocolate."

Running to the kitchen, she grabbed the pan with the burned ingredients on the bottom off the stove. "I forgot all about it."

Standing in the entryway to her kitchen, Derrick watched her dump what looked to be black tar into the sink. Forgetting for a moment that some of his clothes were wet from his trek through the snow, Derrick turned all of his attention to the woman cursing at a piece of cookware.

At their meeting earlier in the week, everything about her had said professionalism. Dressed in an emerald-green suit with matching accessories, her stylish hairdo and makeup, she had presented herself as someone who thrived in a business setting. But tonight, the complete opposite met him. No makeup, hair quite unruly, and the cargo pants and sweatshirt made a business meeting the last place she would fit in. But no matter what was on the exterior, it couldn't affect the true Natalie. Smooth skin, eyes the color of honey, and a smile that could light up a dark room.

"Is there anything I can do?"

Not turning to him, Natalie ran hot water in the pan to begin soaking some of the goo from the bottom. "No. It's already ruined."

Clearing his throat, he started to unbutton his shirt and said, "Don't take this the wrong way, but I've got to get out of these clothes."

Natalie turned to face him and her words died in her mouth as she watched him remove his shirt, the final layer of his clothes. She had never before given a second thought to the terms *expansive, firm, chest,* but those were the exact words that popped into her head when her eyes drank in his dark skin. Watching him begin to unbutton his pants forced Natalie out of her temporary haze.

"What do you think you're doing?" she gasped, raising her brow in surprise.

"I'm getting out of these wet clothes. Twice during the trek up the road that leads to your house I was the unwanted recipient of snow falling from trees. It's very likely that if I don't get some dry clothes soon, I'll catch pneumonia."

As she walked out of the kitchen, Derrick, already standing in the entryway, didn't move, forcing Natalie to turn sideways to pass. Just inches apart, their bodies didn't touch, but a spark of electricity passed between them and Natalie found herself short of breath. Almost in a whisper, she said, "Well, Dr. Carrington, I definitely don't want to be the one held liable for you catching such a terrible illness. Follow me."

Twenty minutes later, Derrick returned from her bedroom looking completely ridiculous, and Natalie couldn't withhold her laugh. Wearing a black sweatshirt with sleeves that stopped about four inches from his wrists and a pair of black sweatpants that stopped halfway down his calves, he made painfully obvious that the owner of these clothes stood nowhere near his six-foot-three-inch frame.

"I'm glad you find this amusing, but I take it by my choice of clothing options, there's no Mr. Donovan."

Stopping her laugh, Natalie eyed him suspiciously. "If your goal is to find out if I'm single, all you have to do is ask."

Leaning against the doorjamb, Derrick crossed his arms at his chest and smiled. Sass. He liked that in a woman. "Are you single?"

"Yes."

That little piece of information pleased Derrick immensely, though he tried not to let that show.

Stepping fully into the kitchen, he asked, "Is it OK if I use your phone? I need to call the hospital. They'll be trying to transport as many doctors as they can, so I'll need to let them know where I am."

"Help yourself. You've only been in town a couple of months and you're already on staff at a hospital?"

Natalie swore she saw a flash of sadness in his eyes, but it disappeared so quickly, she wondered if it was her imagination.

"With everything that's going on with my father and his business, I decided it was time I came back home. My practice in Los Angeles was a partnership, so I'm in the process of selling my share. Not ready to set up another private practice, I signed on with Trinity Hospital two weeks ago."

Listening to him make the call, Natalie remembered the situation with his parents and their business. She couldn't wait to get a look at their books. There had to be something she could do to help them. Reaching for another pan, she decided to try her hot chocolate once again.

Ending his call, he watched her remove the ingredients from the pantry. "Looks like someone likes to make their drinks from scratch."

Setting a clean pan on the stove, Natalie answered, "I can't stand anything instant."

"Everything that's instant is not necessarily a bad thing," he said.

"Are you kidding me . . . instant pudding, instant coffee, ready-to-bake cookies, microwave pasta? Believe me, I'm sure there's not one thing 'instant' you could name that I would consider good for me."

Moving to stand directly behind her, he asked, "What about attraction?"

Natalie froze in midmotion and turned to face him. "What did you just say?"

"You asked me to name something instant that would be good for you. I offer you attraction."

Sarcastically, Natalie pointed her finger at him and countered, "How wrong you are, Dr. Carrington. Some of my worst experiences started with instant attraction. So you see, I'm more prone now than ever to take the slow, unhurried route in that category."

Reaching around her, he took the cocoa and added it to the pan. "You may want to take the slow route, but sometimes the attraction can be too strong. Too potent. Your only option is to react."

Natalie stepped back and realized this conversation had just turned very personal. Watching him gently stir the simmering mixture, she answered, "A sure sign of immaturity is a person unable to control himself. That's why this society of instant gratification and quick fixes will soon reap the results of its juvenile behavior."

Pouring the milk into the pan, Derrick continued to stir and responded without turning around, "So you're telling me you're adult enough to suppress your feelings of attraction for the sake of maturity?"

With a playful laugh, Natalie countered, "Your assumption is that I have an attraction to suppress."

Pouring the steaming drink into two mugs Natalie had placed on the counter, he handed her one. Their hands connected and neither moved.

"Do you, Natalie?" Pausing, he watched her reaction closely. "Do you have an attraction you're trying to deny?"

Taking her mug, she ignored his piercing eyes, sexy voice, and direct question. Heading toward the hall, she said, "I'm going into the living room to watch the evening news. You're welcome to join me."

Neither spoke as they listened to the weatherman condemn them to at least another day together, nor did the subject of attraction come up again. Natalie couldn't stop silently answering his question. It was simple. Yes. She was most definitely attracted to Dr. Derrick Carrington.

For fear of acting on that attraction, Natalie thought it best if she turn in for the night, even it was still quite early. "I'm off to bed. You're welcome to sleep in the guest room. It's the second door on the right at the top of the stairs. And just to let you know, I keep a loaded nine-millimeter by my bed."

Derrick laughed as amusement shone in his eyes. "You can't be serious!"

"Let's just hope you don't give me a reason to prove it."

Sassy, feisty, and full of spunk. Natalie Donovan was becoming more interesting to him with every passing moment. "Good night, Ms. Donovan."

"Good night, Dr. Carrington."

Not ready to face Brandon yet, Tanya sat in the leather chair and twirled around to face the window. Any other time she would have marveled at the beautiful winter picture being painted outside. Mother Nature had made a breathtaking statement with snow-covered trees and hills. Alas, the beauty of the moment got lost in the presence of her circumstances.

Leaning back, she closed her eyes and remembered the last time she had sat in this chair. Brandon had been working nonstop to prepare his closing argument for a major case in which his client had been accused of violating antitrust laws. Understanding the importance of his work in relation to his quest for a partnership, Tanya had supported his efforts by giving him the time and space he needed. But time and space weren't what Brandon had in mind when she brought him something to eat.

Close to midnight, Tanya had worn a silk robe with a black teddy underneath. When she placed the sandwich, chips, and ice water on his desk, Brandon bypassed the food and went straight for the flesh. Reaching his arms around her waist, he turned the chair and pulled her between his legs.

"Brandon, I didn't come in here to distract you."

Without responding, he had tugged at the belt that held her robe together and in an instant, it fell to the floor. With deliberate motions, he reached up and massaged her breasts, feeling them peek through the thin material.

As soft moans emitted from her mouth, she tried to step back. "You're not going to blame me if you botch your closing statement tomorrow."

Ignoring her words of caution, Brandon eased up from the chair and replaced his hands with his mouth. His tongue, in expert fashion, spent time sucking and licking each breast, causing her body to relax and give in to the passion that lovingly consumed her. No words were necessary as he reached across the desk, clicked off the lamp, and illuminated the room in the soft glow of his computer monitor. Without effort, the spaghetti shoulder straps melted away, and leaning back in his chair, he pulled her with him.

Unable to deny the raw sensuality of sexual desire forming in her center, she placed one bronze leg on each side. Straddling him, she confirmed his arousal was full and complete.

Reaching up, he moved a strand of hair from her face and gently kissed her lids. "Your eyes are exquisite."

Kissing her nose, he whispered, "Your nose is perfect."

Softly, the back of his hand stroked her cheek and sweetly kissed her lips. "Nothing in my life matters without you. I love you."

A tear formed in the corner of Tanya's eyes. Those three little words caused her heart to skip a beat. This was the first time he had spoken those words to her.

Uncontrollable heat ripped through her body as she stroked and loved him. As she rode the waves of overwhelming satisfaction, uncontainable joy threatened to completely overtake her. Meeting each thrust with equal intensity, he massaged her breast and whispered those three words over and over again.

"I love you, Tee. I love you so much. You are my every-thing."

The blood pounded through every part of her body as Brandon held her hips and guided her on the ride of her life.

Hours later, in the wee hours of the morning, when he had completed his closing statements, he made love to her again. This time, enjoying taking their time, it was slow and sweet and she felt Brandon's soothing endearments of love like never before. Connecting in every possible way, they lay in each other's arms and she reveled in the level of content-ment. In herself. In life. In him.

Tanya relaxed in his arms after he fell asleep. Sated and satisfied, she searched for words to tangibly describe what she found in their relationship. Happiness. Pleasure. Grati-fication. Completeness. All of those combined to create Tanya's total being.

A successful career, a man who loved her, and marriage and children in the near future. Everything she ever wanted in life seemed right within her reach. Never in her wildest dreams had she ever thought life would be this good. But those dreams had quickly vanished. How could two people that had shared something so beautiful end up apart?

Hearing the knock at the door, Tanya snapped back to re-ality and jumped out of the chair as if something had shocked her. Small beads of sweat formed on her brow, bringing the phrase "hot and bothered" to mind.

"Tanya, you need to eat something."

The grumbling in her stomach served as an annoying re-minder that he was right, but she couldn't tell whether the salivation in her mouth was from the thought of food, or from the thought of making love again . . . with him. Re-membering the closet and the study scene caused her body to crave him.

"Tanya?" Brandon repeated. "Are you going to come out?"

When she had thrown Brandon out of her office after he

confessed to his betrayal, Tanya's goal remained clear. Put him out of her mind and out of her heart. And if someone had asked her last week if she had accomplished that goal, she would have confidently said yes. But that was before she saw him, touched him, smelled him, and rested in his arms.

Opening the door and silently walking past him, she entered the kitchen, sat down, and reached for her fork. Abruptly, all motion stopped. Blinking twice, she looked at Brandon standing in the entranceway and gave a tentative smile. A half dozen chocolate chip cookies from her favorite bakery sat in the center of the table. Lena's Bakery made the best cookies east of the Mississippi and there had been many occasions when she went out of her way to treat herself to the gooey, soft treats. And it was definitely out of the way. The shop was located across state lines . . . in Virginia.

Pleased that he had found a way to make her smile, Brandon took a seat across from her. "I thought you could you use something special after the night you had. I know they're your favorites."

Taken aback by the gesture of kindness, she stammered, "But the snow . . ."

"I went out while you were sleeping . . . before the roads got too bad. I just made it. They were closing up when I got there."

Brandon smiled as he watched her expression. Knowing her so well, he knew she was pleased, but refused to let it show how much the gesture meant to her.

Taking a few bites in silence, Tanya quickly realized how hungry she was, and before she knew it, her plate was empty.

As he was moving to pick up her dishes, Tanya stopped him. "The least I could do is clean up."

"Is this a conciliatory gesture?"

Hearing the sarcasm in his voice, she answered, "Let's just say it's the least I could do for you feeding me."

"Feeding you? What about the ride home, the shower to clean you up, the hangover remedy, the cookies—"

"The shower?"

Brandon, realizing his slip, continued to clean up.

Stepping in front of him, she asked again, "What shower, Brandon?"

Staring in her eyes, he searched for any indication that she was joking. "You really don't know what I'm talking about? You passed out last night after you threw up all over yourself. I couldn't let you sleep in your . . . well, you know."

"Let me get this straight," she said, wondering what else had happened last night that she couldn't remember. "You stripped me naked, put me in the shower, and . . . and what exactly *did* you do?"

Not waiting for a response, she raised her voice and he knew he was in for it. Once Tanya got started, she was next to impossible to stop. And she didn't disappoint him now.

"What is the matter with you? Who told you to bring me home anyway?"

Letting her continue her tirade, he tried to pay attention to what she said, but found it impossible as his thoughts carried him back to last night, when his hands had touched every part of her body. And just as it had been five years ago, it was so last night. Everything about her turned him on. He was unable to control his expression as a seductive smile appeared and he felt his manhood coming alive.

Noticing his expression, she stopped in midsentence. "What are you smiling at?"

Chuckling, he said, "Trust me, you don't want to know."

Hearing the undercurrent of seduction in his tone, Tanya thought it best to end the discussion. "This isn't working."

"What?"

"You. Me. That's what."

"Because you won't let it work," he said, wishing he could knock some sense into her hard head.

"Give me one good reason why I should."

Without a second thought, Brandon said, "Because I love you."

Tanya heard the words and remembered a time when she basked in hearing his voice speak those words to her. She had believed them when he told her five years ago, and her breath caught as she realized she believed him now. But him loving her didn't change anything. Quietly, she responded. "Loving me is a privilege and you lost yours."

Grabbing her hands and raising them, he kissed each finger without breaking eye contact. "You're wearing my gift."

Closing her eyes, Tanya remembered her impulsive move to put the anklet on before she had gone out. Not quite sure why she did it, she found it giving her a sense of comfort she hadn't expected.

"I want my privileges back," he whispered. "Let me love you again."

She felt the tears well in the corners of her eyes. "I can't take the risk again."

Placing her hand around his neck, he then wrapped his around her waist. Coaxing her closer, he molded their bodies together. "Yes, you can. All you have to do is say, 'OK, Brandon, I'll give us another chance.'"

The room became engulfed in silence and Brandon remembered that first rule of negotiation. Hoping at this moment that her mind and heart would line up, he held his tongue to give her a chance to take what he was offering. He would stand in this kitchen with his arms around her until she spoke those magic words that would put the two of them back together.

Watching the struggle of emotions play across her face, he felt his heart constricting when he watched a lone tear fall down her cheek, and Lolita's words ran through his mind. *I hope you find someone you can't imagine living life without . . . and I hope she wants nothing to do with you. Then you'll get your payback for all the wrong you've done to others.*

They say that everything that goes around comes around, and Brandon gulped hard, rigidly trying to hold his own tears in check as he realized the universe could, in fact, be paying him back for his bachelor lifestyle in a big way. All those years of playing the field—treating women like objects. Breaking it off when they got too serious with him had come back to bite him in the butt. Even he would agree that if Tanya turned him down, he might be getting exactly what he deserved, but deep inside, he and Tanya had a love that that was real and true, and they both deserved to share their love for the rest of their lives.

Tanya's eyes remained closed, needing no sight to see exactly what Brandon Ware offered her. As the contours of her body rested perfectly against his, everything she loved about him rushed to the forefront of her mind. His beautiful face, soft brown eyes, and short-cropped hair. His sculpted body, solid as a rock, garnered second, third, or fourth looks from any woman.

Knowing his body intimately, she could recite, without hesitation, all of his hot spots. Places where she knew that one touch or one kiss could set his soul on fire. The spot behind his left ear, the reaction of her touch caressing his chest, or her tongue gently grazing his lips. And he could do the same for her. He knew just the right places to stroke, touch, feel, and kiss.

Moving beyond the physical, Tanya thought of all the other reasons she loved him. Helping her father install his satellite system because her dad had refused to pay the installation fee. Taking on pro bono cases, helping people who could never afford his law firm's fees. Warming her car up on cold winter mornings, and helping her plant flowers in the spring.

Afraid of where her thoughts were taking her, she stepped out of his embrace and discreetly wiped away her tears. With her last bit of strength, she fought to hold on to the last bit of anger that held her heart by a string. "Brandon, a home-cooked meal and my favorite cookies do not change anything. We are not lovers. We are not friends. We are two people stuck together in a snowstorm. Nothing more, nothing less."

Brandon watched her closely, trying to gauge the validity of her statement. When they had separated years ago, it wasn't because their feelings for each other had changed. In his heart, he knew that her feelings had remained as strong for him as his for her.

"Are you sure it's nothing more?" he challenged, stepping right back into her personal space. Of all the women who had been a part of his life over the years, no one had compared to the one standing in front of him. Hoping to bypass her mind and zero in on her heart, he stroked her cheek with the back of his hand and promised, "I can give you everything you want. Everything you need."

Tanya raised her eyes to meet his, and the tug on her heart told her that he spoke the truth.

Having overheard her conversation with Damian, Brandon knew exactly what Tanya wanted out of life. True love. Children. The happily ever after. And Brandon wanted those same things . . . with her. Trailing down her neck with his fingers, he gently stroked her shoulders. "If you let me, I can make all your wishes come true."

His touch, firm and persuasive, enticed her into his arms.

Kissing her cheek, he whispered, "Let me be the husband who loves you."

Kissing her ears, he continued softly, "Let me be the father of your children."

Tanya swallowed hard and let the melodic sounds of his voice take over every part of her, from head to toe.

Kissing her right temple, he whispered, "You name it, it's yours. You dream it, it's yours. Anything your heart desires, I'd move mountains to make come to pass."

Tanya gazed into his eyes and believed the love and commitment. "Brandon—"

"Listen, baby. Tee, I still love you. I still need you. I still want you. I've put everything on the line for us . . . my partnership, my relationship with my brother . . . and I'm willing to do anything else that's necessary to tell you how terribly sorry I am that I lied to you. I've wasted five years of our lives because of my selfishness and immaturity. But I told someone the other day that I was older and wiser. And I promise that if you give me another chance, you'll never regret it. I'm asking . . . no, I'm begging . . . for your forgiveness."

Tanya listened to his words and knew that this was the moment of truth. If she turned him down again, she knew in her heart that he would not ask again.

If I ended all my relationships because the other person made one mistake, I wouldn't have anyone in my life. And that includes you. The words of her mother rang in Tanya's ears.

How could you marry Martin? You're in love with another man. Christine's statement pierced Tanya's heart.

Remember what I said, girl. Give Brandon a chance. Why is it so difficult for you to forgive? Natalie's question struck a nerve.

No matter how hard you try, Tanya, you can't deny love. Damian's analysis left nothing to interpretation. As all these thoughts ran through Tanya's mind, she realized that yes, there was, in fact, a conspiracy against her. Her family and her friends were asking her to do what she'd always found so hard. Forgive.

Suddenly, Tanya's spirit, soul, and body became tired. Tired of being angry. Tired of feeling lost. Tired of thinking. Tired of fighting with Brandon. Tired of battling with herself. Raising her eyes to meet his, she let her shoulders relax and at that moment, the weight that had rested so heavily on them for the past few weeks swiftly evaporated. "OK."

"OK?"

"Yes, OK."

Not wanting to assume anything, Brandon needed explicit clarification. "What exactly are you saying 'OK' to, Tanya?"

"OK, Brandon, I'll give us another chance."

Having waited years to hear those words, Brandon said a silent prayer of thanks before wrapping his arms around her and spinning her around, planting kisses all over her face and neck.

"Brandon," Tanya said, laughing. "What are you doing!"

Not putting her down, he wanted to savor everything about this moment. "Say it again."

"You're being silly."

"So humor me."

"I want to give us another chance."

"One more time, baby."

"I want to give us another chance."

Brandon's lips descended on her, causing her heart to hammer in her chest. The powerful force of love that Tanya had suppressed over the last five years came gushing forward like an open dam. Now that she'd freed her spirit, her heart, and her soul, there was no denying the passion that sparked from the moment their lips touched. Unable, and unwilling, to control the gamut of emotions swirling around her, Tanya leaned into him and locked herself in his embrace.

Over the years they had been apart, Tanya had tried desperately to replace him in her life and in her heart. Dating several eligible men, she'd hoped that at least one of them could invoke a partial feeling of the euphoria that she had experienced during her time with Brandon. No man came close. Every relationship ended with increasing feelings of loneliness. Now that she was back in his arms, she understood the stupidity of her efforts. There could never be anyone who could satisfy her completely except the man in her arms.

Brandon's hands reacquainted themselves with every part of her body. Running his fingers through her hair, down her neck, to her shoulders where he gently squeezed and kneaded. Finally joining his hands behind her back, he happily wallowed in the thought that she welcomed him. All the dreaming of this moment he'd done for the past five years paled in comparison to the jolt of life that had infused his body. He may have been breathing, working, eating—doing all the mundane chores of life, but he knew now that he hadn't been alive. How could he have been when she was missing from his life?

Not wanting air to be able to move between them, he pulled their bodies closer. Tracing the soft fullness of her lips with his tongue, he hungrily consumed her with savage intensity. While some might think that a reunion kiss would be sweet and gentle, this connection was anything but. Powerful. Potent. Intoxicating. Compelling. The commanding kiss caused the blood to pound in his brain, his knees to tremble, and pleasure to radiate throughout.

Leaving her lips, he trailed a path of searing kisses to her cheek, then her ears, and finally her neck. Moans of pleasure echoed throughout, and reluctantly he took one step back, careful not to break complete contact, while he tried to catch his breath. "Tanya, I want you so much right now, but us getting back together was never about this. If you're not ready to make love, it's OK. I understand. Believe me, I'm satisfied just knowing that we're a couple again."

Tanya adjusted her blouse and digested what he'd just said. For the past few hours, the only thing she could think about was the two of them making love. In the closet, in the study—anywhere and everywhere. The need to feel him inside her threatened to make her physically ill. Reaching up and stroking his chest, she boldly declared, "Are you kidding, Brandon? This is the best part about making up! Show me just how much you've missed me."

Taking her hand, he started for the hallway that would lead them upstairs to his bedroom.

Passing the living room, Tanya smiled and gave him a

wicked grin. "No need to waste that warm fire in the living room."

"Your wish is my command." Leading the way, Brandon brought her in front of the fire and eased her down. In that moment, his purpose on this earth entered his mind with amazing clarity. To love, cherish, obey, and honor this woman for the rest of his days.

Lying beside her, he glided his hand across her flat belly. Reaching underneath her shirt, he trailed his fingers lightly upward until he cupped her breasts. In no rush, he took his time exploring, arousing, and giving her pleasure. As he squeezed gently, the soft moans from her lips confirmed the pleasure of his touch. As he moved his body to partially cover hers, his arousal pressed into her. Removing her shirt, he replaced his roving hands with his warm tongue, tracing around her breast, until he reached its core.

With her eyes closed, Tanya relished every touch, every kiss, and every stroke. Trembling from his erotic caress, she no longer wanted to be just a spectator in this moment. Her hand moved toward his pants, and sliding it down the front, she began to gently stroke him. The moment she made contact, his cry of pleasure only served to encourage her. With excited confidence, she reached under his shirt with her other hand and rubbed his sensitive chest and stroked his nipples.

"My life has been so empty without you, Tee."

A bolt of cold air moved between them as their bodies separated to remove the remainder of their clothes and for Brandon to retrieve the small foil packet. Seconds later, they lay skin to skin and heat singed their bodies from head to toe.

Whispering words of endearments and running his fingers through her hair, Brandon stared at the image of fire, passion, and love staring back at him. Coaxing her legs open with his knee, he raised his head and stared into her eyes. "I love you, Tanya."

Brandon entered her and Tanya immediately became

filled with a sense of completeness. This moment defined all that she had been searching for since that awful day five years ago. Shivers of delight swept through her and she moved her body to the rhythm he set. Meshed in exquisite harmony, neither could tell they had ever been apart. Tanya gasped in sweet agony and her heading was spinning as she soared so high, she could have gotten a glimpse of heaven. Moments later, Brandon followed with his own release.

As their heavy breaths returned to normal, Tanya wiped the moisture from his brow before he separated himself from her.

Making the choice to put herself back in his life, she could no longer deny the words that threatened to escape her lips from the moment he stepped into that hospital. "I love you too, Brandon. I love you too."

Martin slammed down the phone and let out a slew of expletives. He had been calling Tanya for the past two days with no luck. Having already left two messages on her home phone and another on her cell phone, he refused to leave another. Where could she be in a city that was shut down?

Calling Christine under the pretense of congratulating her on the baby didn't uncover any information. He thought of calling Natalie but didn't want to appear to be too desperate. Remembering the comfort level of Brandon Ware at her house, he picked up the phone and called Gavin.

"What's going on, Martin?"

"Have you heard from Sanders?"

"You've got to be kidding me, man," Gavin said, unable to hide his growing agitation at his boss's focus on this woman. "It's after eleven o'clock."

"I don't need you to tell me what time it is. Just answer my question."

"Look, Martin, he said he would tail him for a week and

get back to us. I'm scheduled to meet with him sometime on Wednesday."

"Well, I'm changing the plans. You get him on the phone tonight and tell him to give you what he has."

Gavin tried to remain calm and talk some sense into Martin. He didn't like the way this situation was playing out, but he had to choose his next words carefully. If he pushed Martin too far, that would only make him dig his heels in deeper. That was the last thing Gavin wanted. What he really wanted was for Martin to let this thing go. "Listen, Martin. Whatever he has can at least wait until the morning. I'll call him first thing."

Martin switched the phone to his other ear. "Since when did I become the one to follow orders?"

Gavin remained silent for a moment. Rarely did Martin pull rank and it was never over some broad. The two of them had been through thick and thin together. They'd fought racism, other politicians, and the system. They were finally in a place where they could begin to make a difference. Gavin hoped that feeling of apprehension in the pit of his stomach wasn't a sign of times to come. "What is it about her, Martin? We could handle the press on this. Just let it go."

"How can I let it go when I love her?"

"Do you?"

"Excuse me?" Martin asked, standing and pacing the floor. "What kind of question is that? Of course I love her."

"Are you sure you want to spend the rest of your life with her, or is it that for the first time in your adult life, you're about to lose?"

"That's the dumbest thing I ever heard," Martin argued. "I've spent the past year of my life with her. Getting to know her. Falling in love with her. How could you question my feelings?"

Gavin knew Martin better than he knew himself, and he wondered if he was listening to himself. Over the years, he had witnessed Martin develop many different types of relationships. Most of them were out of necessity and very few of them were real and true. Hoping to get his point across, he said, "What you've done is posed for pictures with her, hosted fund-raisers with her, and escorted her to various political functions. You haven't spent more than a few hours alone with her, and according to you, you haven't even slept with her. How much love could you possibly have?"

Martin, rubbing his temples, worked overtime to maintain his composure. "I know it's late, so I'll excuse your questioning of my motives. But what I won't do is wait any longer for my report. Get in touch with Sanders and call me tomorrow at nine A.M. with the info."

Exhaling a perturbed breath, Gavin said, "I'll talk to you first thing in the morning."

Twelve

Tanya awoke early the next morning embraced in the strong arms of Brandon. After having made love again by the fireplace, Brandon carried her up the stairs and together they climbed into bed. Watching the slow rise and fall of his chest now, Tanya slid her fingers up and down his arm, deciding to wake him up the way she used to.

Replacing her fingers with her lips, she trailed soft kisses up his arm, around to his neck, and finally to his face. As she kissed his eyelids, his nose, and finally his mouth, it only took a few seconds before he turned to her and pulled her close.

"Good morning, gorgeous."

"Good morning, handsome."

Such a silly endearment, but when they had been a couple, those were the first words out of their mouths every morning. Tanya seemed amazed at how easily they fell into their old routine. An outsider watching the two of them would never guess that they had been apart for five years.

"Why don't you shower first while I fix us some breakfast?" Brandon offered.

"I have a better idea. Why don't we shower together and then you can fix breakfast?"

Brandon leaned back and laughed. "I see you're still not fond of the kitchen."

"Hey, I cook enough to survive, but when I don't have to . . ."

Kissing her on the nose, Brandon said, "Can't wait to hear those snowplows."

Snuggling closer, Tanya wrapped her arms around him. "I kinda like the world we created right here."

"But in this world, there's nobody here to marry us."

Tanya's expression froze in place and her body stiffened. "Come again?"

Moving stray strands of hair out of her face, Brandon lovingly gazed into her eyes. It hadn't been his intention to propose like this. He'd always planned the intimate dinner, the expensive bottle of champagne, and the ring hidden in the cake. But hopefully, she understood that the feelings behind the proposal were more important than the atmosphere in which it was given.

Pushing back the covers, he walked stark naked across the room and retrieved a box from the dresser. The sight of pure maleness oozed from his confident, strong, and powerful stride, and Tanya found herself temporarily mesmerized.

Climbing back into bed, he presented her with an open small black satin box. "I love you, Tanya, and I want to spend the rest of my life with you."

Tanya cast her eyes downward and covered her mouth with her hand. At least three carats, the emerald-cut ruby glistened against the natural light. Confusion etched her face and she stared at him, eyes filled with unasked questions.

"I bought it the day after I saw you at the hospital, even though I knew you were considering marrying that other guy."

Tanya half smiled at his reference to Martin.

"And from the force of your slap that night, any sane person would have thought the odds of you giving me another chance were one in ten million. But I didn't give up on us. I couldn't give up on us."

Taking the ring out of the box, he reached out for her left hand and slid the ring down her ring finger. "I've waited five

years for this moment. Beneath your anger and my regrets—
there was always the love. Our love."

Tanya stared down at the ring on her finger but failed to
speak.

"We'll have a small ceremony . . . just our closest friends
and relatives. I'll wear a black tux, minus the tails, and you'll
wear an ivory floor-length sheath dress with a short veil that
doesn't cover your face. After the ceremony, we'll share dinner and dancing with everyone at your favorite restaurant.
The cake, three layers, will be designed to look like gift
boxes and we'll save the top layer to eat on our one-year an-
niversary. We'll go to Jamaica for the honeymoon and stay
in that wonderful villa we rented five years ago. We'll spend
our days lounging on the beach and our nights working on
our first baby. How does that sound to you?"

Tanya reached up and stroked the side of his face as the
warm tears fell openly down her face. When they had vaca-
tioned in Jamaica, they'd been lounging on the beach
enjoying the warm air when the topic of weddings came up.
He had just recited back to her the very words she had told
him that day. The words that described her perfect wedding.

She thought of her mother, Christine, Damian, and Natalie. Just a few days ago, she had cursed them all for giving
their unwanted opinions and thoughts on her relationship
with Brandon. Up until yesterday, the feelings of betrayal
had still held reign on her mind. Now, as she stared into his
beautiful brown eyes, none of those words came to mind.
She had truly forgiven him and allowed herself to feel no
shame in that. He had betrayed her once, but Tanya believed
in her heart that he would never betray her trust again.
"Don't I even get my five dates first?"

"Baby, if you say yes, you can have anything your little
heart desires."

"Yes."

At hearing that simple three-letter word, Brandon practically smothered Tanya with his body. "You've made me the happiest man on earth."

Natalie entered the kitchen and stopped short when she saw Derrick setting the table with fluffy omelettes and fresh juice. Her night's sleep had been anything but peaceful as she tossed and turned, thinking of the man who slept less than twenty feet away from her.

As the newscaster recapped the weather situation, it would appear that the county had worked diligently to clear the main roads overnight and then begun focusing on the side streets today. With any luck, her street would be one of the first ones plowed. Her three-bedroom, two-and-a-half-bath home with its spacious living room, dining room, kitchen, and basement suddenly felt too small for the two of them.

Derrick scooted back a chair and motioned for her to take a seat. "I think you'll be pleased with my breakfast. It's the least I could do for inconveniencing you last night."

Natalie took a seat and wondered why she never noticed his slight dimples before. It gave him a boyish feel that indicated he liked to have fun.

"You should approve of everything I have on your plate. I tried to stay away from anything instant or microwavable. I would have churned the butter, but . . . well . . . you know . . . I just didn't have enough time."

Hearing the playfulness in his voice, Natalie decided to play along. "Well, I hope this isn't loaf bread you've made my toast with. There was flour, yeast, and a pin roller in the cabinet. Surely you made this bread from scratch."

Pretending to wipe sweat from across his forehead, he dramatically sat down opposite her. "I have slaved too much this morning. I beg of you to enjoy the fine baking of Wonderbread."

Picking up her fork, Natalie said a quick prayer and dug

right in. After several bites, she had to admit that the food was pretty good and complimented the chef.

"Thanks," Derrick said, adding syrup to his pancakes. "After I graduated from medical school and started my residency, I realized I couldn't go another year with processed food from a vending machine. The dorm food was bad enough, but hospital food took the cake . . . no pun intended. I went to the bookstore, bought a beginner's cookbook, and the rest, as they say, is history."

"Are you telling me you didn't have a girlfriend all too willing to cook your meals for you?"

Derrick paused and his eyes sparkled with amusement. Giving her a slow grin, he asked, "If your goal is to find out if I'm single, all you have to do is ask."

Having her words thrown back in her face, she decided to be just as bold as he had been the night before. Tilting her head to the side, she smiled. "Are you single?"

Caught up in all the teasing they'd done this morning, Derrick had unwittingly walked himself into a corner. Refusing to lie, he gave the only answer he could. "No."

That one word sucked the air right out of her lungs. Not wanting to show her grave disappointment at his answer, she took another bite of her food and held her expression. She had checked his ring finger when he came to Business Strategies, and not only was he ringless, he didn't even have a tan line. But that didn't mean that he wasn't engaged or heavily involved. Feeling a little embarrassed, she dropped her fork in her plate, no longer hungry. "I feel sorry for her."

"Excuse me?" Derrick asked, taken aback by her response.

"You've been flirting with me from the moment you stepped into my house. All that talk about instant attraction. To think she's probably sitting at home worried about your tired behind out in a snowstorm, and here you sit making goo-goo eyes at me."

Derrick tried to hold back a laugh, but couldn't. "Goo-goo eyes? Just how old are you?"

Ignoring his gibe, she took her dishes to the sink, dumping the remainder of her food in the garbage disposal. Without saying a word, she left the room.

Sitting in the living room, Natalie flipped through several channels trying to calm her anger. When he entered the room a few minutes later, she refused to acknowledge him.

Taking the spot next to her on the sofa, he rested his arm behind her but didn't touch her. "Make no mistake, the moment I walked into your conference room, it was an instant attraction."

"How lovely," she answered sarcastically, continuing to channel-surf. "I'm sure your wife would love to hear all about your instant attraction."

"I'm not married."

"Oh, well, let me rephrase that. I'm sure your fiancée can't wait for you to come home and tell her all about this attraction you have for me."

"I'm not engaged."

Throwing the remote on the table, she turned to face him. "Whatever you want to call her . . . girlfriend, lover, roommate . . . it doesn't make a difference to me. All I know is that only a jerk would give off sexy smiles, long stares, and compliments to someone other than that person. And I don't appreciate it."

Watching her eyes grow narrow and her nose flare, he knew he had somehow managed to press all of her hot buttons. "So are you saying you aren't attracted to me?"

Appalled at the audacity of his statements, she stood and headed for the door. "What I'm saying is that the second that plow comes down my street I want you out of here."

Coming clean, he leaned forward and said, "I'm separated."

Not impressed by his statement, she'd heard that line

many times before. "Is that your way of saying, 'My wife doesn't understand me like you do, and if you just give me a little more time—a week, a month, a year, ten years—I'll leave just as soon as I can'?"

Standing himself, he took deliberate steps to her and paused inches from her. "It's my way of saying I married my college sweetheart who couldn't wait for me to graduate from medical school so that she could be called Mrs. Charlene Carrington, wife of Dr. Derrick Carrington. It's my way of letting you know that I lived with a woman for almost ten years who cherished the big house, designer clothes, and social invitations more than me. It's my way of saying that knowing my marriage was on the rocks, I came home early with tickets for a two-week vacation in Maui, hoping to plug whatever leak had drained our relationship. It's my way of saying I opened the door and found my wife in my bed with my so-called best friend. It's my way of saying that the divorce will be final in two months."

Natalie's heart raced as his nearness caused a flutter in her stomach. Never knowing what it was like to fall in love with someone, she could not imagine what it would feel like when that love was betrayed.

For a long moment, neither spoke but studied each other intently. His eyes drew her in and she felt compelled to take a step back, but her brain couldn't connect with her feet and she didn't move.

Gazing seductively over her face, he reached out and twisted a piece of her hair. "It's my way of saying that I think 'instant attraction' is an accurate description of what we both felt the moment we laid eyes on each other."

Natalie watched his head lower toward hers.

Enticing her by rubbing his nose against hers, he whispered, "Open your mouth for me."

She heard the command and amazed herself when she followed his instructions. Tracing her lips first, his tongue intoxicated her senses with its warmth. Wrapping his arms around her waist, he captured her lips with his, and there was no denying that his assessment of an instant attraction was right on target.

Lifting her arms, she locked her hands behind his neck and gently massaged the nape. As she rested against his solid body, the kiss engulfed Natalie, causing her desire for him to expand. Exploring every part of his mouth, she wondered how she had survived almost thirty years and never experienced the pure pleasure that threatened to overtake her. And just when she thought she was ready to take the plunge into blissfulness, the telephone rang.

Startled, she jumped out of his arms and focused on catching her breath. When her girlfriends had talked about kisses that make your knees weak and your body react in every possible sexual way, she thought it was a bunch of crock. She'd been kissed many times, and no one had ever caused this type of reaction—until today.

Needing to put some distance between them, she found her voice. "I'll get that in the kitchen."

As soon as she left the room, Derrick fell onto the couch and leaned his head back. *What in the world did I just experience?* He hadn't planned to kiss her, but the draw was too powerful to resist. It had been almost a year since that fateful day when he walked in on Charlene and James, and he hadn't even had the notion to look at another woman since, let alone kiss one. Not that Charlene represented the entire female population, but the sting of her actions had left him wary of jumping into any new relationships.

When his mother had called and told him about his father, he only intended to come for a week—two at the most. Taken aback by the severity of his father's illness, he had realized that he missed being around his parents. With only professional ties in California, Derrick made the decision to move back to the East Coast. Walking into Business Strategies a week ago got him thinking that he made the right decision. Getting snowed in with the owner of Business Strategies convinced him that he made the right decision. Not only would he start a new practice, he believed it was time to start a new relationship—with Natalie Donovan.

Natalie grabbed the phone on the third ring, trying to calm her racing heart. She had to be at stroke level.

"Hey, Nat, it's Tanya."

"Hi," she responded, not quite having her breathing under control.

Hearing the breathy tones, Tanya thought it sounded as if Natalie had been running. "Is everything OK? Am I interrupting something?"

Finally calm enough to speak, Natalie glanced down the hallway to make sure the coast was clear. "Tanya, girl, you are not going to believe what happened to me!"

"And you are not going to believe what happened to me . . . but you first."

"Do you remember when I told you about Dr. Derrick Carrington?"

"You mean the guy who put the *s* in sexy and *d* in 'damn, that man is fine'?"

Remembering their previous conversation, Natalie grinned. "Well, he just put the *k* in kiss."

"What?"

Natalie explained the bizarre situation to Tanya, from the knock at the door, to the hot cocoa, to the fire-hot kiss they had just shared.

"You have got to be kidding me."

"I'm telling you, Tanya, that man awakened everything in me. I swear, if this phone hadn't rung, no telling what would be going on in this house."

"Probably the same thing that was going on in Brandon's house."

Natalie paused, digesting what was just said. If her analytical skills were still intact, Tanya had just informed her that she and Brandon got busy last night.

"I knew it," Natalie exclaimed. "I knew you wouldn't make it one night with him. That man loves you like there's no tomorrow. It's about time you exercised your option to forgive."

Tanya stretched on the bed and couldn't agree with her friend more. Now that she had made the decision not only to forgive him, but to marry him, everything in her life seemed to fall into place.

"Natalie, he proposed!"

Natalie screamed in excitement and a few seconds later, Derrick came in to see what was going on. "What!"

"He climbed into bed and gave me the most beautiful ring."

Fanning her face, Natalie overflowed with sincere happiness. "I think I'm going to cry!"

Tanya's smile faded and her tone became serious. "Thank you so much, Nat."

"For what?"

"For helping me learn to forgive. For putting up with my funky attitude the past few weeks. But most of all, for calling him to rescue me from that club."

Natalie stopped waving in front of her face and allowed the tears to fall. "Any time, my friend."

Natalie hung up and shared the good news of Tanya and Brandon with Derrick. "I know you don't know these people from the man in the moon, but she's my best friend and they've been apart for five years."

"And they managed to get back together and get engaged?"

The feat did seem quite remarkable. "It lets me know that true love does exist."

The dreamy look in her eyes told Derrick that although she played tough on the outside, inside she was all mush. Moving toward her, he pulled her close. "Now where were we before that phone call?"

* * *

Martin sat in his home office chewing on the end of a pencil. Checking his watch, he saw it was a little before nine. Thinking back to his conversation last night with Gavin, he realized it wasn't a typical characteristic for him to lose his temper and snap at his staff, but something about his situation with Tanya had brought out the worst in him.

When she had hesitated to accept his proposal at her birthday party, he chalked it up to the surprise of the moment. Even when they talked at the hospital, he thought that whatever doubts she was experiencing, he could erase with a little patience. But when he arrived at her home and saw another man, the powers he was up against to get her to say yes just tripled in strength.

He'd run the facts about Brandon Ware through his head a thousand times. And each time, he came up empty. A successful attorney who spent most of his adult life building his career. There had to be something else. Something more to him that he could use to show Tanya that even if she wasn't sure about her feelings for Martin, Brandon was not the man for her.

Without waiting for the second ring, Martin picked up the phone. "What have you got?"

"Good morning to you too, Martin."

Not in the mood for games, Martin said, "Cut the jokes, Gavin, and give me the report."

Finding no comfort in his anxious tone, he responded slowly. "I spoke to Sanders and there's good news and bad news. Which do you want first?"

"Are you for real?" Martin asked, hearing the amusement in his voice. "This is not the time to joke with me."

"Have it your way, but I have the information and you don't. So, which do you want first, the good news or the bad news?"

Hearing the silence on the other end, Martin exhaled. This

was Gavin's way of getting back at him for pulling rank last night. While Martin was the man out front, he needed Gavin to take care of things behind the scenes. And while Gavin had a knack for handling all kinds of situations, it wouldn't make a difference if he didn't have a front man to support.

Giving in, Martin said calmly, "I'll take the bad news first."

Gavin smiled and knew they had reached an understanding. It was Martin's way of apologizing without saying the words "I'm sorry."

"The bad news . . . I found out where Tanya has been the past few days."

At that statement, Martin sat forward in his chair, all his attention focused on Gavin's next words.

"She met up with Natalie at a club on Friday night. Got a little . . . no, let me correct that . . . got a lot drunk and was rescued by a man. Six feet, solid build, and obviously already a friend."

"Brandon," Martin stated, feeling his agitation grow.

"He took her back to his house, the snow came, and they've been there ever since. He left briefly yesterday, before the weather got severe."

"Where did he go?"

"Lena's Bakery?" Gavin recited, never hearing of the place.

Martin snapped his pencil in half. "Damn. That's her favorite place to get cookies."

"How touching," Gavin answered, his sarcasm lost on no one who would have heard him.

"What else you got?"

"That's it for the bad news. He has no idea what they've been doing to occupy their time, but he's sure they've found a way to keep warm during these long, winter nights."

Martin knew he spoke those words to get a rise out of him, but he refused to lose his cool to Gavin. He was sure this tactic of disseminating information served two purposes. One, he wanted to update Martin on what Sanders found. But two, he wanted to make sure Martin didn't go off the deep end over this woman. Gavin needed his congressman to be focused and committed to building his political career. He could not afford to have some love-struck person on his hands.

"Where's the good news?" Martin asked.

"You'll love this next bit of info, boss. Looks like Sanders found a bone."

"Call your mother."

"What?" Tanya asked. They had showered, made love, and showered again and now they relaxed in the living room. Brandon reviewed some case material while Tanya enjoyed the latest issue of *Image* magazine. Not having heard a plow truck, they knew they were still prisoners, which suited both of them just fine.

"I said call your mother," Brandon repeated.

"Why?"

"To tell her about us."

Tanya eyed Brandon suspiciously and wondered why he would be concerned about her mother. "I don't think Mabel Kennedy is sitting around waiting on the latest update in the Brandon and Tanya saga."

Closing his file, he scooted over next to her and handed her the phone. "I beg to differ on that point."

Taking the phone out of his hand, she placed it back on the cradle. "Why do you say that so confidently?"

Brandon slowly leaned back and stretched his arms across the back of the sofa. Placing his feet on the coffee table, he exhaled dramatically and smiled. "Mabel and I have quite a relationship."

"What are you talking about?"

His eyes twinkled with glee. "Any son-in-law worth his title should have a great relationship with his wife's mother."

Picking up the phone, Tanya dialed the number to get some answers to his crazy riddles. "Hi, Mom."

"Tanya. So good to hear from you. I heard about the snowstorm and called you last night but didn't get an answer. Is everything OK?"

"Yeah, Mom, everything's fine. Actually, I'm calling with some news."

Hearing the hesitation in her voice, Mabel braced herself. "What is it? What's wrong?"

"Oh, nothing's wrong, Mom. It's just . . ." Somehow she couldn't get the words out. Turning to face Brandon, she watched him mouth the words "I'm engaged to Brandon."

"You see, Mom, me and—"

"You and what, child? Just spit it out."

"I'm engaged to Brandon," he mouthed again.

"It's like this, Mom, last night I . . . I mean we . . . I mean Brandon—"

"Did you say Brandon?"

Immediately Tanya heard the change in her mother's voice. The tone went from concern to joy in less than a second.

"Yes, Mom, Brandon and I . . ." Taking a deep breath, she quickly threw it out. "Brandon and I are engaged."

For a moment, no sound could be heard.

"Mom, are you still there?"

Overjoyed that her prayers had been answered, Mabel teased Tanya. "Is that what all the fuss was about? All I can say is that it's about time."

Tanya removed the phone from her ear and shook her head. As she put the phone to her ear again, confusion lay in her next question. "You mean you're not surprised?"

"Surprised? Tanya, I'm just wondering what took you so long."

Did Tanya miss a part of this conversation? The last time

she had spoken to her mother about Brandon, she made it quite clear that the last thing that could possibly happen would be the two of them getting back together. Now she was telling her mother that she was engaged and her mother didn't seem the least bit surprised.

"Tanya?"

Still trying to recover from the absurdity of this conversation, Tanya answered, "I'm here."

"Do you like the ring?" she asked knowingly.

"The ring?"

"Yes, the ring," Mabel answered, faking impatience with her daughter. "Rubies were always my favorite. And an emerald-cut! Oh, it must be absolutely breathtaking."

Tanya heard the words and it took several moments for it to register that her mother had described a ring that she had only gotten a couple of hours ago. Slowly she asked, "How'd you know about the ring?"

"Are you kidding?" Mabel started, sounding as if Tanya should already know the answer to that question. "Any man worth my daughter's hand in marriage better ask for permission first *and* have the ring."

Was Tanya the only one who didn't know how this story was going to end?

"There's something else, Mom."

Hearing her change in tone, Mabel sat forward. "What is it, Tanya?"

"Mom, I want you to know that I talked to Danielle."

"And?" Mabel asked hopefully.

"And I think we're going to be able to work it out."

"I'm glad to hear that . . . and, Tanya?"

"Yes?"

"I'm proud of you."

"For what?"

"For following your heart and learning to forgive."

"I love you, Mom."

Mabel blew her a kiss right before she hung up.

Tanya playfully punched Brandon in the arm. "How long have you been having this relationship with my mother?"

In a quick motion, Brandon grabbed Tanya's arm and reversed their positions. Pinning her hands behind her head, he covered her body with his on the sofa. Playfully, he kissed her on the nose. "Jealous?"

"Don't flatter yourself," she said, wriggling her arms to get free.

"I called your mother after I begged you to take me back last year."

Tanya's motions stopped and she stared openly at Brandon with an expression of disbelief. "You did what?"

Releasing his hold on her, he still didn't move. "The guilt of what I'd done was eating away at me. I couldn't stand the fact that after being in your parents' home, eating at their table, and visiting their church, they would think I would cheat on you."

Scooting away from him, she tried to see any logic in his statement. "Let me get this straight. You let my parents know that you never cheated on me, even though there was no chance that we were going to get back together?"

Growing serious, Brandon said, "I never lost hope, Tee. As long as I had breath, there was always a chance for us."

Kissing him, she knew she'd made the right choice.

Thirteen

Natalie met Tanya at the front door and pushed her directly into the kitchen, not even giving her the chance to remove her coat, hat, and gloves. Agreeing to meet at Christine's for lunch, Tanya had no doubts what the main topic of conversation was going to be.

"Girlfriend, have we been waiting for you!" Natalie said, pulling out a chair from the table.

Patting the seat, Stephanie shook her head in agreement and added, "You sit right here and tell us every single detail."

"And don't leave anything out," Christine said. "I've got about an hour before the next feeding and I don't want to miss one word, so start talking."

After another night of her being held up in Brandon's home, the roads had finally been safe enough for them to venture out this morning. Dropping Tanya off at the club to pick up her car before he headed to the office, Brandon had only let her out of the car after reminding her that she still owed him five dates and he planned to collect—starting tonight. He promised to pick her up at seven o'clock and take her to dinner at her favorite restaurant.

Tanya removed her coat and plopped into the chair. Taking off her hat, she ran her fingers through her hair, adding a little height. She was unable to contain the exhilaration at the changes taking place in her life in the past week, and the signs of despair, gloominess, and sadness had now been replaced with jubilation, happiness, and joy. All the feelings that had consumed her in the weeks leading up to her birthday dissipated when she made the decision to allow Brandon to become a part of her life again. Removing her gloves, she prepared to give her friends every single solitary detail.

"Look at that rock!" Natalie exclaimed, grabbing Tanya's hand and pulling it across the table. "This ring is exquisite. I never thought of any other stone than a diamond in an engagement ring, but the ruby looks absolutely stunning on you. It fits you."

For the next few minutes, the women took turns complimenting Brandon on his great taste and individual style.

"That man knows you well," Stephanie said. "Now that I see that ring on you, I couldn't imagine you wearing anything else."

Tanya's light laughter and silly gesturing of her hand showed just how much she'd changed.

"I can't believe this is the same person who left this house last Friday confused, uncertain, and full of doubt. Now, you look like you can take on the world," Stephanie said.

"Just the world?" Christine joked. "More like the universe!"

Leaning back, Tanya fully relaxed and enjoyed the teasing from her friends. "I must say, the past several weeks my mood swings had more twists and turns than a roller coaster. I was even beginning to feel the signs of the green-eyed monster."

All three women stared at Tanya in confusion.

"Jealousy?" Natalie asked.

"You guessed it."

"At what?" Christine asked.

"At all of you," Tanya said, moving her eyes from woman to woman. "I'm ashamed to admit it, but, Christine, you have that beautiful baby girl. And, Stephanie, you've just married the man of your dreams and talked of starting a family." Focusing on Natalie, she continued, "You found your purpose in starting BSI. Watching all those great things happen in all of your lives made me wonder if I was destined to live a life of discontentment."

"And how do you feel now?"

Tanya thought about Christine's question and released a slow smile. Glancing at her ring, she said, "I have a man who loves me, a wedding to plan, and a family to start. Life is almost perfect."

Placing a large bowl of salad on the table along with grilled chicken, Stephanie passed around the pitcher of water and asked, "What's missing?"

"It's not that something's missing per se, it's just that lately I've been feeling restless with my job."

"Wintertime is the slowest time of the year for your business," Christine offered.

"I don't think that has anything to do with it," Tanya responded, searching for the right words to articulate what she felt. "I'm not fulfilled anymore. Some days I wake up and I just don't see the purpose in going into the office."

No eating took place as all three women focused on Tanya's situation.

"What do you think you'd like to do?" Natalie said.

"I wish I knew. Christine, with your interior design firm, and, Natalie, with BSI, both of you are doing exactly what brings you joy."

"You sound like you might be interested in starting your own business," Stephanie offered.

She shook her head in the negative, as that wasn't the first time the thought had entered her mind. "After watching Damian build Ware Construction Company from the ground up, and witnessing what the two of you went through when you set up shop, I don't know if I'm cut out to be an entrepreneur. It takes a serious commitment to start and build your own company."

"And it takes capital," Natalie said. "Especially if you're choosing something that's not home-based. I see it all the time. Businesses that could have been successful—should have been successful—but weren't."

Curious about that statement, Tanya said, "How do so many businesses find themselves in a situation like that?"

"Pick any number of reasons," Natalie started. "Mismanagement of funds, lack of planning, no understanding of the contracts and deals they sign. But one of the major reasons is underestimating the capital they need to keep the business going until they can turn a profit. And when the money runs out, people sometimes make desperate—and bad—decisions."

"Such as?" Tanya said, fascinated by what she was sharing.

"Taking out loans with terms that are not in their best interest. Signing contracts for services with steep discounts that don't allow them enough of a profit to pay their bills. Or they will sell their business at a loss, leaving them in a worse financial situation than when they started."

"It sounds as if BSI's client list could be cut drastically if people made better decisions before starting a business."

Natalie nodded in agreement. "I'm hoping to expand our programs to help people before they find themselves in a situation where they need emergency care. If my grant comes through—and I have it on good authority from a contact at the corporation who's offering the funding that it will—I'll be able to provide these type of preventive services."

For the first time in years, Tanya felt a professional surge of excitement. "I want to help."

"Excuse me?" all three women said in unison.

Tanya jumped up from her chair and circled the table. "Right now, the focus of BSI is to handle clients who are in the midst of business mistakes and trying to recover. You told me you have a long list of companies you're working with."

"That's true. More companies than volunteers."

"Let me work with people who are considering starting a business. I've been a part of building Damian's business from the start. I know everything from writing business plans, leasing office space, preparing budgets, finding funding, and negotiating contracts."

"You'd be interested in doing that?" Stephanie asked, watching her face light up like a child's on Christmas morning.

Natalie heard the enthusiasm in Tanya's voice, and relief flushed through her. This was the woman she used to know. Motivated. Excited. Ready to take on the world. Maybe getting involved in BSI was exactly what she needed to ward off her boredom with her job, to give her a sense of purpose.

"You do have the skills," Christine admitted.

"I promise you, Tanya, as soon as that grant comes through, the job is yours. I'm sure you could work out a deal with Damian on splitting your time."

Tanya sat back down with a million thoughts running through her head on various options for helping new business owners. There could be seminars, training classes, on-line information, and pamphlets of information she could design. "You don't understand, Natalie, I want to get started on this now."

"But the grant—" Natalie started.

"Forget the grant. You work for free, so can I."

"You're serious, aren't you?" Stephanie asked, amazed at the change in her total demeanor since beginning this conversation.

"You're damn right, I'm serious," she declared. Turning her attention back to Natalie, she picked up her fork. "I'll come to the office with you this afternoon. I'm on vacation, so that will give me enough time to get a jump on designing some programs before going back to work."

"You got yourself a deal," Natalie said.

A couple of hours later, Tanya followed Natalie into her office at BSI to pick up an information packet about what the organization currently had in place so that she could begin to think of how she would help fill in the gaps of the services they offered.

Natalie watched Tanya flip through some of her brochures while choosing her next words carefully. "Tanya, I consider us to be really good friends, and I'm only asking because I care."

Hearing the serious tone of her voice, Tanya set aside the material she was reading and focused her attention on Natalie. "What's on your mind?"

"I can see in your eyes that you love Brandon, and I know that you two deserve another chance. But engaged? Are you sure you're ready for that? You've been apart for five years."

Tanya, not the least bit offended by the question, gave Natalie a reassuring smile. "I've asked myself that same question off and on throughout the day, but each time I come to the same conclusion. Damian was right. I've been trying to do it for the past five years, but the reality of the situation descended on me the moment he walked through those hospital doors. I can't deny love. I love Brandon. This really feels right."

Satisfied, Natalie curved one corner of her mouth into a wicked grin. With gleaming eyes, she said, "Then that makes two of us who had—how shall I put this?—a very interesting time being snowed in."

Leaning forward to the edge of her seat, Tanya said teasingly, "What else did you and this mysterious Dr. Carrington do besides lock lips? Inquiring minds want to know."

"No, Tanya, we did not sleep together," Natalie stated emphatically.

"Umm?" Tanya responded skeptically.

"Seriously, it's not like I didn't want to, but I thought it would be a little tacky to give it up on the first date."

"Date?" Tanya jokingly asked. "You two haven't had a date yet. You've just been making out."

Laughing, Natalie hadn't been this excited about meeting a man in years. "This man actually has potential. I really like him."

"You sound like this could get serious."

"We'll see. We're going to dinner tonight."

"I hope things really work out for you, Natalie. You deserve some happiness."

"Thanks, Tanya."

Tanya hesitated a moment, sitting back in her chair, before she continued, "There's something else I've been meaning to talk to you about."

Natalie heard the change in her tone. "What is it?"

"I spoke to Danielle the other day."

It was no secret that Tanya could not stand the sight of Danielle at one point. But over the last couple of weeks, Danielle had really reached out to her sister. "And?"

Standing, Tanya walked over to the window. "She asked to stay with me for a couple of weeks while she auditions for a television show."

Something in the way she made that statement told Natalie that Tanya was at a crossroad with her sister. Holding on to the anger so long had taken its toll on her and she sounded as if she was ready to give their relationship another chance. "What did you tell her?"

"I haven't given her an answer yet."

"Say yes."

The simplicity of Natalie's words struck Tanya. She made it seem as if allowing Danielle back in her life was something akin to picking out what shoes she was going to wear today. Easy. "My mom says she's turned over a new leaf. But it's hard to forgive and forget all the trouble she's caused in the past."

"But forgiving Danielle would complete this journey you've been on the past few months."

Tanya furrowed her brow in confusion. "What's that supposed to mean?"

"It means you need to let go of this last anchor that has tied you to a past filled with bitterness. You've been so unhappy the past couple of months and you continually blamed it on turning thirty-five. But I think it was more than that. It was the anger that was dragging you down—"

"I might have been upset at the way I've been treated by certain people, but I would hardly consider myself being dragged down because of it," Tanya interrupted defensively.

Rising, Natalie walked around her desk to stand in front of Tanya. "Are you kidding? You've been moping around for months! You were mad at Brandon, mad at Danielle, and mad at Martin."

"Martin?" Tanya asked, surprised. "If anything, he was the one bright spot during that time. What did he ever do to me to make me mad?"

"You were mad at him for giving you what you wanted from someone else. You were mad at him because he wasn't Brandon."

Tanya paused a moment as she digested Natalie's words. Her initial response was that Natalie had been reading too many self-help books and watching too much Oprah and Dr. Phil. But the more she thought about it, the more she wondered if Natalie had a point. Could all of her restlessness have been tied to the anger she was holding on to? She had to admit that she'd felt lighter, happier, and more excited about life today that she had in any day during the past year.

She'd forgiven Brandon, renewed a relationship with her sister, and found an outlet to use her professional knowledge to help others. "Well, Dr. Donovan, I will admit that I haven't been this happy in a long time."

Laughing at her reference, Natalie gave her a hug before they sat back down to talk about what programs Tanya would like to implement.

* * *

Brandon stared out the window into the late afternoon sun. After the snowstorm, the beaming sun was a welcome sight to the city. It was also a reflection of his life. Everything in his life shone bright. Back in DC, he had delved into his caseload, which got his intellectual juices flowing more than setting up the office in LA, and now that he was back with Tanya, he couldn't imagine anything making his life better.

"Brandon, you got a minute?"

Turning, he smiled. "Sure, Thomas, come on in."

Motioning for him to take a seat, Brandon noticed the lines of concern across his face. With Brandon's having worked with him for ten years, there was no mistaking that something was terribly wrong.

Placing a document on Brandon's desk, Thomas explained, "I received this notice today, and I'm wondering if you can explain it."

Brandon took the letter and quickly perused its contents. "You've got to be kidding me."

"No, Brandon, I don't think it's a joke," Thomas answered, keeping his voice calm, which directly contradicted his complete annoyance.

Brandon read it again, not wanting to accept what the words on the page were telling him. "But this is impossible. Everything was in order."

Removing his glasses, Thomas rubbed his chin. "Not according to that."

"I'll get Damian on the phone. I'm sure he'll be able to get to the bottom of this."

Rising, Thomas buttoned his coat jacket and headed for the door. "I've already contacted Mark Dunkin. I'm sure the county executive can shed some light on this as well." Checking his gold watch, he continued, "I'm due in court in thirty minutes. Leave me a message and let me know what you find out."

Brandon nodded and glanced at the letter again.

"We've already invested over five million dollars in the land for our new offices. We were ready to begin building in a couple of months. Between your brother and Mark Dunkin, somebody better be ready to explain how our permits could be denied because of zoning and environmental interests."

Brandon heard the words and assured Thomas that he would get to the bottom of this.

After Thomas left the office, Brandon called his brother.

Natalie began sorting through the mail while she waited for her next appointment. After Tanya left, she'd planned to head over to the interior design firm, but got held up in reviewing a case for a client who desperately needed to work out a deal with the IRS. Losing his house was a possibility if they didn't find a solution.

Christine had often asked why she remained at her firm. It was obvious that her first love rested in the work she did at BSI. Natalie had considered the question many times, but always felt she could handle both endeavors. Now, she wasn't so sure. Hiring an executive director would take some of the pressure off and her and allow her to spend more time at the design firm. However, the more she thought about it, the more she realized that she didn't want her role to diminish at BSI. Perhaps, when the grant came through, instead of hiring someone from the outside to run the organization, she would take on the job herself, working at BSI full-time.

As she discarded junk mail and set aside letters to be read later, Natalie's eye suddenly widened at the nondescript brown envelope staring back at her with the Whittington Foundation seal in the corner. This was the information she'd been waiting for. According to her sources, BSI was in the lead for receiving their five-hundred-thousand-dollar grant, but nothing would be official until she received the official award letter. That's what it appeared she held in her hand.

Tearing open the letter, she quickly scanned the contents before her smile faltered and confusion coursed through her. Unable to keep the emotion out of the moment, she felt the tears welling up in the corner of her eyes.

"This can't be happening," she said to the empty room.

Flipping through her Rolodex, she found the number and took a few deep breaths before punching the last few digits.

"Hi, you've reached the voice mail of Sarah Davis of the Whittington Foundation. . . ."

Cursing under her breath, Natalie waited for the beep. In a professional and calm tone, she spoke. "Sarah, it's Natalie Donovan at BSI. I received a letter today stating that the grant we applied for was not awarded to us. I'm a bit confused, as my conversations with the grant reviewer led me to believe otherwise. Could you please call me at your earliest convenience? Thank you."

Natalie hung up the phone and threw the letter on the desk. It would be months before she heard back from the other grants she'd applied for. What was she going to do now?

Applying a layer of gloss over her lipstick, Tanya checked her reflection in the mirror. Singing along with the radio, she slipped her feet into her shoes just as the phone rang.

"I understand congratulations are in order."

Normally, this was the point where Tanya would roll her eyes and think of some excuse to get off the phone, but she no longer felt the swell of anger that appeared whenever they had a conversation. "Hi, Danielle, and yes, congratulations are in order."

"Mom told me about the engagement. I'm happy for you, Tanya. I really am. I always knew you and Brandon belonged together. It's good that you guys finally worked it out."

Taken aback by her kind words, Tanya started to believe

that her sister really might have turned over a new leaf. "Thanks, Danielle."

An uncomfortable silence ensued, and finally Tanya spoke. "Is there something else you wanted?"

"Actually, there is. I wanted to know if you've made a decision about me staying with you. Michelle said she has an old college friend that I could stay with if things didn't work out with you."

Tanya didn't know whether it was the high she was experiencing in reconciling with Brandon, or the fact that she would feel like a heel if her sister came to DC and stayed with a stranger, but she found herself telling her sister that she could stay with her.

The genuine, enthusiastic response caught Tanya off guard.

"Thank you so much, Tanya. I promise I won't be any trouble. You won't even know I'm there."

Danielle not causing trouble would be considered a foreign concept to anyone who'd known her over the years, but with the commitment made, Tanya wouldn't change her mind. But there was one thing she wanted to know. "Are you over Damian?"

The silence on the other end of the phone caused Tanya to be concerned. When Christine and Damian had been dating, Danielle wreaked havoc on their relationship. Insulting Christine, and trying to win back Damian to help pay off her debts, had almost ruined their chances of getting together. There was no way Tanya would expose Damian or Christine to any more pain because of Danielle.

"Tanya, Damian and I ended years ago. It was my pride, ego, and diminishing bank account that caused me to continue to pursue him after he and Christine got together. But you can believe me, I have no romantic interest in Damian and I harbor no ill feelings toward Christine."

Tanya wasn't 100 percent sure that what Danielle had spoken was the truth, but deciding not to dwell on the negative, she opted to let the subject drop. If Tanya could forgive Brandon and give him another chance, then she owed it to her blood sister to do the same. "Then I guess it's settled. I'll see you this weekend."

"Is Brandon coming?"

Tanya hadn't asked Brandon, but admitted that he would most likely be accompanying her.

"Great. Then I'll see you both this weekend."

Danielle hung up with her sister and immediately called her agent, Michelle. This television show had become her lifeline. She needed to get the job as much as she needed the air to breathe. With a little over a year since she'd moved back home, she had yet to do anything of substance to get her life back on track. Everything she'd ever owned had been either repossessed or sold to cover outstanding bills. If it weren't for Michelle, she wouldn't even have had the money for the plane ticket to Georgia.

Her parents hadn't said anything, but she knew she couldn't be a freeloader forever, and if this opportunity didn't pan out, she would be forced to get a job. Just the thought of going to work Monday through Friday from eight to five caused a fearful shiver to rise up her spine. She was not born to live like that. Had she not lost all her fame and fortune and burned so many bridges, she probably would have transferred her career from runway model to television without a hitch. Unfortunately, her reality was quite different. If this situation didn't work out, she would be forced to do what she dreaded most of all. Live what she considered "an ordinary life."

"Michelle Ford."

"Michelle, it's Danielle. I spoke to my sister and I'll be in DC on Sunday. What time should I report to the studio?"

Michelle flipped a few pages in a file and found the info she needed. Giving Danielle directions and the time, she also reiterated the importance of the audition, not only for the job, but for future work. "Listen, Danielle, there is no one in this industry who wants to deal with you. I mean absolutely no one. When I said I called in every favor to finagle an audition for you I meant it. The executive producer is leery of working with you, the writers are cringing at the thought of having to create something great for someone they can't stand, and the director? Well, you know what kind of relationship you developed with the director."

Danielle's relationship—or lack of a relationship—with the director was clear. "I'm not the same Danielle Olivia Kennedy that I was a year ago."

"You better not be," Michelle said emphatically. "I love you like my own daughter, but if you screw this up, you're through."

Hearing the doorbell, Tanya checked her watch. If it was Brandon, he would just let himself in. Unconsciously smiling, Tanya remembered that morning, just over a week ago, when he had let himself into her house and back into her life. It amazed her that she had never changed the locks and she pondered if that was because, subconsciously, she always knew they would end up together.

Dressed in gray wool pants and a scoop-neck, long-sleeved blouse, Tanya grabbed her purse and headed downstairs just as the doorbell rang for a second time. Peeping through the hole, she wondered why he would be coming by. They hadn't seen each other or spoken since the night she gave him back his ring.

"Hi, Martin," Tanya said, stepping aside to let him enter.

"I hope you don't mind me stopping by unexpectedly, but I tried to call you the past few days and couldn't catch up with you."

Offering no explanation of why she hadn't returned his

phone calls, she took his coat and led him to the living room. Feeling slightly uncomfortable at his unexpected visit, she motioned for him to take a seat. "How have you been?"

Martin took a long look at the woman he wanted to spend the rest of life with. Her hair, a sea of curls, framed her oval face. Her clothes hugged her body in all the right places. As he was preparing to respond to her question, his eyes caught the glare from her ring finger.

Tanya caught the look and fought the urge to place her hands behind her back. When she had decided to let Brandon back in her life and accept his proposal, she believed in her heart that she had made the right choice. Therefore, she refused to feel shame or justify her decision to anyone. Including Martin.

"I see my prediction the night you broke up with me proved itself to be true."

Knowing exactly what he referred to, Tanya didn't feel the need to defend her behavior to him. She only spoke the words she believed she owed him. "Brandon and I broke up five years ago after dating for a year. I want you to know that I didn't start seeing him again until after you and I ended our relationship."

A spark of anger ignited in Martin and he worked hard to contain his tone. "Is that explanation supposed to make me feel better? Is this the part where you expect me to say congratulations? Am I supposed to just happily accept that the woman who turned down my marriage proposal a couple of weeks ago is now engaged to someone else?"

"Martin, I didn't mean to hurt you," Tanya said. "You have to know that the reasons we broke up had nothing to do with Brandon."

Martin leaned forward and fought to keep his tone even. "First of all, Tanya, let's be clear about the circumstances surrounding the end of our relationship. *We* did not end our relationship. *You* ended our relationship. Second of all, you expect me to believe that after being apart from someone for five years, he can just step back into your life for a couple of weeks and you're ready to commit your life to him?"

The sarcasm in his statements wasn't lost on Tanya and, taking into consideration that he was still recovering from the broken engagement, she cut him some slack by maintaining a calm demeanor.

"Of course I expect you to believe it," she said, staring him directly in the eyes. "If you didn't, that would mean you were accusing me of cheating on you."

Martin's silence at her statement infuriated her. Was he actually accusing her of having an affair?

Standing, she headed for the door. "I think this visit is over."

Martin didn't move. "How long do you think it will be before Brandon shows his true colors?"

Placing one hand on her hip, she narrowed her eyes at his cryptic statement. "What is that supposed to mean?"

Martin leaned forward, and his lips curved into a sly smile. "Come on, Tanya. You know as well as I do what type of man Brandon Ware is."

Through clenched teeth, she answered, "No, Martin, I don't know. Why don't you tell me what type of man Brandon is?"

"He's the type of man who won't be able to commit to you for the rest of his life."

"Excuse me?"

Relaxing in his seat, Martin shrugged as if what he was saying made sense. "All you have to do is look at the facts, Tanya."

"Exactly what facts are you talking about?"

"How about the fact that he's had more women than you or I could ever count?" Martin pulled a folder out of his briefcase. "Your fiancé has been quite busy in the five years that you've been apart."

Tanya watched him open a file and wondered exactly what he was up to.

"Let's see, there was Anita, Sharon, Carolyn, Erika, Stacy, Abbey, Rachel, and Lolita."

Flipping the page, he scanned the information before he continued. "And how could we forget about Rose, Cathy, Marsha, and Robin? Looks like your new beau has a long list of previous loves behind him. You really think he's able to commit himself to just one woman?"

Martin watched her eyes, trying to determine how much his words had affected her. "Granted, the one woman who he's committed to is beautiful, kind, successful, and would make any man a wonderful wife. She just won't be getting the same in return. Brandon Ware is not what anyone would consider husband material."

Tanya's patience had expired. "Martin, I don't need a recap from you about who Brandon may or may not have spent his time with in the past five years, and I will not sit here and discuss my relationship with Brandon with you." Moving toward the door, she hoped Martin would pick up the hint that it was time for him to go. Hearing the list of women didn't sit right with Tanya but she refused to let Martin see her discomfort. The faster she could get him out of her house, the sooner she could clear her head of all those names swirling around in her mind.

Standing, Martin ignored her hint that he leave and instead went to stand directly in front of her. "Then maybe you'd be interested in who he may or may not have spent time with since he got back from LA."

Feeling her personal space invaded, she fought to maintain her position. The last image she wanted to portray was that she would back down.

With a smug look on his face, he continued. "You are so beautiful, Tanya, and I love you. You may not want to marry me, but I guarantee you can do better than Brandon Ware.

You can bet money that once a player, always a player." Kissing her on the cheek, he dropped the folder on the table. "My proposal is still open. If you want a marriage with someone whose commitment you'll never have to question, call me."

She stood in the same spot for several minutes after she heard the door shut. Turning her attention to the folder, she stared at it, a part of her wanting to look, another part wanting to throw it in the fireplace and burn it.

Curiosity got the best of her and she sat on the sofa. Opening the file, she stared at the images. The first picture was Brandon sitting in a restaurant with a very attractive woman. The second picture showed them leaving and the third had them outside what appeared to be her apartment complex kissing. The next sequence of pictures showed her entering her apartment and then coming out. The date on the pictures indicated they were taken just over a week ago.

As she stared at the photos, a million questions swam through her head. Not wanting to believe that Brandon would be claiming to love her and seeing someone else, she searched her mind for every perceivable explanation. But as the minutes ticked by, she couldn't come up with one reason why he would be in these pictures with this woman.

Hearing the front door open, she knew Brandon had let himself him.

Walking into the living room, he opened his arms to greet her. "Hey, baby. Ready to paint the town red?"

Getting no answer, Brandon immediately knew something wasn't right. "Tanya, what is it?"

Still getting no response, Brandon sat beside her on the sofa and saw the pictures. As he flipped through them, there was no mistaking the flash of anger in his eyes. "What the hell is this?"

Turning to him, Tanya couldn't hold her anger any longer and exploded. "It's exactly what it appears to be. You having dinner and then going home with a woman. I'm sure you've noticed the date on them. I believe it's the same day you claimed to love me and want me back."

"I know you aren't accusing me of seeing another woman."

Picking up the photos, she threw them at him. "I don't have to accuse you of anything. Everyone knows a picture is worth a thousand words."

Walking past him, she ran up the stairs and slammed her bedroom door.

Less than a minute later, Brandon stormed into the room with the pictures in his hand. "Where did you get these from?"

Ignoring his words, Tanya turned to face him, eyes blazing, and held her hand out. "Give me my key."

"I'm not doing anything, including leaving this house, until you tell me where you got these pictures from."

"What difference does it make where I got them from? The point is, you can't seem to kick your old habits."

Taking deep breaths, Brandon moved to stand directly in front of her. "Where did you get these pictures?"

Raising her chin defiantly, she refused to be intimidated by his stance. "Martin gave them to me."

"Martin!" Brandon screamed. "You broke up with the man. Don't you think he would do anything to come between us?"

"That's where you're wrong, Brandon. He didn't do anything—you did. You claimed to love me while you were obviously seeing someone else. Some things never change."

The disappointment in her voice was evident and Brandon felt her slipping away. "Explain to me how a man I have only met once manages to have pictures of me."

That caught Tanya off guard. How did Martin get these pictures? Why did he have them?

Seeing her expression, Brandon asked incredulously, "It never crossed your mind to ask?"

"Oh, excuse me, I was too busy watching the man I planned to marry heading to another woman's house."

"Planned?" Brandon asked, hearing her use the past tense of that word. "What are you saying?"

Tanya's emotions were at an all-time high and she once again questioned whether she had moved too fast in rekindling her relationship with Brandon. Her heart wanted to believe that the man standing before her wasn't capable of making love to her while seeing another woman. But what else could she think? "Can you explain these pictures?"

"Why should I?" he said, throwing the pictures on the bed. "It looks as if you've already drawn your own conclusion."

Trying to diffuse a tense situation, Tanya took a deep breath and gave herself a moment to collect her thoughts. Taking a seat on the bed, she lowered her eyes and stared at her hands. Evenly, she said, "Brandon, just tell me the truth about the woman in the picture."

Brandon worked to control his anger at the situation. Clasping his hands in front of him, he said, "You say that as if I've lied to you."

Tanya remained silent for almost a minute. Finally, she raised her eyes and stared for several seconds at him, her look unwavering. "Have you?"

Brandon saw the mistrust in her eyes and knew he was fighting a losing battle. He took the stairs two at a time and slammed the front door on his way out.

Martin ducked down in the front seat of his car until Brandon's car disappeared down the street. With a satisfied grin, he glanced at his watch. Just seven minutes. Not bad. Starting the car, he made a quick U-turn and headed home.

Fourteen

Natalie sat in her office the next morning rereading the letter for the third time. Each time she read it, she hoped somehow the words would change, but they didn't. On this one page, all the hard work she'd put into BSI seemed to be for nothing. All the plans and hopes she'd had for programs, for training sessions, seemed dissipated now. *How could this happen?*

"Natalie, Dr. Carrington is here to see you."

Folding the letter, Natalie put it back in the envelope. "Thanks, Jea. Give me a few minutes and then you can show him in."

Hearing the weariness in her voice, Jea hesitated. "Is everything OK?"

Forcing a smile, Natalie pushed back in her chair. "Sure. I've just got quite a few things on my agenda today." She saw no need to worry her staff about the grant. Their positions were still secure, there was just nothing to use now to build the organization.

"Well, there's no better way to lose the stress of a day than spending time with someone as fine as that man standing out in the lobby. And he's carrying a lovely bouquet of flowers. I guess dinner went well last night."

Jea, a twenty-three-year-old graduate student at American University, had no intentions of settling down any time soon. But that didn't stop her from rooting for Natalie. Every time a new man came into Natalie's life, Jea said a silent prayer that he would be the one. Natalie, the nicest woman she'd known, served as a strong role model for her. Educated, professional, and willing to give back were all the qualities she thought necessary.

As Natalie remembered those mind-blowing kisses she and Derrick had shared at her house, and the ones they had shared last night, her cheeks grew warm. It had been years since any man had caused her to blush. "Let's just say that things are definitely looking up for me in the romance category."

"I couldn't be happier for you," Jea said, giving her a hug.

A few minutes later, Derrick entered her office offering her the flowers and a large accordion file with his parents' business information inside.

She thanked him for the flowers, but the sparkle in her eyes that he had become accustomed to seeing was no longer there. "You seem to be preoccupied with something."

"Actually, I received a letter yesterday that carried some disappointing news."

Leaning against her desk, he reached out for her hand. "You want to talk about it?"

Natalie appreciated the concern in his voice and found it refreshing that someone actually cared about what was going on in her life. For so long, she had dealt with all of life's situations on her own. It was nice to be able to share the load with someone else, even if there was nothing they could do about it. "I applied for a half-million-dollar grant about nine months ago. Tracking the process and talking with my contacts at the foundation, it seemed as if we were a lock. This money would have allowed me to increase staff and implement training and business workshops around the area."

"Don't tell me, the grant didn't come through?"

"You guessed it. I tried calling my contact at the foundation, but no luck. I spoke to her voice mail twice yesterday and once this morning. I even tried to get in touch with Martin Carter."

"The congressman?"

"Yes. He's the one who pointed me to this grant."

Moving to kneel in front of her, he gently stroked her hand. "I'm really sorry, Natalie. I'm sure there'll be other grants."

Feeling the warmth of his touch travel to every part of her body, she reveled in the quiet strength and support he was offering to her. "I know. It's just that the process can be so time-consuming. The next grant I could possibly hope to be awarded won't be ready for issuance for another six months. In the meantime, I'll have to continue helping all these business owners with limited resources and staff."

"Natalie," Jea said over the intercom, "sorry to interrupt, but Tanya is on line two. She's says it's urgent."

Natalie listened carefully as Tanya's mouth was running a mile a minute. "Slow down, Tanya, what's going on?"

After several minutes, Natalie got the gist of Tanya's words.

"I can't believe this is happening. How could he do this after claiming to still love me?"

Natalie's anger swelled at the thought of pictures of Brandon with another woman. After all of the pushing she had done to get the two of them back together, she knew something like this could break Tanya once and for all. "Don't move, sweetie, I'll be there after work."

"Everything all right?" Derrick asked after Natalie got off the phone.

"Let's hope so."

Walking her to her car, Derrick kissed her sweetly on the lips. "How about I pick you up around eight tonight? I'll cook for you."

"Aren't you staying with your parents?"

Reaching in his pocket, he pulled out a set of keys. "I rented an apartment this morning. You can help me christen it."

His suggestive tone wasn't lost on Natalie and she smiled, "Eight it is."

Tanya opened the door and Natalie followed her into the living room.

Getting comfortable on the sofa, Natalie noticed the ring. "I see you're still wearing it, so that must mean something. Have you talked to him?"

"No. He hasn't called and neither have I."

"Tell me what happened."

Tanya recapped the story and Natalie had only one question. "How and why did Martin have those pictures?"

"I don't know and I don't care. The only thing that matters is that they exist and it's Brandon in them."

Hoping to help Tanya through this, she said, "Has Martin been following Brandon? Has he been following you?"

At the thought of someone watching her or Brandon, Tanya's entire demeanor changed. What kind of person would take photographs of other people without their knowledge? What game was Martin playing?

"Why would he do something like that? What would he have to gain?"

"It's obvious, Tanya. He wants you back."

At the sound of the doorbell, Tanya glanced at Natalie, her eyes defying her words and showing hope that it was Brandon on the other side.

Looking through the peephole, she sighed. A double whammy.

Damian and Brandon followed Tanya into the living room and Natalie made room for Damian on the sofa.

"We've got a major problem, Tanya," Damian said. His eyes, red and slightly swollen, indicated that he hadn't gotten much sleep last night.

Thinking this visit was about her situation with Brandon,

Tanya defiantly said, "No, Brandon has a major problem. He can't seem to let go of his philandering ways."

Standing, Damian began to pace the floor. "Forget about you and Brandon's childish behavior. This is serious."

Tanya started to object but noticed the sheer frustration in Damian's eyes.

"Our permits didn't come through on the Morgan and Rock project."

"That's impossible!" Tanya exclaimed. Standing, she joined Damian on the other side of the room. "I handled this project myself and everything was in order. The only thing we were doing was waiting for the process to take its course."

"Well, the process has some questions about zoning and environmental studies," Brandon said, speaking for the first time. He came tonight only because Damian had insisted they needed to put their heads together if they were going to solve this problem. But how could he think when the woman who made his life worth living stood less than ten feet from him acting as if he didn't mean a thing to her?

The moment she had answered the door, the only thing he could think of was taking her in his arms and kissing her until neither could stand it. With her dressed in jeans and a fitted sweater, her sexiness had still shone through.

"Environmental? That's crazy."

"It's not the only thing crazy around here," Brandon mumbled, the words harsher than he had intended. How was he expected to be polite and civil when the only thing he wanted to do was shake some sense into her?

"Did you call the planning commission?" Tanya asked, turning her body away from Brandon. By her movement, one would have thought she couldn't stand the sight of him. In reality, it was just the opposite. In his blue jeans and turtleneck, his arresting good looks could only be described as lethal. Feeling her body react, she decided that her only option was to turn her attention to the other people in the room.

"You're damn right I called them," Damian answered. "Not only is the Morgan and Rock project in trouble, but it seems that two more of our projects slated for permits may be held up as well."

"This is absurd," Tanya said, mostly to herself. Sitting, she thought of what their next step should be. "We need to call Mark Dunkin and find out exactly what's going on. We've never had a permit problem before."

"I did. And the county executive had some very interesting news for me," Damian said. "It seems there's been some pressure to hold up this project, and the politics of the situation won out. His hands were tied."

"Pressure from who?"

"He wouldn't say, but I would give you only one guess," Brandon said.

The room fell silent and all eyes faced Tanya. "You can't be serious. You think Martin has something to do with this?"

"Don't you?" Brandon said. When he left her house last night, his first thought had been to find Martin and punch him square in the jaw, but a call from his brother with the news from the county executive changed everything. Martin intended not only to destroy his relationship with Tanya, but also to put his brother's business and his position at the firm in jeopardy. He needed more than a physical blow. Brandon needed to hit him where it would hurt for a long time: his career. He just had to figure out a way to do it. "Only someone with his kind of power could accomplish something like this."

Feeling the tension level rise to astronomical proportions, Natalie stood. "Everybody, calm down. This has been a very trying day for all of us."

"What's been trying for you?" Tanya said, suddenly concerned that she had been so absorbed in what was going on in her life, she hadn't given Natalie a chance to update her on what was going on in hers. Friendship was a two-way street, and lately, Tanya realized, it was very one-sided.

Natalie informed them about the grant and the fact that her programs were now put on hold indefinitely. When she mentioned that she had called Martin, all three pairs of eyes stared in silence.

"Your little ex-boyfriend probably had something to do with that too," Brandon sneered at Tanya. His sarcasm wasn't lost on anyone.

Looking from Damian to Natalie and finally resting her eyes on Brandon, she found it hard to believe what they were suggesting. "All three of you must be out of your minds. Why would Martin do something like this? What would he have to gain?"

"Revenge," Brandon answered.

"For what?"

"Don't play dumb, Tanya, it's not attractive on you."

Ignoring his dig, she said, "You think Martin would go through blocking Natalie's grant, and screwing with our permits?"

When no one answered, she knew they all agreed that Martin had something to do with this.

"Don't be ridiculous," Tanya said. "What proof can any of you offer?"

"We can start with those pictures," Brandon said, stepping right in front of her. "What was he doing following me?"

At the reminder of Brandon with another woman, Tanya snapped. With her hands on her hips, she challenged him right back with a question of her own. "What were you doing with that woman?"

"If I told you, would you believe me? Or is your mind already made up?"

"Have you been lying to me all this time? Are you really able to commit to one woman?"

Insulted at her insinuations, Brandon lashed out. "You have the nerve to ask me something like that after I ask you to marry me?"

"Look, you two," Damian said, "this isn't going to get us anywhere."

Frustrated, Brandon agreed. "You're right, big brother, so let's do something that will be productive. Where does that bastard live?"

"Don't call him names," Tanya hissed.

"Are you defending him now?" Brandon asked, throwing his hands up at the absurdity of the situation.

"Call it what you want, but I'm not telling you where he lives."

"The hell you aren't," Brandon yelled. "If you're going to break it off with me over those damn pictures, then I deserve the chance to go over there and kick his—"

"Brandon, calm down," Damian said before turning his attention to Tanya. "Look, Tanya, I need to talk to Martin. I have to find out if he's behind this permit issue. If we don't get this straight, Ware Construction Company stands to lose a considerable amount of money and a couple of large clients. I can't run my business like this."

The desperation in his voice was not lost on Tanya. The fact remained that his company's ability to operate could be in serious trouble if they didn't get to the bottom of this. The ramifications of permit problems could be astronomical. Tanya plopped on the sofa and rested her head in her hands. Could Martin really be responsible for all of this?

"Natalie?" Tanya said, raising her head and looking to her friend for advice.

"They're right, Tanya. Somebody's got to talk to Martin, and the sooner the better."

Shaking her head in agreement, she said, "OK, but I want to be the one to talk to him—alone."

Brandon objected immediately. "No way are you going over there by yourself. It's obvious that man can't be trusted."

"Don't even go there, Brandon," Tanya answered. "You are the last person to talk to me about trust."

Damian stepped between them before their argument escalated. "I'll give you tonight to talk to him. But if you're not successful, then he's all mine."

"And mine," Brandon added.

"Call him," Damian said, handing Tanya the phone.

Natalie, Damian, and Brandon listened as she dialed his number and told him she needed to talk to him. Getting permission to come over, Tanya hung up, indicating that she would be there within thirty minutes.

Damian headed for the door. "Let us know what you find out. Call as soon as you get back. Let's go, Brandon."

"I'll be right out."

Damian glanced at Tanya and waited for her to object. When she didn't, he nodded and said, "I'll be in the car."

"I'm right behind you," Natalie said, as she grabbed her jacket, purse, and keys and headed for the door.

Alone, Brandon moved to stand in front of her. "We need to talk. Can I come by when you get back? I think after we both have a chance to calm down, we can work this out."

Tanya felt her heart rate increase as he invaded her personal space. With concentrated effort, she refrained from reaching out to him as memories of the passion they had shared just a few short nights ago infiltrated her mind. Quickly, a flash of Brandon in another woman's apartment replaced those thoughts. "I'm already calm."

Relief flooded through him that she finally understood. "Then can we put this whole thing behind us?"

Turning away from him, she said, "I said I was calm, not stupid."

"Excuse me?"

"I agree that Martin had no right to invade your personal life, but he didn't force you to pose for those pictures."

Walking up behind her, he put his arms around her and felt her body tense. "Think about it, Tee. I've been after you from the moment I got off that plane. Don't you trust me?"

His question was met with silence and Brandon took a step back. "Tanya?"

"Tell me you didn't meet that woman at a restaurant and go home with her."

Brandon had promised her he would never lie to her again. "I can't do that. But—"

Cutting him off, Tanya took off her ring and held it out to him. "Just go."

"Tanya, you have to let me explain about that night."

"That's where you're wrong, Brandon. I don't have to let you do anything. Now, please go."

He opened his mouth to speak, but no words came, as he knew she wouldn't listen to any explanation of those pictures.

She watched him walk out the door, without taking the ring. Only when she heard the car drive off did she allow her tears to freely fall.

Tanya stood at the door preparing the words she would say to Martin. She raised her hand, but the door opened before she could knock.

Martin stepped aside and motioned for her to enter. "I was looking out for you. Let me take your coat."

Tanya walked past him and into the living room. "I don't think I'll be staying that long."

"Are you sure? I can uncork a bottle of your favorite wine."

"This isn't a social visit, Martin."

"Really?" Martin asked with a sly grin. "I would think after finding out what type of man Brandon turned out to be, you would be more than willing to make this a social visit."

His sleazy tone only served to annoy Tanya even further. "Did you or did you not have something to do with blocking the permits for the Morgan and Rock project?"

Pretending to be insulted by the question, Martin said,

"Tanya, what would I have to gain by taking part in such an unfortunate set of circumstances?"

"How about the grant for Natalie's organization? If I remember correctly, the Whittington Corporation was a strong contributor to your campaign."

"If Natalie's organization failed to receive the funding they needed, I'm sure that it has more to do with her grant-writing skills than with any relationship I may or may not have with that corporation."

"Are you denying that you had anything to do with these two situations? Are you calling it a coincidence?"

"I'm not calling it anything. But I will tell you that now that I am aware of these difficulties your employer and friend are having, there may be something I can do about it. Perhaps a call to the county executive or a meeting with the head of the Whittington Foundation?"

Tanya tried to contain her fury as she listened to him act as if he were doing them a favor, when in reality he was probably the one that had caused the damage to begin with. "I'm sure if there was anything you could do to help rectify this situation, you would be more than willing to do so."

Casually walking across the room, he took a seat on the sofa and said, "What about you, Tanya? What would you be willing to do to help rectify this situation?"

"Excuse me?" Tanya asked, listening for the hidden meaning in his statement.

"You want something and I want something. Maybe there's a deal to be worked so that both of us get what we want."

"It's quite clear what I want," Tanya said, wanting him to spell out exactly what he was asking, "but why don't you say clearly what it is you want?"

Popping the cork on the bottle of wine that sat on the table, he acted as if he had all the time in the world. "The answer to that question is very simple. I want you."

"Are you out of your mind? You actually think you have a snowball's chance in hell to get me to agree to something like that?"

"All I'm asking is that you give me the opportunity to show you how great we can be together. Before playboy Brandon showed up, don't tell me you weren't going to accept my proposal."

Tanya thought back to that fateful night at the hospital. There was no arguing that Martin's statement was true. Before she ran into Brandon, she had had every intention of walking down the aisle and right into the arms of Martin Carter. Even though her relationship with Brandon didn't work out, Tanya still believed that Martin wasn't the man for her either.

"Martin, it wouldn't matter if we spent the next year together, it wouldn't change the fact that you and I do not belong together."

"I love you, Tanya."

"How can you say you love me when you're destroying my friends' businesses?" she cried, trying to maintain her composure.

"All I'm trying to do is make you see that we could have a wonderful life together."

"I'm sorry, Martin, but you and I will not get back together, no matter how you use your power."

Walking past her toward the door, he said, "Then I guess this conversation is over."

Not moving, she couldn't believe that Martin would let it end like this. "You would destroy people's livelihoods, what they've worked so hard for, just because you can't get your way?"

"Once again, my darling, you are mistaken. I'm not destroying anything, you are."

* * *

Tanya arrived at Damian's house a little after ten and quickly updated him and Brandon on the results of her visit with Martin.

"That man must be completely mad," Damian said, trying unsuccessfully to hide the worry in his eyes. "Doesn't he realize the impact of his actions?"

"I tried to reason with him, but he wouldn't budge," Tanya said.

Brandon listened without responding to Tanya's replay of what had happened at Martin's. Having spent the past two hours pacing the floor, Brandon had tried to maintain calmness while waiting for Tanya to return. Visions of her alone with Martin had embedded themselves into his mind, and Damian had had to stop him from following her.

"Who's his right-hand man?" Brandon asked, speaking for the first time.

"Who?" Tanya asked.

"Who's the man who's always there? The one who could get you to Martin when no one else could?"

Tanya hesitated a moment before saying, "I guess that would be Gavin Blake. He was Martin's campaign manager, now his chief of staff. They've been together since college."

Brandon grabbed his coat and headed for the door. "I'll touch base with both of you in a couple of days."

"What are you going to do?" Damian said, confused.

"I'm going to beat Martin at his own game," Brandon answered, before focusing his attention on Tanya. "And after that, I'm going to settle this issue between us."

Tanya felt her body shiver at the intensity with which he stared at her. The last twenty-four hours had been a roller coaster for her emotions, and finding out Martin could be so cold had stripped to the bare minimum her trust in the men she'd chosen. There was no way she was going to allow herself to be manipulated again. "The issue is settled. The

Morgan and Rock project is the only reason we'll have to communicate with each other."

Brandon heard the words of dismissal and forced his responding words down his throat. Now was not the time or the place. Once he'd taken care of Martin, only then would he turn his attention to Tanya. And once he put his focus on her, there would be no way he would let their relationship end.

A few days later, Brandon waited patiently in his car until the black Mercedes Benz pulled into the driveway. The gentleman got out of the car and took a quick look around before walking up the walkway to the front door. Picking up the folder in the passenger side, Brandon flipped through the pages one last time before tossing it to the side. Just as the man started up the steps that led to his brick town house, Brandon casually got out and walked across the street.

Forgoing the suit and tie that normally made up his work-week attire, he wore jeans, an oversize sweater, and a black skullcap, making him fit in more with the streets than the boardroom. Casually and comfortably, Brandon walked up the asphalt just as the man stuck his key in the door.

"Got a minute?" Brandon called out in a friendly tone.

The gentleman turned at the pleasant voice, but was met with an expression that was anything but. Brandon's eyes, dark and purposeful, demonstrated his true feelings. The last thing this meeting would be was a social visit.

The man picked up on his expression, and the corners of his mouth curved into a sly grin. "I guess I should be surprised, but I'm not. What can I do for you?"

"From the pictures you had taken of me, I would say that you've done quite enough."

"I understand those pictures caused quite a stir with your girlfriend," he answered innocently. "What did it take? About seven minutes to send you on your way?"

Brandon's jaw tightened when he realized someone must have been watching her house if he knew how long he was there. Ignoring the man's condescending tone and the obvious pleasure he'd received witnessing Brandon's relationship with Tanya fall apart, Brandon shoved his hands inside his coat pockets to keep him from knocking that silly grin off his face. "I'm not here to talk about Tanya."

"That's a shame. I understand she's one of your favorite topics." Pausing a moment, he continued, "So then, to what do I owe the pleasure of this visit?"

"I'm here to discuss permits and grants."

Glancing at his watch, the man shrugged nonchalantly and turned toward his front door. "I know nothing of what you're speaking of, and as much I've enjoyed our little tête-à-tête, I believe you've wasted enough of my time."

Brandon stood silent as the gentleman placed his key in the front door to the upscale town house. Right before he stepped completely inside, Brandon cleared his throat. "Speaking of time, I did some interesting reading earlier today. Quite an interesting story."

Stepping inside, the man shut the door halfway before saying, "Good day, Mr. Ware. Have a nice life."

"Talked about a young man arrested on drug charges. From what I gather, had it not been for some savvy political moves, he would be serving about a seven-year sentence for possession." Turning on his heels, Brandon headed down the walkway toward his car before yelling back, "But like you said, I've taken up enough of your time."

Before Brandon could reach the sidewalk, the man stepped back onto the porch and squared his shoulders. "What do you want?"

Brandon smiled in victory before he turned around. "To talk."

A few minutes later, Brandon sat in the living room with Gavin, ready to cut a deal.

Looking around, Brandon made note of the area Persian rug laid on top of shining hardwood floors. The rich wallpaper and window treatments accented the room, which could easily be used for a cover of *House & Garden*. It was obvious—Gavin liked the finer things in life. With a cryptic smile, Brandon said, "Nice place. You've gotten quite accustomed to the good life. Would be a shame to lose it all."

Not taking a seat, Gavin refused to be rattled. "Cut the crap, Brandon, and spit it out."

As he leaned forward, Brandon's smile left his face. "Look, Gavin, I'm going to be straight with you, I couldn't care less about what happened to you in Atlanta seven years ago."

Gavin remained expressionless as he admired his tactics. With that sentence, Brandon made it abundantly clear that he wasn't bluffing. The information he had on Gavin was tight and accurate.

"How did you find out?"

Relaxing, Brandon shrugged. "I'm a highly paid corporate lawyer. I play the game better than anyone."

"Then I'm sure you know that all the records of that incident were destroyed. It would be your word against mine." With confidence he added, "And I wouldn't underestimate the value of my word."

"And I wouldn't underestimate the value of the almighty dollar," Brandon countered. "Nothing is ever completely destroyed. If you'd like to see a copy of the police documents, I'd be happy to show them to you."

Gavin didn't answer right away, contemplating his next move. He could call his bluff and let the chips fall where they may, but with Martin's political career so young, it would be a high-risk move. "I'll ask you again, what do you want?"

"Get your boss on the phone."

Brandon listened as Gavin walked across the room and dialed Martin's private number. Turning his back on Brandon, he relayed the situation in a low voice. Not able to make out all of his words, Brandon knew they tried to figure out a plan of action in a matter of minutes.

"OK, Brandon," Gavin said, facing him, "Martin's all ears."

Without hesitation, Brandon demanded, "Tell him I want those permits executed tomorrow."

Gavin turned his body away from Brandon and gave his boss the message. After a few seconds of silence, he answered. "It will take several days, but consider the permits issued."

"Two days tops," Brandon countered.

"Done," Gavin said, slightly annoyed.

"Number two," Brandon said. "Natalie Donovan and BSI get that half-million-dollar grant."

Gavin heatedly discussed this situation with Martin in a hushed voice before he faced Brandon. "That particular situation is a little tricky."

"Then I guess what you're telling me is that you're a magician."

The humor only incensed Gavin more, but he understood he couldn't lose his cool. The last thing a new congressman needed was a story in the paper involving drugs, prostitutes, and his chief of staff. "What I'm telling you is that the award letter went out to another nonprofit organization. It's virtually impossible to take that grant away and give it to BSI."

"I'm not interested in *how* you do it. I just know that by the end of the week, a confirmation letter should be delivered to BSI informing its founder that she should expect a half million dollars by the end of the month. It doesn't matter to me where it comes from. Perhaps out of Martin's personal account?"

For a few seconds, Brandon could hear the curt whispers of Gavin as he relayed the messages.

"We'll take care of it. Anything else?"

"Yes," Brandon said, standing to head for the door. "I want that FBI flunky in the four-door sedan to leave me alone. If

I so much as think I see a tail on me, or anyone else I know, I'm sending what I have to the *Washington Post*. Got it?"

Through gritted teeth, Gavin spoke with his boss one last time before disconnecting the call. "You can see yourself out."

With a gentlemanly nod, Brandon stepped into the hallway and walked to the front door. "Nice doing business with you, G."

At the last minute, Gavin quickly caught up to Brandon and moved to stand in front of him. Bigger than Brandon, Gavin doubted that he would lose a physical fight.

"Don't even think about," Brandon declared, never blinking an eye. "They'll be cleaning up your blood for days."

They stood nose to nose, neither cutting his eyes away.

After several seconds of sizing each other up, Gavin said, "One word of that incident in Atlanta turns up anywhere, we shut your brother's business down before he knows what hit him."

Stretching out his hand, Brandon waited for Gavin to the same. Hesitating, Gavin finally clasped his hand in Brandon's and they shook. "Have a nice day."

Once Brandon stepped onto the porch, Gavin slammed the door behind him, letting out a string of expletives.

Fifteen

Tanya packed the last of her items and closed her suitcase. Leaving on an early morning flight, she planned to spend the night at Natalie's, who had volunteered to take her to the airport. Even though Tanya's love life was a complete mess, she was truly happy for Natalie. The relationship with Dr. Carrington continued to develop and Natalie believed that in him, she had found something real and lasting. Tanya had never seen her happier.

Leaving for Georgia couldn't have come at a better time. The more distance she put between herself and Brandon, the better. Remembering the morning he had slipped the engagement ring on her finger almost caused the tears again. With all her heart she believed that the words of love he spoke were true. How could she have been so wrong?

Damian had called Tanya a few hours ago and happily informed her that the permits were issued that morning and that the Whittington Foundation had made a discretionary contribution to BSI in the amount of five hundred thousand dollars. He emphasized that if it wasn't for Brandon, things might have turned out very differently.

Dragging her suitcase down the steps, she stopped at the bottom when she heard the doorbell ring. Without looking through the peephole, she instinctively knew who it was. He'd been calling her the past few days, and finally he decided to come to her house. Setting her bags in the living room, she waited for what she knew would come next.

Just as she predicted, she heard the key slide into the lock a few seconds later. This time, it wouldn't turn. The locksmith had left an hour ago. Brandon Ware could no longer step into her life whenever he pleased.

A minute later, her phone rang. Glancing at the caller ID, she didn't pick up. He was calling from outside her door. Starting to leave the room, she didn't want to hear his voice. But her feet wouldn't follow the command of her brain.

"Tanya, I know you're home, because your car is in the driveway. Please pick up."

Tanya didn't move.

"OK, at least hear me out. I admit, that night at the restaurant, I did leave with that woman and go to her apartment."

Tanya heard the words she had begged him to admit, but instead of bringing her a feeling of relief, they pierced her already wounded heart. Sitting on the sofa, she closed her eyes and rested her head in her hands.

"I was in the midst of a pity party because you weren't willing to give us a chance. It doesn't excuse my behavior, but you have to know, nothing happened."

Tanya shook her head and almost laughed at the tired excuse. Did he honestly think she would believe him?

"The minute I stepped into her apartment, I thought of you and what you meant to me. All I'm asking is that you take a good look at the pictures. Just look at them. You'll know I'm telling the truth. Please call me. I'm heading to the office. I love you."

The line went dead and a few moments later, she heard the sound of his car pulling off.

He must think I'm a complete idiot. Nothing happened? How dare he insult my intelligence? They were holding hands at the restaurant. His hand was on the small of her

*back as he escorted her to her car. She kissed him outside
her apartment building before he followed her in.*

"Sorry, Brandon. The evidence is stacked against you and
there is no cause for reasonable doubt," Tanya muttered to
the empty room, heading back upstairs to finish packing her
carry-on.

An hour later, she picked up her keys and slung her purse
over her shoulder. The faster she got out of DC, the sooner
she could lick her wounds and get her life back together.

Grabbing the handle of her roller bag, Tanya caught the
blinking red light of her answering machine out of the corner
of her eye. The only way to erase the message would be to listen to it. Pushing play, she was prepared to push erase as soon
as he started talking. But something stopped her and she found
herself listening to the entire message a second time.

"All I'm asking is that you take a good look at the pictures."

The folder sat on the coffee table with the wrinkled photos inside. She'd planned to take them with her to Georgia,
so that when her parents or Danielle asked about Brandon
she could just present the file to them and end all conversation about how she and Brandon should be spending the rest
of their lives together.

Letting her curiosity get the best of her, she touched the corner of the file with the tips of her fingers and flipped it open.
All she saw was this woman smiling in Brandon's face at the
dinner table. Setting that photo to the side, she looked at the
next one. The two of them standing by the coat check. As jealousy and anger mixed inside her, she stacked the pictures back
up. She'd seen enough. Just as she closed the folder, she finally
saw what Brandon hoped she would. How could she have
missed it? Suddenly, it all made sense. He did go to her house,
but Tanya now knew, without a shadow of a doubt, that nothing happened. Unspeakable joy swept through her.

Opening the front door, she stepped onto the porch as she put on her coat, almost slipping on some of the snow that had turned into small patches of ice. She could have called but wanted to tell him in person that she accepted his apology and his proposal. He still had to explain some things, but sleeping with another woman wasn't one of them. Because he didn't do it.

Tanya stepped off the elevator and walked right past the receptionist as she signed for a package from a courier. Turning the corner at the end of the hall, she moved past the empty secretary's station and pushed open his cracked door. Just as she opened her mouth to speak, she froze in her tracks. Right before her eyes stood a very attractive woman with her arms wrapped tightly around Brandon's neck.

"Have you missed this as much as I have?" she asked in between kisses.

Blinking several times, Tanya needed a moment for her mind to process what her eyes were seeing. Feeling sick to her stomach, she silently stepped back and leaned against the wall. Catching her breath, she raced down the hallway. Pushing the elevator button several times, she prayed it would arrive before her eyes released the water it fought to hold in its corners.

Tanya stood at the rental counter patiently waiting to be served. Declining her mother's offer to pick her up, Tanya had hoped the ninety-minute ride to Dankerville would begin the healing process. They say history has a habit of repeating itself, and here she was, once again, heading to her childhood home after breaking up with Brandon, trying to restore her soul, repair her spirit, and mend her heart.

As she headed out of the hustle and bustle of the city traffic, Tanya relaxed as the four-lane highway turned into a two-lane country road. As she inhaled the fresh air, her neck began to loosen up, her shoulders began to relax, and the stress of her failed relationship began to dissipate.

Turning into the long driveway that would lead her to her parents' house, Tanya prepared herself for the questions about Brandon. She had only told her family that he wouldn't be joining her on this trip, and that they probably wouldn't be seeing each other anymore. They hadn't asked her to elaborate, but she wasn't foolish enough to believe that they would not press her for more information once she arrived.

As she parked the car, the front door opened and her mother, her father, and Danielle stepped out on the porch to greet her. Adam Kennedy, at sixty-one, and Mabel Kennedy, at fifty-eight, maintained the active lifestyle of couples half their age. Both had retired three years ago from teaching elementary school, but managed to fill their days with church activities, gardening, and volunteering in a tutoring program for high school students. Fashionably dressed in jogging suits and Nike tennis shoes, they excitedly waved to her as she stepped out of the car.

Pasting on a smile, Tanya determined to maintain her composure and not break down in uncontrollable tears, as she had done twice on the plane and once in the car. She'd survived Brandon Ware before, and she would do it again. With her arms open, she approached her mother first, and then her father, getting bear hugs from both of them. Finally, her attention turned to Danielle.

Neither moved for several seconds, staring openly at one another. Giving a tentative smile, Tanya opened her arms and they gave each other a genuine hug. "It's good to see you, Danielle."

Mabel, pleased that her children had finally made amends, opened the screen door and motioned for Tanya to enter.

Stepping into the house, Tanya heard the door shut behind her and turned to her family standing on the outside.

"We have an errand to run. We'll be back in about an hour," Mabel said.

Confused, Tanya started to ask how they could leave just as soon as she arrived, but they were halfway down the porch and heading for the car before she could get the words out.

"Tanya?"

She spun around at the sound of his voice. Brandon stepped out of the living room and into the foyer.

"What the . . ."

Contacting Mabel, he had explained everything that happened between them, leaving nothing out. The desperation in his voice and the heartfelt words of love he expressed for her daughter convinced Mabel that the sincerity she heard in him was true. Since Tanya refused to see him in DC, Mabel suggested he come to Georgia. "I called your mother last night and she told me what time you planned to arrive. I caught an earlier flight so that we could talk."

Fury would not begin to describe the emotions that surged inside her, but amazingly her voice remained calm. "There is nothing to talk about."

As she attempted to walk past him, he reached out for her hand. "Nothing happened between me and the woman in those photos. If you look at the pictures—"

"If you look at the pictures," she interrupted calmly, "you can tell by the clothes you're wearing that after having dinner at Lenny's, there is no way you could have arrived at my house that night at nine forty-five if you had spent any amount of time with her."

Relief swept through Brandon as he pulled her close, but when she jerked away from him, still agitated, he was confused.

"I'm sorry, Tanya. I know it was a mistake to leave the restaurant with her but you have to know you're the only woman in my life."

Fighting the tears threatening to overtake her, Tanya declared, "After everything we've shared these past few weeks, if you had told me those words yesterday, I would have believed you."

"And now you don't?"

As she stepped away, all the calmness she had tried to maintain left and she found herself almost yelling. "I saw you yesterday."

"You saw what?"

With a cryptic laugh, she answered, "Now don't you play stupid, Brandon. It's definitely not becoming on you."

"Then stop talking in riddles and tell me what you're talking about." The desperation in his voice was evident. The past few days had been the worst of his life. Being apart from her only solidified his need to be with her. She wouldn't talk to him, wouldn't see him, and it was breaking his heart.

"I came by your office yesterday to tell you I wanted to marry you, but you were otherwise occupied."

Brandon's lips curved into a slow smile, and he stepped closer to her, wrapping his arms around her to block her escape. He whispered in her ear, "If we are going to be husband and wife, you are going to have to have a little more faith in me."

Overwhelmed by the feeling of contentment she found in his arms, she forced her words out of her mouth. "The night of the snowstorm, I believed that we were destined to be together. Even after seeing those photos, I realized that your love was true. But don't insult me by telling me that after watching you kiss another woman, I should have a little faith. You destroyed that yesterday."

Instead of answering her, he stepped back and pulled out his cell. After dialing, he punched several numbers and placed the phone to her ear.

"Brandon, this is Lolita. I . . . umm . . . I wanted to apologize for yesterday. I was completely out of line. I guess I didn't want to believe you when you told me you were one hundred percent committed to your fiancée. I thought that once I kissed you, you would be willing to . . . well . . . you know . . . But I gravely miscalculated your dedication to your relationship. You didn't even kiss me back. Whoever she is, she's one lucky woman. I've never had a man, committed or not, turn me down. Anyway, I know my partnership vote is coming up this year, and, well . . . I hope you'll vote on my work and not my lack of judgment in my personal life. Good-bye."

Brandon clicked end and waited for Tanya's reaction. Reaching for her hand, he got down on one knee, never taking his eyes from hers. "I love you, Tee. Nothing is more important to me than you. Marry me."

Looking into his eyes, Tanya saw the truth in his words and felt his love in her heart. "OK."

Not wanting to take anything for granted, he asked, "OK, what?"

"OK, I'll marry you."

"Thank you, thank you," he said, rising and flooding her with kisses. "I promise to make you happy every day of your life."

"I know you will, Brandon. I know you will."

An hour later, Tanya, her family, and Brandon sat around the kitchen table enjoying a homemade meal of fried chicken, mashed potatoes, macaroni and cheese, and collard greens. The laughter resonated throughout the house as Danielle told stories of her crazy antics as a model, unable to believe that she had really acted that way. Adam and Mabel, thrilled at Tanya and Brandon's reconciliation, talked nonstop about weddings and grandchildren.

As Tanya listened to the joy and happiness around her, she reached for Brandon's hand under the table. With the man of her dreams by her side and her new endeavors with BSI, Tanya didn't think life could get any better.

Just then, Brandon slid a business card in her lap for only her to see. The name of the company read *Cherished Cherubs*. Leaning in to her ear, he whispered, "I spoke to Dottie yesterday. I put an order in for the nursery furniture. If we start tonight, the furniture and our baby should arrive about the same time."

Her cheeks grew warm from his suggestive tone and she couldn't help saying a silent prayer of "Thank you." All her childhood birthday wishes had finally come true.

Epilogue

Danielle stood outside the studio door taking deep breaths. This was it. The moment she'd been waiting for for the past year. The chance to prove herself and get her career back on track.

The competition for this job would be fierce. There were at least fourteen other people being considered to host this show. Gathering up every bit of confidence she could, she glanced in her compact one more time.

Her hair, hanging straight to her shoulders, gave her a youthful look. Her makeup, meticulous without being over-bearing. Her outfit, a Vera Wang ensemble compliments of her agent. With a few silent words of self-encouragement, Danielle pushed open the door.

To her surprise, the studio appeared dark and empty. "Hello?"

All of a sudden, the lights came on and a shadow stepped out from behind a wall. "Good afternoon, Ms. Kennedy."

A swarm of butterflies entered her stomach. "I thought I was scheduled to meet with the executive producer. What are you doing here?"

Walking toward her, he stopped just a few feet from her. "I thought it would be advantageous for us to have a little chat before the formal audition process began."

Danielle fought from running out the door. She wasn't prepared for this—for him. The *Fashion Week* live show wasn't her first encounter with this director, Xavier Johnston. As a matter of fact, up until that night of the show, they'd shared a very personal relationship. But her behavior had ended it when he couldn't believe she'd jeopardize his show with her own self-centeredness.

Almost four months ago, when she had come to New York to audition, the fact that he was the director was purposely withheld from her. After she completed her reading, he informed her in front of the crew and other cast members that in no uncertain terms would he work with someone as difficult, immature, and juvenile as she. He continued by saying that many people in the industry felt the same way, and for those who didn't, he was sure he could change their minds.

Leaving the city embarrassed and defeated, she had found the results of her selfish ways sinking in. On the plane ride back to Georgia, she had decided that she didn't want to be that person anymore. Always taking, never giving. She had ruined her career and ruined her relationship with Xavier.

Many would call it an "aha" moment, but Danielle considered it just a decision. She decided to change. At that moment, she had felt lighter and freer than she'd felt in years.

"Your agent must have friends in very high places, because if it was up to me, you wouldn't get another audition for the rest of your life."

"Then I guess it's good that it's not up to you."

Xavier whole-heartedly laughed and said, "Still have that smart mouth."

"Look, Xavier, all I'm asking for is a fair chance. Don't blackball me on this." Danielle held her breath while she waited for his answer.

"Fine. But if you screw up, you've used the last of your favors."

Danielle watched him disappear out the door and exhaled a deep breath. True excitement that she would receive a fair shot was only one part of her relief. The other part was that Xavier Johnston had left the room. Standing so close vividly reminded her of what she had found so attractive about him years ago. His hazel eyes, close beard, and deep voice had her knees shaking. But she had ruined their chance the night of the fashion show. The only thing she focused on now was this audition. Not even someone as fine as Xavier would get her off her mission. She'd studied the show's concept and understood the market. This was the perfect job for her.

Xavier shut the door and leaned against it. Danielle had remained just as gorgeous as the day he met her. Ever since he'd known her, she'd been a pain in the neck. But her agent seemed to believe that she had turned over a new leaf. He meant what he told her—he would be fair with the auditions. But if she had changed, and got the job, how would he be able to resist her?

Dear Readers,

I hope you enjoyed reading the story of Tanya and Brandon. I want to thank all of you who have taken the time to write or e-mail me to let me know how much you've enjoyed my stories. It is truly appreciated.

Please visit me on the web at www.doreenrainey.com or e-mail me at doreenrainey@prodigy.net. You can also write me at P.O. Box 1263, Alexandria, VA 22313.

Until next time,

Doreen

ABOUT THE AUTHOR

Doreen Rainey graduated from Spelman College and resides in the suburbs of Washington, DC, with her husband. Currently, she works as a human resources manager for a CPA firm. Her other works include *Foundations for Love* and *Just for You*.

Doreen was named Best Multi-Cultural New Romance Author of the Year by *Shades of Romance* on-line magazine and received the EMMA Award for Favorite New Author at Romance Slam Jam 2003.